Bonds & Bones

A Witches & Immortals Series
Book 4

Stephanie Vorwald

Editing by Whitney Morsillo of Whitney's Book Works
Cover Design by Etheric Tales & Edits | Mc Damon

This finale is dedicated to my very own past, present, and future. My world has been flipped in ways that were unimaginable, and because of some of those moments, Witches & Immortals was able to come to life. I will forever be grateful for the fans that have followed this series and look forward to writing more in the future. The Mississippi River will continue to have my heart and be my home away from home.

Through blood, sweat, and tears, I give you the finale...
Bonds & Bones.

Contents

Stephanie
VORWALD
ESCAPE FROM REALITY
YA FANTASY

Chapter 1

Freya Chamberlain

I sat there, trying to wrap my head around the fact that Isadora had just walked into my home, uninvited. And the mere thought that she decided upon herself to sit in my dad's seat made me grind my teeth. I met her gaze and wanted to wring her neck the moment she showed her face. But, of course, she didn't remember any of what she'd done. She had no idea the amount of shit she caused in my life or what she had done to my family.

My inner peace was raging, and I wished that I would've killed her back at JFK. Now, I was heavily regretting the fact that she was still breathing as I watched her chest rise and fall without remorse for what she had done. I glared at her and hoped that she could feel my personal daggers piercing her evil soul. I sat quietly at the table, knowing very well that if I opened my mouth, fire would escape it, charring her to ash. I looked around the table and studied everyone's face to try and distract myself.

Margo and Callum sat side by side, smiling and holding hands, at the table across from me, and the pit in my stomach lessened knowing that they were alive and happy in this moment. I truly was happy that someone finally could smile. It seemed that in Crystal Rock only one family could be happy at a time. Maybe this place truly was cursed, and every founding family that came from it was cursed too.

Eric sat next to Margo, opposite end of the brain mushed, ex-Immortal, his ex-lover and ex-partner. He was staring straight back at me with a glare screaming 'shut the hell up.' I knew that he wanted me to stop brewing in my thoughts and calm my temper. But the only thing holding me back was the fact that my magic was still gone. If I had my fire, I would've roasted her from my seat. I snickered out loud and caught myself in my own thoughts as Eric rolled his eyes and shook his head.

I looked away from him and whatever plan he had rotating in his head. I turned next to me and looked at my mom. My lonely, saddened mom, who wished her husband and other daughter were here celebrating with us. We were finally together again after all these years with all secrets out, and here we were, back to square one. A broken family. Her blank gaze never left her plate of untouched food that Eric had dished up. She had spent the last few weeks in bed, frying her brain, trying to think of anything and everything to find them. Every locator spell came up with nothing. And even the stupid map that was used with the dagger centuries ago was just as worthless. Her heart continued to ache as the map would start to trace them and then vanish in a poof of smoke. I watched her closely over the last few weeks, and each failed attempt, broke her further. I didn't blame her one bit for wanting to lay in bed and mope at this point. She had finally been happy, and just like that, that bitch across the table took it away from her.

My glare moved back to the famous 'Izzy,' the nickname Margo and Eric were calling her. 'Isadora' was now long gone in her own head and burning somewhere in the depths of hell while 'Izzy' was able to start a fresh new life and not remember the trauma of the last few months that she's caused each and every one of us. I pitied her, really. I almost wished that I could've had a quick erase for myself two years ago when Jaxon was gone. The pain would've been much easier to carry. But then again, I would not be where I was today, and that thought instantly vanished the pity of having my memories being toyed with. It would have been a disaster waiting to happen.

All I could smell was Izzy's ambered vanilla perfume, which now seemed to be filling the room. I had never noticed it before... Maybe I was too focused on fight or flight mode whenever I was around her. Or she just never lingered this long in our presence. At least, I surely didn't try and keep her company any longer than needed.

I pulled my stare away from her and looked back to Jaxon, sitting next to me. He watched me intently as my eyes had made their rounds and grabbed my hand, pulling it under the table and resting it on his leg, squeezing it tight and rubbing my palm. I knew he was trying to calm me, but from the inside, I was burning to get the hell out of my own home. I hadn't even realized that I was bouncing my leg and fidgeting with my shirt, in hopes of my necklace still being there, but it was gone with Haven, wherever that was. I could feel Jaxon trying to calm my nerves, but I was going to need more than his love right now to make my brain settle.

"Pass the wine," I demanded.

Jaxon turned to face me, confused. He leaned over and whispered into my ear, "Babe, since when do you drink?"

I glared across the table and nodded. "Since your very own mom dragged *her* into my home," I said loudly enough to disrupt the table from their chatter, and everyone looked back at me in shock. Eric with warning in his eyes. My mom broke her gaze from her plate and looked up with a smirk. Then, I knew, for the first time in a long time, she and I were on the same page. Her temper was boiling just under the surface too. I nodded toward her and stood as I grabbed the bottle of Rosé and walked over, grabbing my mom's arm, along with her fragile broken heart. I paused and let her grab the oversized blanket off the back of the couch and slung it over my shoulder before taking her arm again and biting the cork off the bottle. Spitting it across the living room and walking outside with the bottle raised high to the sky, I gulped it down.

"Happy Thanksgiving, assholes," I said, wiping my lips with the back of my hand, letting the warmth consume my insides and liquid courage grow within me by the minute.

"What's her problem?" Izzy asked innocently, as I slammed the door behind us.

The cool night air was the only thing that was making my fiery rage subside a little. My mom and I sat huddled next to each other with the bottle of wine passing between us, keeping us warm. I could feel the alcohol sloshing around in my empty stomach as my body relaxed for the first time in weeks. I could feel the sober me trying to reach through to take care of the drunk me. I pushed her back and let the feeling of numbness kick in. I just needed a switch to turn off every feeling I had inside me for a little while.

I looked up and realized my mom was looking back at me, silent but watchful.

"Happy Thanksgiving." I lifted the bottle and drank it before passing it to her. She gave it back to me for the last sip before cheers-ing the sky and whoever was listening to my slur.

Eric stepped outside and clicked his tongue at us both. Anger filled his eyes as I began to laugh. He turned and walked back in silently.

"We're going to need more of that stuff," my mom yelled back to him, as she exhaled, and we both giggled. I watched as her shoulders lowered and her breathing became more steady.

"I'm sure Eric will be back out shortly to scold my behavior to our 'guest,'" I laughed, wishing he would come outside so I could have him become our butler with another bottle.

She shrugged. "Oh well. Margo could've warned us. Or even Eric." She inhaled heavily, and I watched as her chest shook, trying to hold her emotions together. "I had been strong for so long—"

"Mom, don't."

"Damn it, Freya. I have done everything possible to keep the ones I love out of danger for eighteen years, and now, here we are... What have I done so wrong in life to be dealt all the wrong cards? Is the true price of love just pain?" She leaned forward and began to sob into her hands.

I quickly sat up and let the sober me try to reach the surface as I wrapped my arms around her. "Mom, this isn't your fault. Isa—," I exhaled slowly. "Izzy did all of this, but I swear I am going to fix this."

She continued to sob as the door opened, and the wind blew the ambered vanilla scent toward us with an unwanted guest holding another bottle of wine.

"I'm just setting this down for you. The others said you had enough, but I beg to differ." Izzy stepped an inch closer and set it on the ground before turning and walking back inside quickly.

Her face was full of fear, as if she had woken a bear. I sat dumbfounded with my mom still crying in my arms. I stared at the bottle of wine and willed it to explode, for a new one to appear, untouched by her. I lifted my palm toward the bottle and pushed my magic to break it. When nothing happened, I stood and grabbed it, bringing it back to our seats. My mom had finally begun to catch her breath and let the tears dry, so I showed her our new bottle, deciding not to tell her who had touched it, hoping that her crying had drowned out the words of our enemy.

She half smiled as she took it and faced her palm in front of the cork to make it pop off without a corkscrew. Izzy probably did that on purpose too. Leaving us to struggle to open the bottle without the tools we needed. Thankfully, my mom still had her magic. She lifted the bottle and drank quickly before passing it to me.

I watched as her beautiful doe eyes' dried their tears and her cheeks flushed. I closed my eyes and copied her guzzle.

I knew I would regret this in the morning, but something inside me said I needed this tonight. The door opened again, and I kept my eyes closed, not wanting any part of Izzy's conversation. I laid my head back on the swing and let my mom's head rest on top of mine.

"Will you be coming back in?" Eric asked.

Keeping my eyes shut, I shook my head. "Not while she's here."

"I...," He started as his footsteps got closer and then he hesitated. "I want them back too." He inhaled quickly as I opened one eye and wondered if it was the drunk me seeing his emotions or if he actually was letting himself *feel* something. "Freya, I made a promise to you and your mother, and I intend on keeping it. I will get them back."

I closed my eyes and just nodded, not sure if I agreed with him or if I just wanted him to shut up. The cold air on my face was helping to balance out my reddened, wine flushed cheeks. The world began to spin as the wine did its job and made me not give a damn which way it spun.

Freya, we're still here. Please, focus on my voice.

"I hear you," I slurred.

Haven's voice faded as fast as it came.

Chapter 2

Jaxon Oakes

I watched carefully as Freya stood and walked outside with her mom dragged behind her. I debated on going with, but looked over and saw my mom's pleading eyes across the table for me to stay. I knew it wasn't because she wanted me away from Freya at this point but because having her sister back in her life the last few weeks had been draining and she was trying to hold herself together without letting Izzy know the amount of hate she still held toward her.

"Did I do something wrong?" Izzy asked.

Eric walked into the kitchen, shaking his head. I was unsure if he was answering Izzy or if he was pissed off at Freya's exit.

I smirked to myself, agreeing with Freya for not wanting to even sit six feet from her. I didn't even like the idea of Izzy being in the same house as my parents, which was why I kept staying here, trying to be as far away as possible.

"I shouldn't have come, should I?" Izzy asked, as her eyes welled with tears. "My head is so confused. I don't know which way is up today. I think maybe I should head home."

"No, you are fine, sister. Just sit and eat. Freya and her mother have suffered a great loss recently, and they are grieving." My mom patted her shoulder while keeping her distance, as if she was waiting for Izzy's switch to flip and her evil side to come back out and cause havoc.

Eric walked outside, then back in angrily, straight past all of us and to the backyard. Whatever words were exchanged, I decided I wanted no part in it.

"Well, looks like it's just us left." I laughed as I grabbed the turkey and mashed potatoes and plopped them on my plate.

Izzy looked up and smiled at me. "Good thinking, can't let this food get cold."

I ignored her smile and nodded as I passed the potatoes to her, trying to let my own tension with her go, as my scar on my side started to burn with the reach.

Don't let her win.

I half smiled and grabbed my fork, filling my mouth with food to smother the words I wanted to say. Because I already knew that biting my tongue would no longer work with her. She had taken everything from all of us at one time or another, and I was not having it.

Just shut up and eat.

"Do you think they will want another bottle?" Izzy asked innocently, nodding her head toward the front porch.

My dad finished his plate and stood up, grabbing my mom's already empty plate, and headed for the kitchen.

"I'll help you." My mom jumped up too quickly to get her own taste of freedom, leaving both Izzy and I alone at the dining room table.

Eric yelled from the backdoor as he walked back in just in time to answer her. "Do not give her another drop," he said sternly, as he walked upstairs, slamming the guest bedroom door. Izzy slumped down in her chair, and watching her intently, I realized she felt more out of place than anyone here. She was trying to fit in and only being pushed away.

Good.

Izzy was playing with her fork and the gravy on her plate, swirling it around. "I think I might set this outside, just in case," she whispered, grabbing the bottle of wine and standing. She moved too fast for me to stop her, but I kind of wanted to see if she would even survive out there for a second. I shook my head as I sat back and watched her step into her own death trap, listening intently.

When no fire ignited and no tornado blew her away, I stood to get closer to the door, bumping into Izzy as she rushed back inside, shuddering from the cold.

"Oops." She stepped aside quickly, trying to steady herself. "Sorry." She walked past me to the living room and sat down quietly.

I looked past the doorway and saw the bottle get accepted. Knowing that a second bottle was definitely going to mean that Clara's healing tea would be needed in the morning, I decided to let Freya sit for a little longer out there and have her peace with her mom. She needed the bonding time with the only family she had left. Instead, I walked upstairs to see where Eric had disappeared to.

He was in Freya's parents' room getting the bed ready for Alex. His thoughts matched mine, knowing that we were going to be carrying them back into the house tonight.

"Here." I handed him the last pillow on the side of the bed with Jim's shirt tied around it. "She hasn't slept without it since that day."

He grabbed the pillow and stared at it. "We need to distract them. They are falling apart, and we still have the Ragnar issue to deal with and the souls. We need to give them each a task to focus on outside of getting their family back."

I still didn't like Eric the best, but over the last few weeks, he'd started to grow on me. He had been very careful around Alex the moment Jim and Haven disappeared. He had carried her broken self from the field all the way home, refusing any car that had tried to help. I think he needed the walk just as much as she needed to be carried.

I nodded. "What do you have in mind?"

"Tomorrow morning, Freya's going to help me return the souls to their rightful places."

"She's not going to like it without her magic."

"Exactly why she needs to do it. She needs to step out of her comfort zone and be around everything magic to see if something will trigger it."

I thought about it for a minute and realized that all of us had been tiptoeing around with our magic to try not to upset her more than she already was. "What about Alex?"

Eric smirked and tossed the pillow back to me. "That's going to be your job. Take her and come up with clues to track down Ragnar or just keep her busy. I don't give a damn."

My brows furrowed. "Why don't you take Alex and I go with Freya?"

He looked down quickly, "You can't return the souls." He fidgeted with his palms before looking back up to me and exhaling slowly.

Defeated.

He huffed. "I need some space from her. She's my brother's wife, and I can see why my brother is so intrigued with her."

Shock ran through my veins. "You're falling for Freya's mom?" I immediately started to shake my head in disapproval. "Dude, no, that can't happen."

"I know." He glared back at me. "Maybe it's her power of persuasion, but something about her pulls me in. I just want to keep her safe for my brother's return, okay? I owe him that much."

"Maybe you should go stay with Lynn for a while. I'll be here, so I can watch them both."

Eric looked away and contemplated. "I don't want to bring danger to Lynn, either. It's best I stay here for now. I just need a day away."

I nodded, knowing that he meant well. "It has to be her magic," I reassured him, swallowing hard, hoping that was all.

"I hope so." Eric finished getting the bed ready and walked past me, stopping in the doorway. "You need to keep that between us." He turned and glared. "Don't make me kill you. Freya wouldn't be happy with me." He smirked and then walked away.

I froze and then rolled my eyes. Just when I was starting to like the fucker a little bit, he said something stupid like that. I shook my head in annoyance. Maybe he'd get sucked into the soul world tomorrow and disappear. Smiling at the thought of it, I walked down the stairs to carry Freya into the house.

Chapter 3

Freya Chamberlain

I woke up in my bed. Last thing I remembered was sitting on the porch with my mom... *drinking?* Drinking. I looked down and realized I was out of my hoodie and in shorts and a tank top. I didn't remember changing, either. I instantly regretted sitting up as the hangover was real and took over. My head spun as the vomit rose. I turned over and grabbed the garbage can that had been conveniently placed for this exact moment before heaving into it.

Jaxon woke beside me, pulling my hair out of my face and rubbing my back as I made a fool of myself. Red wine on an empty stomach was not a good combination. I regretted not enjoying some of the Thanksgiving meal that had the house smelling good all day yesterday. I groaned as my stomach emptied, laying back down with my arm covering my eyes from the bright sun coming through. I replayed all of yesterday again in my head, trying to fill in all the blanks that I could.

"I'm sorr—" I whispered to Jaxon before he stopped me.

"No need." He stood up, still in the outfit he wore here yesterday, and walked toward the door.

"Did you change me?" I asked, embarrassed.

He turned and smirked. "You attempted it yourself. Luckily, I caught you before you cracked your head open." He laughed softly.

"I made a fool of myself, didn't I?"

Jaxon laughed. "Not at all. Let's just say that you were quite relaxed, and I carried you in here, and you complained that it was too hot and started to strip naked before passing out again."

My eyes bulged at the thought.

"So, I grabbed those pajamas and helped you dress." He shrugged. "Even though I know you are a strong, independent, fully capable woman and could've done it yourself in time." He winked. "Now sit still. I have the healing tea downstairs, great for hangovers. Your parents should really think about selling it at the bar." He quickly froze as he realized the mention of my dad was not a good idea. He turned with an apologetic look as I waved it off.

"That's a great idea." I grinned back at him before he walked out.

I sat up, laughing at my own stupidity.

Great, and that is exactly why I don't drink.

He returned with the tea and handed the steaming tentacles mug to me. I smelled the aromas, grateful for the herbs that grew here. I remembered our painting day and let the happy memories grow back inside of me. I sipped it quickly, hoping that the faster I drank it the better I would physically feel.

Jaxon leaned against the headboard and waited patiently for me to recover.

"So, what's on the agenda for today?" I asked once I emptied the cup, feeling motivated to accomplish something more than a shower. My head was already starting to feel better.

"Great, I was hoping you would ask." He smirked and leaned forward, pulling the mended dagger out from behind him and laying it across my hand carefully. He seemed to think I would toss it and shatter it again. "It's been a few weeks, and we have souls that have homes to get back to." He placed his hand on top of it and half smiled. "I know it no longer has the prison world inside it, but I figured it would help motivate you to save the ones that came from it."

I stared at the dagger that betrayed us at JFK with his own bloodline and grimaced. The obsidian no longer had a shimmer to it and seemed like nothing more than an antique Viking soul sucker that was now powerless. My hope of a good day deflated with the weight of the world back on my magic-less shoulders.

"Do we have to do this today? I don't even have magic," I mumbled.

"Eric can help with that. I just need you to go with him and make sure they are being taken care of properly."

I looked up at him and studied his face, "You're not coming with me?"

He shook his head. "Nope, I have mom duty today. Your mom." He smiled reassuringly. "I need her to help finish painting the bar. We need that place reopened, otherwise Jim will strangle me when he is back."

Not if, but when.

I half smiled at his confidence and then shivered at the thought of the last time we were at the bar... The thyme spell with Haven that shattered our lives before she disappeared.

"I don't think that's a good idea for my mom."

"Trust me, Clara is coming too. We're having some bonding time today."

I grimaced at the idea of spending the day with Eric and away from Jaxon, but then he reminded me of all the souls swimming at Jaxon's home still, and I agreed that it was time. They were waiting for us to set them free. Each and every one of them. Plus, with Ragnar still out there somewhere, releasing them would be the best idea to keep them out of his hands. He was now our biggest threat, and yet, we knew nothing about him.

"Fine, but promise me that you'll make my dad's famous burgers at the bar later tonight for us? I think that will make my mom smile."

He nodded and came in for a kiss, but I dodged out of the way. "Sorry, hangover mouth and all. Be back in five."

I quickly ran to the bathroom and brushed my teeth, jumping in the shower and scrubbing the alcohol from my skin. It would be a long time before I touched that stuff again. The thought of the liquid made my stomach turn again, and I quickly poured the Juniper shampoo over my head and let the smell help me relax in the peaceful steam. I let my thoughts settle and focused on my mission for today. I had no idea how to do it, but Eric had set Grace and Nora free. At least, I knew *he* could do it, and maybe, just maybe, it could spark something inside of me.

I hoped.

I got fully dressed in the bathroom, ashamed of making a fool of myself last night in front of Jaxon. Of course he was a gentleman and babysat me. I shook my head as I lifted my long sleeve sweater over my head and headed back to the bedroom to face the man I loved with a more clear head. I jumped on the bed and kissed him, letting him tangle his hand through my freshly washed hair and bring me closer to him.

"Do I really have to spend the day with Eric?" I pouted. "I mean, after last night, he's going to be glaring daggers at me all day. Literally." I picked up the dagger as he laughed.

"Yep, you made a promise, and those souls are waiting. So, do it for them."

I groaned but felt the guilt grow. "Fine. But only because I keep my word."

He smiled and kissed me once more before we headed down the stairs where Eric had coffee brewed and empty mugs waiting to be filled.

"Good morning," he said without even looking at me.

"Morning, I'm not a hundred percent sure it's a good one."

"Well, did you get it all out of your system?" He turned and smirked, facing the now embarrassed me.

I nodded and rolled my eyes. "Brand new again."

"Good. Grab an egg sandwich, and let's get going." He nodded at the freshly made breakfast as he grabbed his jacket.

"Is my mom awake yet?" I asked, looking around the room.

Eric smirked. "Jaxon's going to let her sleep in a little longer."

I turned and watched as Jaxon nodded in agreement. "Clara should be here soon. I'll have her do the hangover honors and wake her up." He grabbed a kitchen chair and sat. "You two have fun." He chuckled quietly as he poured himself a cup of coffee.

I huffed like a child before walking outside into the cold air. Looking over at the front porch, I was happy to have had a bonding moment with my mom there last night but regretted the alcohol that went along with it. Eric walked past me and left. I joined him silently.

"Now that the souls are in our physical world, I should be able to release them. It was getting them here that was the hardest part," he said, mostly to himself because when I looked up at him, he was still facing forward and seemed to be in deep thought.

"What is your plan with Izzy?" I asked him, disgusted that she had a new name for her new life that she would get to live now.

He continued to walk and finally looked down at me. "I think she knows where Jim and Haven were sent to."

I stopped walking.

He paused and turned back around, facing me. "When I was changing the course of her memories, something was blocking me from seeing everything. I think that something was her father."

I stood, confused, and waited for more. Eric had no intention of elaborating, though. He turned and kept walking in the direction of the house.

"That's it?" I asked, as I ran up to meet him. "You're not going to explain?"

He exhaled sharply, frustrated. "It's only a theory. Give me time."

"Time hasn't really been on our side for anything, Eric," I snarled. "In case you haven't noticed."

He turned quickly, and I instantly regretted getting out of bed this morning.

His glare said more words than he had to.

I curled into my own skin with my hands up in surrender. "I'm sorry," I whispered.

"If you don't think for a second that I am not angry with this whole situation, then you are foolish and can go back home and leave me to do this alone. I do not need to hear another word from your mouth that tells me the disgust you have for me. I have enough of that from myself as it is."

We both breathed heavily as his words sank in.

He hates himself enough for the both of us.

Before I could open my mouth, Callum opened the door to the home and waved us in.

"Hey, I hear we are soul surfing today. Cowabunga." Callum laughed and quickly realized the tension between us and turned to walk back inside, leaving the door open for us to follow.

I watched as Eric's frustration consumed him as he shook his head and walked in. I waited an extra minute to collect myself and grow up before joining them. We had a job to do. A job that I had promised to fulfill weeks ago despite Eric's scrutiny.

Chapter 4

Haven Vine

Journal:

I'm starting to lose track of the days. I feel as if we have been here for months. My heart aches to see Ezra and my family again. I know my dad is feeling the same way, although he is not being very verbal about it.

He continues to work on that car in the garage. He seems to be determined to get it running. I recognized the green paint and racing stripes from Freya's mind when we completed our Marks. I keep watching my Mark and waiting for it to fade that way I would know when the end is near, but nothing changes. My magic is strong here and it seems

that I can syphon still since JFK. I hope that Freya can still do the same. We definitely were stronger together that day. Unfortunately, Isadora ruined yet another day for us. I'm ready to go back home, if we ever get to. I have to admit, my hope is dwindling a bit.

The Jasper fossil was with me when we were transported, and now, it sits as a paperweight on this very desk. I keep willing it to do something, anything to send us home or at least show its magic. But whatever it <u>can</u> do, it is <u>not</u> doing right now. I wish Ezra were here to tell me more about his family secrets. I actually just wish he was here. Had I known that we weren't going to be together...

I couldn't continue. I needed a good cry, and today was finally that day. It had been weeks... months? I didn't care anymore. I closed the stupid journal and just let the tears flow. I had been strong for too long, and in this moment, I decided it was time to finally be weak.

To feel.

"Hey, kiddo. Hey." My dad rushed into my room, covered in grease and oil as he made his way across to hug me tight. "It's okay," he whispered, as he let me sob like the child I was.

I sniffled and wiped my tears.

"Hey, how about just us two go on a walk?"

I laughed and wiped my cheeks free of tears. "It's only us two here."

He laughed and elbowed me gently. "Perfect, couldn't ask for a better person to be here with." He winked, which made me smile. "Wherever here is?"

I looked around the room and decided that these four walls were not going to trap me here any longer. "Let's get out of here."

He stood and pulled me up, patting my back.

"Where to then?" I asked.

He shrugged. "Let's head toward Clara's house. We don't have to go inside if you don't want to, but I think it would be good to see what else there is to explore here. Maybe she has some of that tea simmering on the stove."

I thought about it for a minute and panicked when the thought of an empty house, or even an empty plot being there when we arrived, terrified me.

"Plus, I have a surprise to show you."

I looked up at him, confused, and waited.

"Come on," he said, as he started walking down the stairs, dragging me along.

We walked out of the front door, and I stood on the front porch, shocked. "You got it to start?" I rubbed my eyes and waited for the mirage to disappear.

His Camaro was parked out in the driveway, roaring with life. I joined him in excitement as I ran to the passenger side. He opened my door and ushered me in. This world was different here, yet the same. The grocery store always had food and supplies as if when the sun rose, then the world reset itself, but to have a car to get around quicker was going to be nice. I sat down and buckled up as my dad ran around to the driver seat.

"How long have we been here?" he asked, as he shifted the car in drive.

"Well, if my calculations are right, considering that this place doesn't run on normal time, I'm guessing close to two months or so in the real world."

"Huh." He raised his shoulders. "After all this time, I could've fixed this baby back home in less than a month."

I laughed. "Well, to be fair, you have been busy with the bar, your sweet ex-wife, your favorite daughters, and even learning how to be a badass Immortal. It's been kind of crazy. I don't think you would've had the actual time."

He smirked, winking at me. "The original Immortal. But now I know how to fix it when we get back."

Not *if* we get back, but *when*.

I nodded and felt a little bit of hope grow back inside me. The break was definitely needed to get out of the house for a little while and breathe the fresh air today. A whole month without Ezra has felt like a lifetime. I hoped that he hadn't left Crystal Rock and was still trying to find us. I hoped that he hadn't given up on me yet.

I looked over at my dad, who was smiling like a giddy child with a new toy, and quickly wiped away the tear that was trying to show its ugly face today. I decided that today was not the day for sadness. Tomorrow I could cry. I rolled down the window and let my hair fly in the wind, blinding me as it went everywhere. The sun shined down on my face, and I enjoyed the peaceful and much needed moment.

We made the final turn before the dirt road to Aunt

Clara's home, and my stomach started to clench as the closeness made me feel so far away from everything. We drove up the winding bluff, and I exhaled as the little cottage came into view. My heart became happy to see the home I had been missing so much, only wishing that Aunt Clara would run out to greet me today, but at least the home was standing. My dad wrapped his arm around my shoulders and pulled me in with excitement.

"The car made it!"

I laughed. "Did you even doubt it for a second?"

He looked over and laughed. "I actually was shocked that it even started this morning."

The car came to a stop in front of the house as we both waited patiently, examining our surroundings before stepping out and walking to the front porch. I grabbed the railing and made my way to the door, twisting the knob and pushing the door open. I gasped when I realized we were not alone and immediately let my vines extend from my palms, grabbing the lady standing in the hallway and whipping her into the wall, pinning her hard against it.

Her body was just as shocked as my brain was as she tried to release herself from my grip.

"Who are you?" I yelled, inching closer to her, squeezing the vines tighter.

She gasped and struggled to speak. Her face became frightened. I slowly loosened the vines' grip slightly, enough to let her talk but not even think about escaping.

"Nicolai Cambridge," she choked out, as she was struggling to touch the ground with her feet.

"Cambridge?" I stood confused as my father grabbed

my wrists and slowly lowered them, letting the vines retract as he syphoned from me.

"Lady Cambridge," he said, as he squinted and walked closer to the mirage that we were surely seeing. "Izzy and Margo's mother."

My brain started to fire rapidly as I tried to fill in the holes of my own memory.

"Jimmy Greystone?" she asked, as my father nodded.

"Well, Jim Chamberlain now, but yes, back then."

"Immortality looks good on you. Your mother surely succeeded then." She grabbed her wrists and rubbed them before straightening her dress.

"Oxana, actually."

She was from a different time, and that I was sure of, considering her clothing. I stared at her silk navy dress, embroidered with a floral pattern, and an apron lining the dress and cuffs made of an animal hide that wrapped tightly around her forearms.

"Isadora's mother?" I asked again, confused. "Ragnar's w—"

"That bastard is nothing more than an enemy that is hiding somewhere in this place, plotting his next move against me." She scoffed as she glared back at us.

My eyes bulged as I realized she had no idea that Ragnar had been released into our world.

"You're going to want to sit down for this," I said and pointed toward the living room. "I'll go make us some of Aunt Clara's tea."

Her eyes followed me as I walked away, and I could hear her whispering to my dad about immortality. I smiled when I reached the cabinets of my familiar surroundings with the ingredients right where they should be back home.

Home.

I just wanted to get us home. It was time. Hopefully, our enemy's mother could help us, but I was not holding my breath if she was anything like Isadora.

Chapter 5

Aisling Meadows

The mirror's reflection did not look like me at all with the scar formed across my abdomen. I glared back at the betrayal that my own bloodline caused. I hated to admit that the healed wound still felt wide open and pain radiated from the site, but with everything else going on, I figured my pain was the least of our worries.

Isadora had ruined so much, and yet here she was, alive and breathing on the same Earth as me. And now, Ragnar had been released.

What was she thinking?

My own blood to set him free.

What a joke.

This whole time I thought my blood could kill an Immortal, when in truth that rumor was just spread to find an heir to release that psycho from the dagger prison world.

I hugged myself tighter, trying to hide the wicked scar and hold myself together so I didn't crumble. We needed to find Haven and Jim to mend Freya. My own pain and self-loathing could wait, but I knew one thing was for sure. I was going to kill Ragnar myself. I grabbed my green flannel off the bed and wrapped it around my body to help hold me together before heading down the hall to face Aunt Lynn and the boys.

I took a deep breath and let my own emotions go, putting my game face on to conquer today. I walked toward the kitchen where the coffee was brewing and aromas filled the entire house.

"Morning, babe," Declan said, as I reached the cabinet.

"Morning." I smiled and filled my mug to the brim, not leaving any room for the creamer or sugar that were patiently waiting for me on the table. I leaned back against the counter and studied the weather, trying to distract myself from being bossy to Declan for not already being dressed and ready to search the east side of Crystal Rock for any signs of Ragnar's disgusting self.

Aunt Lynn smiled back at me and stood up, wrapping her robe tight around her body as she reached me and rubbed my shoulder before sitting down in the living room.

Ragnar had to be laying low because in the past few weeks, we had only spotted him once, and it was from the back of his head, but I knew it was him. I could *feel* him trying to weasel his way into my head. Eric warned me that he could do that with or without his magic. He had a way of manipulating the mind, and that was for sure not going to happen to me. He already used me for my blood, and that was enough.

Ezra walked into the kitchen, dressed and ready for the search. "You guys ready?"

"Well, some of us are." I smirked as I watched Declan

roll his eyes. "Do you plan on going back home anytime soon? You know Aunt Clara misses you."

He inhaled slowly and seemed to want to avoid the question all together.

"Ez, seriously, we are safe here. You can take the protection shield down now. You are draining yourself trying to keep out the poor little spiders from getting in." I laughed as he walked next to me and leaned against the counter, mimicking me with his filled mug. It seemed as if caffeine was our new daily meal these days.

"Can't I just stay a little longer?" He looked at Declan with pleading eyes. "I just don't want anyone else getting hurt. Clara has her own protection spells on her house and pottery shop. She is probably safer than any of us with no blood relation."

I stared at him and waited for him to meet my gaze. "Ez, you can stay as long as you want. But under one condition." I looked at Declan as he smirked. "Stop intruding on our date nights." I laughed as Aunt Lynn choked on her coffee from across the table. Declan's smirk grew into a smile when he realized what I had said out loud. He had been wanting to say it himself the last few weeks but hadn't dared to upset me while recovering. And Ezra had been so protective since the fight that he didn't mind having the extra protection over me.

"Fine, just don't make me hang out with Freya. That still hurts."

I watched as he fidgeted with the coffee mug before refilling it. I winced for him, understandably so, considering that they were twins. She was a constant reminder of Haven. I nodded and patted him on the back.

"Good, now let's go hunting."

Declan stood and walked to the bedroom to change.

"Hey, you know we haven't checked over the bridge yet, near the pottery shop and casino. Maybe we start there today?" I asked Ezra.

He froze. "Casino is a good idea," he answered, as he turned to wash his now empty mug. "I'd like to check on Ember."

"And the pott—"

"No." He slammed his fists down on the countertop, breathing heavily. "Please, just not there."

"Ez, you have to get back there someday."

"Just... not yet. Please, Ais, it just hurts to go where she's not. You being my Anchor is the *only* thing keeping me here, and if I keep reminding myself that she's gone from the places she's supposed to be, then I'll end up breaking. Okay?" He exhaled heavily as he rubbed the countertop.

"Okay, Ez," I said, rubbing his shoulders. "We can skip the pottery shop today. But please talk to Clara. She could really use some company." I hugged him. "She's hurting too." Then, I walked away faster than he could argue with me.

I knew I was right, and I knew he needed the comfort from her just as much as she did.

I stepped outside and left the front door slightly cracked as I waited on the porch for the men to join me. I listened carefully as I heard Aunt Lynn chime in.

"She's right, you know."

Ezra inhaled and exhaled slowly. "I'm an asshole, aren't I?"

She laughed. "Far from it. If anything, you are too nice. I've watched how you protect my niece these last few weeks, and I must say that I give you tremendous applause for your dedication to her. I know you are hurting, but Clara misses Haven too. I spoke with her earlier, and she really could use your help back at the shop so she can focus on finding them too."

The door opened as Declan joined me on the porch.

"Spying on them?" He smirked as he elbowed me.

I huffed and crossed my arms in my own stubbornness that would surely be the death of me one day. "I just know I'm right."

He smiled as he reached for me and closed our distance. "Aren't you always?" He lifted me into his arms and kissed my lips. I could feel his smile growing between us.

I laughed as I nodded. "Of course I am."

The door opened. "Alright, alright. Come on, you guys. Let's get going. Casino and pottery shop it is," Ezra said, as he walked between us, separating the two of us to an arm's length. "I'm driving. Y'all can make out in the back seat, sick-o's."

I laughed as Declan shook his head and lifted me into his arms and carried me to the car, opening the door before setting me down and hopping in the front seat by Ezra.

"Hey." I reached in my pocket and handed Ezra and Declan each a bracelet that Aunt Lynn and I had worked on last night. "Here, just in case we find Ragnar. This should keep him out of our heads." I exhaled. "*Should* is the key word here, boys."

Declan stared at the piece of leather and sniffed it

before wrenching his neck back in disgust. "What the hell is that?"

I laughed as I slipped my own on. "It's supposed to ward off evil."

"Well, I thought I was a good person, but it sure as hell is warding me off too." He laughed as he grabbed the door handle and pretended to be pulled out of the car by an unnatural force. I wanted to laugh, but this was not the time.

So, instead I glared back at him.

"It's been soaked in a Sea Holly plant thingy. I don't know if it's even gonna work. But Aunt Lynn helped me marinate them last night as a possible theory."

"Has she tried it on my dad?" Declan asked, as he slipped the bracelet on.

"Why would she try it on him?" I stared at him, confused.

He shrugged. "I figured since he could manipulate Isadora's mind that somehow he had the whole mind invasion thing too."

Ezra's eyes grew wide. "Ew, do you think he's related to him?"

I rolled my eyes. "Definitely not."

Declan glared back at Ezra.

"He must've mind melted your brain too, Declan, otherwise you'd be a lot smarter." Ezra laughed as Declan shoved him in an annoyed, brotherly way before we all laughed together.

My mind wandered as I thought of Jim and Haven missing still, all while Ragnar was free because of my own blood. My scar burned as I thought of him, and I wanted to rip my insides out and not have any part of that blade ever being in me to begin with. I glared out of the window as we drove, knowing that I needed to be the one to kill him. I needed to take back my pride and not feel like a vulnerable child.

I am from the original bloodline. I am stronger than him.

I watched as Ezra opened his phone and called Clara.

I heard the relief in her voice when she heard him and smiled to myself.

Chapter 6

Jaxon Oakes

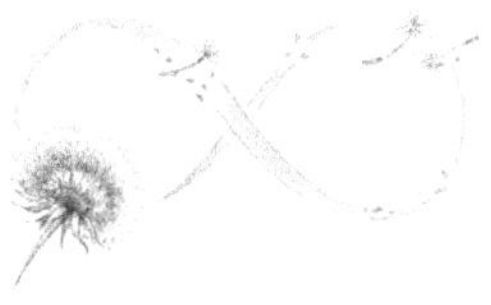

The urgent knock on the door made me jump, even though I knew Clara should be here by now. I looked down at my watch and got up to open it. Something inside me told me to stop as I felt tension between me and the doorknob. I hesitated and took a step back as another knock came through. I inched over to look through the blinds and froze. I walked back over and opened the door.

"Hey, Ember. Sorry, I thought you were someone else."

She smiled and giggled like a child. "Nope, just me. Is Freya here?"

I shook my head and invited her in. "Also, just me. Sorry to disappoint."

She frowned as she walked into the home and made her way to the kitchen, making herself comfortable as if she owned the place.

"Is there something I can help you with?" I asked, as I grabbed her a mug and filled it with coffee, but when I turned, she was gone. "Ember?"

I looked around and wondered what the hell just happened.

Was I seeing things?

I heard the stairs creak, and out of panic, I ran to them and halted when Alex came walking down the stairs sleepily.

"Who were you talking to?"

I turned around and searched the house one last time before scratching the stubble growing along my jawline. "Huh. Ember was just here."

She looked past me and pointed with her brows furrowed.

I turned and followed her stare and saw Ember on the front porch, staring out into the street.

"Coffee is hot in the kitchen," I told Alex. "I'll be right back."

She nodded and walked past me.

I inched my way outside, cautiously watching Ember's stance. "Are you okay?"

She jumped as I reached her, turning with her eyes wide and filled with tears before collapsing into my arms and sobbing.

I stood awkwardly, trying to figure out what the hell was happening as I embraced her. "Ember, please talk to me. I can't help you if I don't know how to fix it."

"Why do you always want to fix things?" She pushed back away from me and wiped her tears. "Everything is the same here but so different. I just want my old life back."

I stood, confused. "What are you talk—"

"I thought you were the smart one." Her face changed from sadness to annoyance. I had only known her for a short while, but she had never acted like this before. I watched her cautiously as I lowered my hands behind my back and let the magic flow from the gravel near me to connect with my intentions of protection.

"Ember, look at me."

Her doe eyes looked back to mine, then glared. "Where is it?"

"Where is what?" Before I could make another move, she teleported and disappeared from my sight.

I let my palm lower and the connection to the earth settle before I looked up and down the street and walked back inside.

"What was that all about?" Alex asked, as I contemplated what had just happened behind the now closed front door.

"I have no idea."

Alex studied my expression and froze. "Ragnar." She gasped. "Do you think he's messing with her head?"

"I doubt she has been the one to find him after all of us have been searching without luck."

"Then, what did she want?"

I looked up at Alex and shook my head. "I'll text Freya and see if she knows anything."

"Good idea. I'm going to go lay back down."

"No, absolutely not." I jumped up and blocked her way to the staircase. "We have painting to do." And with that Clara came walking through the front door without knocking, smiling for the first time since Haven vanished.

"I had a vision," she announced. "They're alive. I saw them driving that silly old Camaro."

Without hesitation, I ran for the garage where I had

stored the Camaro to be repaired as my promise to Jim. I had been lucky that the semi driver donated the car back to us after our encounter with him as a thank you for saving himself and his family from Izzy's compulsions. I swung the door open hard, ready for it to fly off the hinges if they were inside it. Flicking the light on, my hope disappeared as the car was still sitting in the garage, still waiting to be repaired. It was definitely not drivable in its state. I leaned against the doorway, crossing my arms and debating on going back to bed myself. Today was turning into a shitshow.

I walked back into the house and watched as Clara and Alex stood hopeful for news that was not going to be what they wanted. I stayed silent, unable to find the words, and instead just shook my head.

"Okay, well, it means something. My visions are not perfect, but they do work." She paced back and forth. "We're not doing any good standing here while there is paint that needs to dry. Why don't we go brainstorm at the bar?" Clara smiled, and hope didn't leave her, which made me feel it too.

I nodded and smiled back at her. "I'll drive us." I swung my keys around my finger and headed for the door.

The bar was exactly as we had left it. I flicked the switches and let the lights make the place seem alive again. I walked to the jukebox and played *all hits* before walking to the office and grabbing the paint cans.

Alex and Clara stood close and were whispering while I ignored them and got to work. I needed to open this damn bar back up for Jim. Or maybe it was a new distraction for me, considering that JFK was tainted now, and a home there for Freya and I seemed long gone. She couldn't even make herself go to the field since that day. I just needed something more to keep my hands busy. I was just as pissed as everyone else, but I had to keep quiet, just like I did while I grieved for my parents. I could handle my own pain in silence while the others fell apart around me. But damn it, I missed them too, and it killed me knowing that I could've saved them had we not rushed the thyme spell. There had to have been another way. I set down the paint cans, faster than I had anticipated, and one bounced before it spilled.

"Damn it!" I yelled and grabbed the rag from my back pocket while bending down to wipe it up.

Alex cleared her throat and stood in front of me with the paint can, levitating it in front of my eyes as she used her free palm to redirect the paint back into the can, erasing the mess.

She grabbed the now full can and reached her other hand down for me.

I grabbed it and shook my head. "Sorry."

Her eyes seemed to twinkle as she moved her hand to my bicep and rubbed it gently. "No, *I'm* sorry, Jaxon. I have not been myself, and I think you are right. Jim wants this place open again." She inhaled slowly and nodded. "So damn it, we're going to get it back up and running. Thank you for bringing me here."

I didn't know if she used her juju on me or what, but a calm came over me. It might have been just the motherly moment I needed to give me a little more hope for myself that not everything was ruined. I smiled and nodded as she pulled me in for a hug.

She stepped back and grabbed the brushes, handing one to Clara and giving me the roller before emptying the paint into the tray. "Let's get this done."

We all exhaled and headed for the wall with wet brushes of seafoam green—the color that they picked out as the only compromise with Alex's choice of sunshine yellow and Jim's navy blue. I laughed when they first showed me the color, but now standing with the paint in hand, the seafoam green reminded me of the Mississippi River, and that reminded me of home. So, in my opinion, it was a good choice after all.

Chapter 7

Freya Chamberlain

Callum headed for the kitchen where Margo was still unboxing their belongings, settling back into their old home, hoping this time it would last forever for them. She looked up from the last box of pans and walked over to hug me. My body stiffened, not meaning to upset her, but closeness from anyone right now had me on edge.

"I'm sorry," I stepped back. "I'm just—"

"Hush," she said, as she smiled again. "I get it. This is not how things were supposed to turn out, and it seems unfair to have happiness and closeness while you don't know if your father and sister are alive."

She took the words right out of my mouth.

I nodded as I looked back down at the ground, ashamed that I felt that way but happy to know someone understood.

"We're going to get them back." She rubbed my shoulder cautiously. "I promise."

Irritation grew inside me with the promises everyone kept making that didn't mean shit until we knew more. So, instead, I just looked up and tried to smile.

"Let's just get to work."

She nodded as Callum walked next to me with his hands full of jars filled with spices, candles, and a black cat perched on his shoulder.

"Say hello to Tinker. She's our mascot, and with all the bad luck we've been having, I figured she could help balance out the superstitions. Plus, she has been hanging around the backyard ever since we got back."

I leaned in to scratch her ears as she purred excitedly before jumping into my arms. I couldn't help but smile, and a slight happiness came over me that had been missing for the last few weeks. Margo looked up and smiled.

"Hi, Tinker," I said, as I walked into the living room with the souls overhead. With Miss Furball still in my arms, I stared up in wonder and watched the souls swarm above us. Tinker inched her way closer to the ceiling and stretched her neck out as high as she could, sniffing curiously. She purred loud as she watched them move along in a synchronizing dance.

I wondered if she knew someone up there. I shook my head as daydreaming was not in the cards today. I had a job to do. Tinker leaped from my arms onto the floor, good timing so I didn't have to be the jerk to send her away.

"You ready?" I asked Eric, as he straightened his suit and stepped away from the cat who tried to rub against his leg. He shuddered in a way that made me laugh. "Are you afraid of a cat?"

He looked back at me, annoyed. "Black cats and me have a slight history of not getting along."

"The big bad Immortal is afraid of a tiny, four legged,

harmless, purring cat." I snorted as I watched him shoo her away from him.

"You'll see why soon enough." He raised his eyebrow and smirked. "If you can even find the slightest magic to help with these souls. A witch who doesn't have magic." He tsked as he shook his head before looking back at me.

"Harsh."

"Leave my cat fear out of this, and I will leave your lack of magic out too."

I rolled my eyes as I spit and brought my hand out his, ready to shake on the pact that I didn't want being brought back up today. "You act like a child, but deal."

He laughed. "Let's move along now, sweet niece of mine."

As soon as his hand came out and touched mine, my entire body shifted into another dimension as the room spun and disappeared. Panic cinched in my gut like a vision was coming on, only instead, the living room came back into view with the souls swimming melancholy above.

"What the hell wa—"

"Shhh..." he whispered, pointing to the souls. "We're here, so pick the first one that we want to help along to peace. Their magic will flow to their heir of choice once complete."

I looked around the room wide-eyed when I realized we were not in our world anymore. We were somewhere new, even though it looked like Jaxon's home.

"I don't understand. Where are we?" I asked, genuinely concerned and trying to wrap my head around our whole situation. I could feel my nausea grow. I grabbed my stomach as Eric steadied me.

"It'll pass."

I nodded and swallowed hard.

"We're in the middle. It's a safe space I created centuries ago, and it's helping hold the souls together. They'll be able to choose their destination, almost like a fork in the road."

"Like heaven and hell?"

He laughed. "Not exactly. The souls had unfinished business when they were brought here by Izzy. Their souls had the choice to follow their loved ones along until the business was complete or they could run along to peace if they felt fulfilled."

I crossed my arms and tapped my foot. "You're bullshitting me."

He shrugged. "Are we going to waste all day chit-chatting? Ragnar is still free, out there roaming the earth. The more time we waste, the more opportunities he has to regain his magic and plot against us."

"Fine, let's start."

I looked up and studied the souls above but was drawn to one in particular that was bouncing excitedly. I had the strangest feeling that this was the one that I needed to start with. I pointed to the soul, and as soon as my finger locked onto the small whimsical light, it attached to my palm with an electric blue string, as if I was fishing in the river and caught it. I jumped back, shocked at the magic coming from my fingertips without my trying. I looked over to Eric, who nodded and waved his hands.

"It's normal."

"My magic?"

He shook his head. "This soul world is a little different

when it comes to the supernatural. We're still working on your magic part."

I looked back down, worried that I was hurting the soul.

He nodded again and motioned for me to reel it in. I shifted my wrists and waited to catch the soul in between my palms. When the bouncing soul reached me, I slowly enclosed it in my palms and felt it tickling as it bounced around.

Eric's hand hovered over mine as he closed his eyes.

"This next part will feel sort of like a mirage or a dream. Just stick close to me."

I followed suit, and before I knew it, a small jolt zinged through me. Opening my eyes, I was astonished that we were yet again somewhere else, except this place seemed peaceful and full of life. I smiled when I saw a middle aged man standing in front of us. Something about him was so simple that it gave me no fear. I knew instantly that he was the soul I had picked.

"Howdy, I'm Levi. I think you met me cat, Tinker." He spoke with a heavy southern accent that was hard to understand.

He tipped his cowboy hat down and lowered his upper body into a bow.

I smiled. "Hi, I'm Freya, and this is Eric—"

"Yes, I know who he is." Levi glared at Eric before turning back to me with a much kinder face.

"Hey, I kept your stupid cat alive, as promised. Even though she's scratched me more times than I'd like."

The man snorted, slapping his leg. "That's my girl. She never did like other men."

"Wait, that cat is yours?"

The man nodded.

"How old is she?" I studied his fringed leather cowboy hat and red bandana slung across his long sleeve button down that seemed to have a pungent smell, as if he'd not had a clean pair of clothes for years, if not centuries.

The man looked up and grinned. "Eh, what would we say, Eric? About three hundred years now?" He shrugged. "Time runs differently here. I'm not exactly sure."

Eric muttered under his breath, "Too long," before looking back at Levi. "Sure, somewhere around that."

"That cat is three hundred years old?" My jaw dropped as I remembered her in my arms seeming as if she was just a kitten still, playful and limber. "But, how?"

Levi studied my dumbfounded look and laughed. "Ain't you a witch?" His heavy cowboy accent made the words seem to slur together.

I nodded.

"Magic, my dear. Magic in yer world can do anythang if you know what yer' doing with it. And, mind you, with good intentions. Evil hearts will always destroy themselves before the world." He winked.

I stood, confused, wondering how much time in a prison world it would take to make you lose your mind.

"Alright, Levi, we've got a busy day ahead of us. Let's get to it," Eric said.

Levi nodded. "One more thing." He walked closer and hugged me. "I think Tinker likes that Callum guy a lot. Do you mind keepin' an eye on her for me?"

"For as many years as I'm alive, sure."

He grinned. "I will take down her life spell and let her

live a normal cat life minus the extra nine she's been given from here on out."

"You mean you could've done that years ago? Do you know how much cat food she goes through?" Eric asked in annoyance. "Declan became fond of the damn thing, but she would always come and go as she pleased."

Levi laughed, giddy like a child winning a game. "Course, I know."

I laughed with Levi at the harmless game he played, and to be fair, Eric probably needed that constant company for the last three hundred years while dealing with a psychopath. Poor Tinker, though, having to rely on him to feed her.

Eric put his hand on Levi's shoulder and reached his other hand out for mine. I hesitated for a moment before giving in. I held on tight while watching Eric's expression soften as he gave me a reassuring nod.

"I've got you, Freya," he whispered, as he rubbed my palm gently.

Instantly, a sense of calm washed over me. As much as I wanted to hate the man, he was my uncle, and he really was protective of me and my family. And for the first time, he reminded me of my dad. I exhaled slowly, closing my eyes. Seconds later, a cooling tingle rushed through my entire body. I opened my eyes just in time to watch Levi start to glow with a million tiny orbs surrounding him. He smiled, mouthing the words "thank you" as he started to float away, and in the blink of an eye, he was gone, and we were back in the room, looking up at the swarming souls above us.

"You good, kid?"

I nodded before staring back up at the souls, feeling a warmth of euphoria rush through me as the excitement of helping a soul find his way back home made me feel magical in my own self.

"That was amazing." I smiled and jumped up and down with a giddiness that I hardly recognized. "Let's go again."

Eric laughed and pointed toward the ceiling, extracting a soul of his choice this time and bringing it down between his palms. "Hold on for this one. She's a little feisty." He inhaled heavily, bracing himself. "Laney."

I held my breath as I grabbed onto his arm and waited for the next adventure.

Chapter 8

Haven Vine

Lady Cambridge's story made my head spin. I sat quietly, sipping on Aunt Clara's overload recipe, and tried to understand the full story.

"So, you created the dagger world to trap your own husband but got sucked in with him?"

She nodded. "Sacrificed is a better word. I knew I had to get him out of our world before he destroyed it. He was one of a kind. He had his chaos magic surfacing. It was a magic so dark and evil that it—"

"Wait... chaos magic? I've never heard of that. Not even in any of the books or grimoires that I've studied."

Lady Cambridge nodded. "That's a good thing. Chaos magic is only gained by murdering your bloodline and consuming their souls. It is the darkest of all forms of magic. He tried to make Izzy do the same with her sister." Lady Cambridge began to tear up, and I realized that she didn't know that Margo was alive after all. "It is nothing to be proud of. The power he held could split the grounds of

Earth and raise hell itself." She shook her head. "Such an unnecessary power for anyone to hold. He wanted to be all powerful and destroy all others that had magic. That was, of course, before we had daughters born with power. His power was... 'Lost' is the best way to describe it. And he had been on a mission ever since, trying to gain the chaos back so he could destroy our world and rule. He wanted to be the only powerful one. He wanted to choose who stayed in our world. He thought of himself as a god. He was one selfish bastard, to say the least."

"Why marry someone like him?" I asked.

It was my dad's voice that surprised me. "She did it to kill him."

I looked back at him, confused.

Lady Cambridge nodded. "I was sent to marry him and kill him in his sleep."

My eyes bulged as I processed. "Well, something went wrong, obviously. Because you have daughters with the villain."

She nodded again. "His mind control forced me into commencing on our wedding night. I had no choice. I underestimated him. His mind control was more powerful than I had planned on, and sadly, our village's plan to rid him was destroyed the night of the wedding when we conceived. An unplanned event that weakened me from my full magical potential to overthrow him while carrying the twins. The twins were syphoning my magic and made me weak in a magical sense but strong in a motherly one. I do not regret them for a second. I only wish that I wouldn't have underestimated his power."

"You lived with him, though. You had so many chances."

"I did. The day my girls were born, his chaos disappeared from him, and he only had his mind games left, which seemed to deteriorate more until my final days with him. Plus, I learned how to keep him out of my head over the years."

"What did you do?"

She smiled. "As a woman and mother, my mind was stronger than his." She lifted her wrist. "And this bracelet soaked in this pungent herb helps too."

"He's free now in our world, did you know that?" I frowned. "How do we fix that?"

She frowned and shook her head. "I assumed so when I could no longer find him here." She huffed. "First, we need to get out of here."

"Where exactly is 'here?'" my dad asked.

"Jimmy, do you remember when you were a child and your mother used to tell you the story of the middle for soul safety?"

He nodded. "Eric used to bring us there when I was scared."

She smiled and nodded. "This is considered the middle. We are not in a prison world but not dead, either. I was left in the dagger world while it was crumbling, but then a burst of light appeared, and next thing I knew, I was transferred here."

"But the middle was a place for souls to rest until unfinished business was completed before Valhalla. We used to search for our sister there."

She nodded. "This is no prison world. I lived in that other one for nearly a thousand years. This one is peaceful. Plus, here I can do this again."

She smiled, lifting her hands, letting pink energy dancing in her palms as she created an orb.

I lifted my palms and let the vines grow in mine, shaping them into a flower silhouette.

"Let's go back home," I said excitedly, feeling hope finally grow for the first time in weeks, months, years. However long we've been here.

She looked at my dad and studied his expression. "Jimmy, do you not remember how to leave?"

My dad's eyes bulged as he realized he was the key to leaving this place.

"Why me? Can't you use that pink twirling stuff to send us home?"

Panic began to make my heart race as I realized there was nothing more I could do to get us home after all. It depended on my dad who was still relearning his magic.

She laughed. "Oh boy. This is going to take longer than I thought."

She stood up and walked over to him.

"What is he supposed to do?" I asked.

"Well, for starters, he and his brother helped make this place. When they were children, they would come here to hide when war would break out before Eric was old enough to fight in them."

My dad stood and shook his head. "I don't remember how to leave."

Lady Cambridge rubbed his shoulder. "That's because

Eric would bring you here. I just always assumed that you knew how to get in and out yourself too."

Hope deflated as I realized we were right where we started, only with an extra companion this time. "Well, let's get to training, Dad."

He nodded, and without hesitation, Lady Cambridge followed us out to the Camaro.

"JFK?" he asked, and I nodded as he revved up the engine. We took off to our training grounds where we were going to learn how to get back home.

* * *

"Again," Lady Cambridge yelled at my dad while pushing back against him with a pink rage, forcing him to the ground.

"Hey, maybe you should take it a little easy on him," I said.

"Fear is what led Eric to opening this window. So, whether it was Eric at the scene that transferred them or somehow Jim opened this place to save you, then we need to trigger that same fear to get something to unlock," Lady Cambridge yelled while I sat quietly under the tree.

I knew she was right, and the thought of going back home seemed much more intriguing than another day watching the sun and moon rise and fall from the Mississippi River.

My father nodded. "She's right."

I laid my head down and stared up at the branches of the lone tree, then froze as I watched the shimmer of them expand and start to glow brighter with a million colors dancing among the leaves. I blinked rapidly, trying to focus my gaze on the mirage above me.

The shimmering glowed brighter and began to swim through the bark of the tree. I sat up and turned quickly, ready to break my back at the sight.

"What the—"

Before I could say anything, Lady Cambridge was beside me, staring at the glow. "How did you do that?"

I shook my head, jaw still to the ground. "I didn't do anything." I stood up just in time for my dad to reach us, dusting off the remaining JFK field that he was buried into a second ago.

"Dad, did you?"

He shook his head. "Wasn't me, kid." He walked cautiously closer to the bark and raised his hand, merely inches from it before touching the tree. "Whoa, it's tickling." He raised his other hand and touched the glowing tree.

Lady Cambridge followed suit and leaned against it. "Who's magic is this?"

I closed the feet between me and the glowing tree and laid my palms upon it. Within a second, my body jolted from the tree, my eyes closing as I flew through the blue sky and waited for impact.

The electricity flowed through me as darkness consumed me. The blue sky faded, and the impact never came as everything around me disappeared, and Jaxon's home appeared for the briefest moment.

"Freya?" I whispered, as I saw her and Eric standing

under the souls reaching for one. Freya froze and turned toward me, eyes as wide as the ocean.

"Haven?" Her tear filled eyes looked back at me before the entire room was gone and the impact of JFK finally rushed against my body as I skidded across the field and the world, whichever world I was in, went dark.

Chapter 9

Freya Chamberlin

I dropped to the ground as my body began to shake uncontrollably. Tears rolled down my cheeks with no time to wipe them. Eric dropped to his knees and tried to keep me from breaking apart.

"Hey, hey, hey, what's happening? Freya? Look at me. What happened?" He frantically shook me, trying to get me out of a trance that I didn't realize I was in. I sucked in a big gulp of air and looked around the soul room, trying to see her again. But it was only Eric and I and the ceiling filled with souls.

I wiped the snot running from my nose and grabbed my hair, trying to keep whatever sanity I had left in me together.

"Haven," I sniffled. "I saw her."

Eric sat down as he tried to process.

"Freya, it's just you and me here." He shook his head and huffed in defeat. "Maybe you've had enough soul saving today."

I shook my head.

He exhaled. "Yes, let's call it for—"

"No!" I yelled. "I'm fine. I want to keep going."

"Listen, kid... I need to keep your strength up, and with all this soul stuff, I think it's messing with your emotions right now."

"I said, I'm fine." I stopped crying and glared back at him. "I saw her. It was Haven."

"That's not possible. We're not even in our world. This is the middle. A safe space for..."

He froze and his brows furrowed.

"What did you just call this place?" I stood up.

Eric's frozen state continued as the wheels began to turn in my own head.

"A safe space..." He jumped up and ran outside of the home. "Jim? Haven?"

I followed after him and stood on the front porch, watching him run down the empty street. "Jimmy! Haven!" He yelled, looking up and down the street frantically.

Both hope and adrenaline started to flow through me, and for a brief moment, I felt a tingle of magic try to ignite inside me. I looked down at my palms and made a tight fist before whispering, "Ignis," then opened my palm slowly.

Nothing.

Ugh. I rolled my eyes and ran after Eric. He finally stopped at the end of the block and crouched down in the middle of the road, trying to catch his breath.

I reached him and sat down next to him, breathing heavily. "What's... going... on?"

He inhaled sharply and looked at me, seeming vulnerable in his state of hysteria. He laid his back flat against the empty road and stared up at the fast rolling night's sky, stars shining brighter and coming through faster than in our mortal world. His silence made me begin to panic.

I took a deep breath to try and calm my nerves before laying my head back, counting to ten slowly against the rough asphalt, and joining him in the silence, looking up at the stars shimmering. Minutes passed that felt like hours, and still, he said nothing. My mind started to consume itself with fear and loathing at never seeing my dad and sister again. My palms began to sweat, and I needed to clear my head before I made myself sick.

"The middle is a safe space," he finally broke his silence.

I held my breath and listened.

"We're in the middle right now. I was wondering if your father was able to open this world seconds before that blade came down on him and Haven." He inhaled sharply. "It gave me a small moment of hope that maybe, just maybe..."

I sat up quickly and looked around. "You think they're here?"

He inhaled sharply. "I had hope."

"Had or have?"

He sat up and leaned his elbows against his knees, his emerald eyes staring back at me with defeat. He looked like a young teenager, lost and trying to find his way. He put his head back down and inhaled sharply again.

"I made a promise to your father to always keep him safe. And right now, I'm not doing a hell of a good job at it." He shook his head and stared down the empty road. "I want to say they're here. I just can't do that to you or your mom or myself right now. I can't give you hope on a false lead." He ran a hand through his hair. "I should've checked it out on my own. I'm sorry for my outburst of emotions."

I huffed. "Are you kidding me?" I grabbed his arm and pulled him off the ground, hugging him tight. "You just gave me a rush of emotions, and that was the first time I've felt *anything* besides sadness in weeks. Any form of hope, I will take. And you just gave it to me." His body relaxed as he hugged me back.

"Freya, I really do want them back too."

I looked into his eyes. Sincerity filled them. "I know you do. And we will get them back. We're just one step closer now." I looked down at my palms as the tingle came back in my fingertips.

Maybe they were here after all?

I glanced up and down the road again with a new hope that hadn't been with me in a while and smiled. "Let's get home and start again tomorrow."

He looked down at me and smirked. "Now you've had enough?"

I laughed. "I want a clear head tomorrow for the reuniting of our family."

He smiled and nodded.

We started walking back to the soul house, but he stopped me in the middle of the road. He fidgeted as he tried to find his words. "Hey, kid. I know I may not be the hero in your story, but I sure as hell don't want to be the villain, either." He looked away quickly as he gathered his composure.

I laughed, hoping to clear the air of the tense emotions brewing within him. "You lost the villain card when you wrote me that letter." I winked and nudged him to keep walking.

He smirked as we continued to walk together.

As we stepped through the doorway, I hesitated. "Hey, do you mind not telling my mom about this?"

He raised his eyebrows.

"I just don't want to give her false hope, either. She's pretty fragile right now."

He nodded. "Probably a good idea." He waved his hand in front of him and had me lead our way back to our world.

Chapter 10

Jaxon Oakes

I turned the bar open sign on and turned off the fans that helped dry the paint. I stood back and admired our hard work for the day. The sea foam green actually worked for the atmosphere. Something about it gave the new fresh start it needed. Now I needed to end the night with making Jim's famous egg burgers and opening the door for Jack and the regulars to come back in.

It felt like coming home.

Alex turned to me and hugged me tight. I couldn't move my arms around her as she had a grip around me, keeping me still. She laughed as she realized and loosened her grip.

"Sorry," she whispered.

I smiled and hugged her again. Only, this time properly. "Are you kidding me? No apologies needed. You were right about this color. It looks good."

She looked around the newly painted bar and smiled. "Seafoam green reminds me of the river. Makes me happy."

"Happy is good." I let her go and kept one arm around her shoulders, keeping her close.

"Jim will love it." She smiled, and for the first time, she didn't use his name in the past tense. Whatever happiness she was feeling, I was going to let it keep growing.

The front door opened, and I felt relief when Freya walked in with Eric following behind her. Both smiling too. Whatever tonight was going to be... happiness was definitely part of it.

Clara walked in from the kitchen, "Hey, Jaxon, I don't know what the heck I'm doing back here." She laughed with whole eggs in her hands as she raised them up and shrugged.

"I'm coming." I laughed. "Give me a second."

She nodded and smiled.

The bar just had a good vibe, and nothing could change that tonight.

I walked over to Freya and lifted her before she even made her way to the bar stools. "Hey, beautiful." I carried her into the office and set her down on the desk, not caring whose eyes followed.

She smiled and kissed me. "I missed you today," she whispered and then kissed me again.

Something good happened. She knew something.

I grabbed her face and drew back. "Good day?"

"Amazing." She smiled and pulled me between her legs, holding me tight. "The soul freeing was such a good feeling. We saved about fifty of them today. Oh, and that cat is part of your family now." She laughed. "It's a long story for another day... But hey, let's get to making Dad's burgers."

I nodded and smiled. "Aisling said that her and Declan are with Ezra on a lead so they won't make it until later."

Freya shrugged. "I may have a lead. But I won't know for sure until tomorrow." She put her fingers to my lips and closed them from questioning her further.

I wanted to know more, but I was happy to see her smiling today. I knew that whatever had happened she would tell me when she was ready. I smiled and kissed her lips once more. "Alright, come on, let's get in that kitchen before Clara burns dinner."

She nodded as I helped her hop down, kissing her one more time and walking behind her with her neck cradled in my arm.

Walking into the bar was a moment that felt right. Lynn walked through the door and came over to Eric as he smiled from ear to ear. Clara and Alex were sitting at the booth now, laughing. They all looked up as Freya and I walked through the office door toward the kitchen. Then, the door opened again, and we all froze, staring at the doorway, blinded by the sunset making its way in. We all exhaled heavily as Jack and his other buddies walked through the door.

"About damn time you guys opened the bar back up. I was about to move out of Crystal Rock to the next hole in the wall," Jack said, as he walked straight to the bar and took his usual seat. "Where's Jimboy been?" he asked Freya, as she walked over to him with a beer, trying to open the glass bottle and freezing as he asked.

"He's... Um..."

I quickly interjected. "Jim's been away on business.

He's trying to bring on that new seasoning mix he made to get a label for it. He'll be back soon."

I watched as Freya inhaled slowly with relief. Secrecy and small lies for now would be what we needed to tell the town until Jim was back behind the bar. We couldn't let this town in the know about all our magical mishaps lately. We had to keep everyone safe.

Jack nodded and shrugged. "About damn time. Been telling him to sell that stuff for years."

I smiled as I grabbed Freya's hand and pulled the beer gently from her, flicking the top off before handing it to him. "He finally listened to you, Jack."

Freya nodded and walked away as fast as her legs would let her.

"This one's on the house. Welcome back."

Alex nodded toward the office as she walked behind the bar. "Hey, Jack. Good to see you." She smiled as she poured herself and Jack a shot of whiskey. Lynn came walking up behind me and grabbed the glasses to pour, putting her hand on my shoulder with a smile.

"Check on her, please. Lynn offered to help us out here," Alex whispered while wiping her lips of the liquor that surely would be burning her throat and warming her insides already.

I nodded and walked back to the office. I closed the door behind me, seeing Freya pace back and forth. I was sure she was debating on how long we would all have to lie to the locals about their favorite bar owner and fishing buddy. I walked up next to her and grabbed her arm, pulling her to a halt.

"Hey, one day at a time." I turned her to face me and

watched as her state of emotions were whirling inside her pretty little head. I grabbed her face and tried to make her focus on just me. "Hey, Freya, look at me." She huffed heavily trying to control her tears from spilling over. "Today is a good day, remember? We are not giving up." She nodded and sucked in a heavy breath.

"It's a good day," she repeated.

I nodded and smiled. "How about you come help me in the kitchen? Your mom is training Lynn behind the bar."

She smiled and grabbed my hand, squeezing it tight. "Thank you."

I pulled her closer to me, letting our fingers interlock. "I didn't do anything."

"Trust me, your presence is beyond helpful. Plus, every minute I have with you is always going to be bonus time that I never knew I was going to have back." She reached up and kissed me, lingering while on her tippy toes.

I smirked and lifted her up, kissing her with more urgency. I lifted her weightless body and walked back to the wall pushing her against it. Our kissing quickened. I could feel my heart beating a mile a minute, just like hers was. I just wished we had a damn minute alone.

I groaned.

"Let's head to the beach." She pulled back from my lips, whispering against them.

I smiled as she read my mind and then slowed my kisses and laughed because logically, it was not summer anymore. "It's freezing out."

She smiled. "You can keep me warm."

My hand squeezed her thighs as I wished it were possible.

"Babe, it's the middle of winter, and we have a villain on the loose."

She laughed. "You won't protect me?"

She toyed with my desires of need and being smart. I looked back at her and saw that excitement in her eyes. I didn't want to be the one to take the wind out of her sails tonight.

I kissed her again before setting her down and walking over to the closet, grabbing a blanket from inside. "How are we going to get out of here unnoticed?" I nodded toward the door.

"Just go out the back door, I'll meet you in a minute."

I frowned.

"It'll only be a minute." She scrunched her nose and pointed to the door, demanding me to lead the way.

I walked back to her and brushed against her lips. "Promise?"

"I promise," she said, as she grabbed me. "Now go."

"Fine. One minute, otherwise I'm coming back in after you." I smirked, walking out of the office and stepping back into the chaos of the bar. I kept close against the wall and headed straight to the kitchen where I watched as Eric took over making dinner, laughing with Clara. I figured it was now or never to sneak out of here, so I slipped out the back door.

* * *

The sand was cold, but the moon was bright enough to light the beach and the stars were flickering more than usual. The night sky was beautiful. Freya's lavender scent brought back so many memories as I laid on the beach with her. I hoped that my body was keeping her warm as we snuggled inside the blanket wrapped around us like a burrito.

"What are you thinking about?" I whispered, as I tucked her hair behind her ear.

She nuzzled closer, letting my body's warmth keep her from shivering. "Just that it's nice to be alone with you."

I chuckled. "The sand is a new one for me."

She laughed. "Well, with Eric practically living with us and most of us staying in groups for safety, I'd say the beach getaway was definitely worth it."

I sat up and grabbed my shirt, pulling it back over my head and handing her hers. "As much as I don't want to break this up, we really need to get back."

She frowned. "Reality is calling?"

"Yep."

She nodded as she stared at me, her cheeks burning red as she smiled. I laughed nervously, wondering what I had done as I buttoned my jeans and grabbed my shoes.

"What?" I asked.

"I love you."

I stopped tying my shoe and looked up, smiling. "I love you too, babe."

"I know. I'm a lucky girl." She blushed again and quickly grabbed her shoes.

I tossed mine aside and jumped on top of her, laying her back gently and kissing her lips. "I'm. The. Lucky. One," I said between kisses as she let my lips follow her neckline and back up. I grabbed her sides and began tickling her, letting the warmth of excitement run back through her, making both of our bodies forget about the cold November air.

"Alright. Alright." She laughed as she tried to get away from my hands. "You win," she yelled, still laughing.

"I win?" I asked with a smirk.

She laughed and nodded. "Just. Stop. Tickling. Me."

I smiled and stopped, lifting her off the ground. "Love you, Freya."

"You too."

I stood and grabbed her shoes, walking them back to her. We both sat and tied our shoes before soaking in the river's view for one more moment before heading back to reality.

"Those burgers are most likely cold by now, and Aisling and the boys should be back too," she said.

"Yeah. Let's get back before the world crumbles."

She inhaled quickly with panicked eyes, and I realized I ruined the moment.

"Only kidding," I said quickly.

She exhaled and nodded.

"Hey," I grabbed her hand and rubbed it. "Today is a good day."

She looked back up to me and smiled.

"Yes, yes, it is."

Chapter 11

Aisling Meadows

*I*t's him.

Every bone in my body knew who was lingering straight ahead of us.

Ragnar.

A sickness came over me as my stomach began to turn. The scar that helped send him free started to burn the closer we got to him. I paused and let him get a little more distance between us until the burning sensation disappeared. Surprisingly, he hadn't noticed us yet, which made me think that maybe he wasn't as strong as the stories we were recently told. I twisted the mind protecting bracelet as we inched our way closer.

Declan looked over to me with his brows furrowed.

"Do you feel that?" he whispered. "The head rush?"

I nodded. "He's trying to get in our heads. He knows we're here."

He nodded and twisted his bracelet.

I looked back at Ezra who looked back at us, confused.

I pointed to our bracelets and smiled, mouthing the words "they work" but he stared back at me and shrugged.

I rolled my eyes, annoyed that he wasn't on the same page as us. And instead, he seemed uninterested with our mission for today.

Ezra had been almost more attentive toward me the last few weeks, and for some reason, today, he decided to not care anymore. I turned around quickly and waved back to them to keep getting closer. The goal was to find him and see how close we could get without him mind melding our brains. Or really, it was my personal goal. Everyone else in the group told us to locate and not engage. Which, technically, we were 'not' engaging, just getting a closer look. I knew it was a dangerous move, but I needed to *see*, or better yet, *feel* what we were up against.

"Just let me go first," Declan said, as he halted us. "My Anchor isn't here so I can't be harmed."

Realizing he was right, I nodded. "Please be careful."

He smirked as he walked closer. I held my breath as he started to close the distance between them and exhaled slowly when I realized Declan was still unharmed by Ragnar, only an arm's length away from him now.

I jumped as Ezra's hand grazed mine, interlocking our fingers.

I turned toward him, glaring, and pulled our hands apart. His eyes seemed distant, like he was off in space somewhere.

What was I missing?

"Hey, you okay?" His pupils seemed to be extra large as he stared blankly back at me with a look that confused the hell out of me. "Ezra?"

Shit.

Ezra smirked as he didn't hesitate to make a move. He pushed me back into the alley and against the wall as his lips crashed into mine. His tongue tried to spiral its way into my mouth, and I wanted to gag but he was so strong.

"Ezra, stop," I screamed. I tried to contain my anger but was too upset. Then, I was even more mad at myself for drawing attention to us. I tried to push him off, to lower my voice and stay stern. "Ezra, stop now."

His lips continued to graze along my cheeks and lips while I kept dodging my head around. In the midst of trying to unlock his hand from mine, and his bruteness, I saw his pupils flicker a green that was not his normal shade. Then, I realized what was going on.

"Damn it, Ragnar." I grabbed Ezra's arms, needing to get out of this. "I'm sorry, Ez. You'll thank me later," I said, as I kneed him in the stomach and pushed him back out of the alleyway.

He crouched over and held himself. "Ais, what the hell was that for?"

"You kissed me!" I yelled louder than necessary. Then, I looked down at his wrist and anger boiled inside of me. I ran to him and grabbed his wrist, lifting it into the air. "You idiot! Where is it?"

His bracelet was nowhere to be found. I looked down at his eyes, and his pupils were back to normal. He seemed genuinely concerned about what he missed.

Now, guilt loomed over me as I wished I hadn't yelled so loud. Declan was already on his way back to us and his face was furious. His blue eyes were filled with rage, and I knew what was coming next. I tried to stay between them, hands up in surrender. But Declan dodged past my pleading arms while his fists came pounding down on Ezra, still kneeling and trying to put the moments together in his head.

"Get the hell away from her," Declan yelled, as he threw another fist at Ezra's jaw.

Ezra stood up, his muscles pulsing as the rage grew inside him. He blocked Declan's punch and pushed him back. The two started to brawl in the middle of the street. Luckily, the cool November air kept many onlookers inside the coffee shops. I waved the few off and tried to play off as if it was normal play.

I honestly could have stepped between the two, but they had both been on edge with each other recently. I felt like this was something that was necessary for them to grow up. I leaned back against the wall and crossed my arms in annoyance. But I froze as Ragnar turned around, scarred face and smirking from ear to ear. He lifted his arm in the air and dangled something in front of him, shaking his head. He dropped the object and pointed to his head before disappearing in thin air. I swore I saw a glimmer before he was gone. My insides turned as I realized his magic must be coming back, and we were running out of time while we played detective finding him. In reality, we needed to kill the bastard.

I gasped and ran between the boys fighting and pushed between them. "He's gone," I screamed and pointed to the end of the street. "We lost him. Thanks to you two."

Declan and Ezra stopped throwing fists and looked up in the direction Ragnar had been.

"You two let *him* get in between us." I smacked the

back of both their heads. "And, Ezra, where the hell is *your* bracelet?" I snarled through gritted teeth.

He looked down at his wrist and froze. "I swear I had it on. I thought I put it on in the car..." His expression became distant while he rummaged through his memories. "Well, actually, I don't remember putting it on. Wait..." He pointed to the sky, confused. "When did the sun set?"

"Shit," I said, pacing back and forth. "This whole time we thought we were tracking him, but he'd been following us since we left the house." I kicked the garbage can on the sidewalk, knocking it over and spilling empty coffee cups and napkins across the street. "This is all my fault." I grabbed my stomach and rubbed the scar, wanting that whole night to disappear. I looked up and gasped as I realized what my own selfish anger had done. I took a deep breath in and let go of my stomach, trying to repair the damage I had caused.

Ezra and Declan froze.

"Damn it." I tried to bend over and pick up the can, but Declan's hand stopped me as he hovered over me and lifted me into his arms, hugging me tight. Ezra rushed to collect the garbage and set the can back upright.

"Hey, it's not your fault. None of this is your fault." Declan hushed me as my emotions started to finally break the surface, making me feel vulnerable and on the verge of a mental breakdown, but I no longer could hide it anymore. I needed to let the tears flow. So, I did just that and sobbed like a baby. Uncontrollable, emotional tears streamed down my cheeks, trying to freeze from the cold air hitting them. If any onlookers were left, they would surely think we were all meant to be locked away or highly sedated somewhere far away from Crystal Rock. The town had no idea how much danger we were all in. Hell, we didn't even know.

Ezra stepped back and walked over to where Ragnar had disappeared. Declan lifted his sleeve and wiped my face, pinching my nose and removing the ugly snot running down my face. He laughed softly, making me chuckle at the small gesture that really made me feel like a child. He was the protector of my heart. I slowed my breathing and nodded while watching Ezra through my clouded vision as he bent over and picked up the object that Ragnar had dropped. Declan pulled me back in and held me tight, pulling my head under the crook of his neck and finally helping my mind relax. I closed my eyes and inhaled heavily to catch a solid breath of cold air.

Declan tilted my chin up as he moved my hair out of my face. "I'm sorry I got jealous."

I snorted as I wiped more tears. "Ezra had his tongue nearly down my throat. I almost punched him myself."

Declan smirked as he turned around and watched Ezra come back. "I shouldn't have punched him. He wasn't him." He shook his head as if disappointed with himself. He pulled my face closer to his, letting our lips meet, and I threw my arms around his neck.

All the tension that had been building the last few weeks dissipated, and for a moment, everything felt normal again.

He leaned back and then kissed my nose. "Those lips are mine."

I felt the rush of blood meet my cheeks as I nodded and smiled. "Yes." I grabbed his head and rested our foreheads together. "Only yours." I kissed his lips again as his shoulders relaxed, and he laughed quietly.

Ezra cleared his throat as he met us in the middle of the street. "Hey, guys, does this look familiar to you, or has my mind melted?"

He opened his palm, and low and behold, a bracelet laid perfectly in a circle. Only this was not the bracelet that was meant to protect our minds, this was a locator bracelet that my Aunt Lynn had given each of us weeks ago. I grabbed the locator bracelet and shook my head.

"I don't understand." I twirled it around between my fingers. "Why would he need a tracking bracelet?"

Declan cleared his throat as if he didn't want to state the obvious. But I was truly clueless.

I squeezed the bracelet in my palm and crossed my arms, waiting for an explanation.

Declan hesitated. "Has anyone talked to Ember lately?"

My eyes grew wide as the pieces of the puzzle started to come together.

Chapter 12

Haven Vine

"Please, let's just check," I pleaded while holding the ice to my forehead. "I know what I saw. At least... I think I do?"

My dad laughed as he drove us back home for the night or day or whatever time it was. "Sure, kid, we can go look."

Lady Cambridge whispered from the passenger seat while I laid back down in the back. "She did hit her head pretty hard, but in this place, anything is possible."

I lifted the ice pack off my head and watched as my dad's hands tightened around the steering wheel. He accelerated and let the engine roar to life.

Lady Cambridge gasped as the speed continued. "I have to admit, I've never actually been in one of these before." She reached for her seatbelt and pulled it tighter. "I mean, it's definitely much faster than a ship or horse but it's still a big hunk of metal without much protection."

I snorted as I realized her timeline was much different than ours. She had been locked away in a prison world for almost a thousand years and had had very little communication, if any at all. I sucked in my giggle and became empathetic for her loss of time. I wondered if the real world full of people would terrify her when we got home.

I froze as my mind said *when* instead of *if,* and I quickly shook my head as to not give myself false hope.

My dad laughed. "Oh, we can go much faster." The engine purred as Lady Cambridge squealed like a child on a roller coaster ride with excitement. He slowed the car, and they both laughed together.

She looked over to him and smiled. "I guess you were able to grow up in a more fun time than wars and sickness. You were very lucky, Jimmy."

"Lucky was me being able to marry my wife and have my girls. The fast cars were just a bonus over the years."

I smiled as I listened to their small talk, reminiscing of the past and what the future seemed to be now.

Minutes passed as we got closer to Jaxon's house. Their conversations had stopped, and the car ride became silent with nothing but the lull of the engine.

"Do you believe Izzy was killed?" she asked quietly.

My dad slowed the car to a halt as he pulled up in front of Jaxon's house, putting the car in park and not releasing the steering wheel. He grit his teeth before clearing his throat.

I sat up quickly before venom could be spilled. Regardless of the hate we had toward Isadora, this was still her daughter, and we truly didn't know the whole story. I touched my dad's shoulder. "We have no idea. The fight was still going on when a bright light came in and swept us away."

My dad stared out of the windshield silently.

Lady Cambridge nodded as she opened the door, but before stepping out, she turned back to face us. "I'm sorry. Our timelines are a little different. She was only a child when I brought Ragnar into the dagger world."

I nodded empathetically.

She stepped out and started to walk toward the house.

I patted his shoulder and tried to calm him. "She doesn't know all of the terrible things Isadora has done. Her biggest villain was her husband."

He inhaled slowly as he nodded. "I just can't forgive and forget. Now that I remember her trying to kill Margo, it was the same night that Lady Cambridge took Ragnar out of the world and brought him to the dagger world. I remember everything. And we wouldn't be here had Izzy never gone crazy with her father to begin with."

I nodded. "Let's just focus on getting back home. We can deal with that whole situation another time. You know... since we have plenty of *time* here." I smirked, making my dad laugh.

We stepped out of the Camaro and made our way to the porch to meet Lady Cambridge. The house seemed unoccupied, and nothing seemed out of the ordinary. I grabbed the door handle and turned it slowly, waiting for electricity to shoot me across the street.

Nothing.

I exhaled and pushed the door open.

Disappointment filled me as I walked into an empty house. I ran to the living room where I had seen Freya and expected something to be out of place, but instead, there was only a table with a lamp on it in the corner. I walked into the middle of the room where the souls were swimming and closed my eyes to listen carefully.

"Empty," my dad said, as they joined me.

"Shhhh..." I said, keeping my eyes closed. "Freya?" I whispered. When there was no response, I yelled her name louder and peaked my eyes open for a sign.

The lamp turned on suddenly and began to glow, making me jump back. The brightness blinded us, filling the entire room for only a brief second before it exploded, and I swore I saw a glimpse of the souls swimming above us for a fraction of a second before the room went dark again.

I jumped up and down. "You saw that too, right?"

My dad and Lady Cambridge stood speechless.

"Right?" I asked again.

They nodded, eyes wide.

"See, I told you something was going on here." I sat down in the middle of the room and contemplated my theories. I grabbed a pen and paper and started drawing quantum physics and tried to figure out where the loophole was.

A few minutes passed as my dad paced back and forth and Lady Cambridge stood silently.

"I bet they're releasing the souls, and somehow, they are connected with the middle here."

My dad stopped pacing and stared at me. "If we're in the middle, then Eric can find us."

"How will he know we're here?" Lady Cambridge asked. "What if he doesn't come back?"

"There were so many souls in my vision."

My dad nodded. "She's right. They can't be done already. They have to come back."

I stood up and paced. "We just need to send them a sign that we're here. Anything to grab their attention in case they're done."

"And how are we supposed to do that?" Lady Cambridge asked.

My dad and I paced around the room, which made me smile to realize where I had inherited that trait from. I tried to think of a spell that would reach another world and shook my head. Then, I thought of a grimoire in this place that had to have a secret or two. I stopped pacing as I thought about books and froze as a lightbulb went off in my head.

"Freya's journal." I adjusted my glasses and debated on the magical barrier we were up against. "She was using a journal while Isadora pretended to be her therapist. It was a magical journal that copied everything she wrote into a matching one." I tucked my hair behind my ears and sat cross legged on the floor. "I have that journal here. I've been writing in it."

My dad stopped pacing and looked to Lady Cambridge who nodded back to me. "Does she still write in it?" my dad asked.

"Well, no." I huffed.

"So, how do we get her to look in that journal?" Lady Cambridge asked.

I bit my lower lip. Hope deflating as I remembered how pissed Freya was when she found out. Maybe she had already destroyed the book. "I mean, it's a long shot, but if we could just get a message to her that we're here, then maybe they can bring us home."

"I might have something to help," Lady Cambridge

said. "I don't know if it's going to work, but I have one left so we will have one shot to get noticed."

I stared back at her and waited.

She flicked her wrist, and the pink orb floated from her palm as it transformed into a hummingbird, wings fluttering a mile a minute. I stared in awe as I tried to understand her magic.

"It's the last bit of my transporting magic that I used against Ragnar to bring him here. It's not strong enough to teleport any of us, but maybe a journal could be levitated or illuminated with this." She stared at the tiny bird and smiled. "I have been holding on to you for far too long now. I believe it's time to set you free." The bird fluttered before Lady Cambridge closed her palms and safely put it away.

I looked up and nodded. "I think it's worth a shot."

We made our way back to my family's home. I headed straight for Freya's room, hopping up the stairs two at a time, trying to reach the journal as fast as possible. I lifted the half Jasper stone off the journal, kissed it, and set it aside. Freezing, I watched the Jasper stone glow for a brief second, making me focus on the broken half's edge and wishing Ezra would've given me more information about the stupid, beautiful stone. The tiny dragon fossil seemed so fragile even though it was thousands of years old. I picked it back up and rubbed it in my palm, grabbing the journal as I began to write.

Please let this work.

Journal:

Freya or anyone... If you are seeing this,

then please, meet us in the "middle." Eric will know what this means. Please, I beg you, get this message to Eric. We are alive!!! He can bring us home!

My pen lifted itself off the paper as hope and doubt both consumed me equally. I reread my words too many times and felt stupid for thinking this might work at all. I shook my head, trying to delete the negative thoughts and only hold onto the hope. I squeezed the Jasper stone harder and continued to write.

Dad and I are safe, and we have an extra person to bring back with us. I just hope that someone can read this message. Freya, if I'm alive here and Dad is, then you and Eric MUST be alive. There is no other way that we are still breathing if you two are not. I'm assuming, or hoping, that means we have won. I hope Isadora is rotting deep in the earth, and life is nearly normal again. I miss you all, and if you see Ezra, tell him...

Tell him I love him.

I tried to catch my lone tear, but missed as it dripped onto the page of the infinity journal. My eyes bulged as the wet page began to glow for a millisecond before dulling again.

Woah.

I grabbed the journal and ran down the stairs where my dad and Lady Cambridge were sitting at the table. They both looked back at me, confused.

"Sorry," I said, trying to catch my breath, laying the journal down. While holding Ezra's stone in my other palm and praying that we were one step closer to home, I swallowed hard and flipped it open to my entry. "It glowed with my tears." I shook my head in disbelief after saying it, feeling a little more like a mad woman. "I mean, I was a little emotional thinking about home, and a tear slipped past me and fell on the page, and it glowed. That has to mean something, right?"

It has to work. Please work.

Lady Cambridge stood and walked closer to me, pulling me into her chest and rubbing my arms. "Emotions are high right now for everyone, and there is no shame in feeling all of them at once."

I exhaled heavily, not realizing I was even holding my breath, and nodded.

"Now let me take a look at this journal." She gracefully traced her hand over my handwriting and slowed over the spot where the tear had now dried. "There is definitely something to these pages. I can feel a pull of something. Maybe it's linked to the other world, or maybe it's pulling to the other book here in this world." She shrugged. "Either way, it's worth a shot." She lifted her palm and let the pink hummingbird reappear. "Jimmy, is there anything else you want to add to the letter?"

He sat back, and I watched him as his wheels turned. "Yeah, actually." He leaned forward and grabbed the book.

He snatched the pen from my grip before leaning over and writing. Once he finished, he handed the book back to me with the page open for interpretation.

"That bar better be seafoam green by the time I'm back home?" I looked back up at him with questioning eyes. "I don't get it."

He laughed. "Your mother will, and I'm sure it will put a smile on her face."

I frowned, trying to connect his dots, but figured that some things were better left unanswered. "Alright then." I shrugged. "I guess it's ready."

Lady Cambridge grabbed the journal and carefully lowered her glowing pink hummingbird onto the page. She bent over and whispered into the bird's ear, and it perked up and chirped one last time before she slammed the book closed. The pink glow brightened the entire book as it began to levitate before it dropped back onto the table, the glowing subsiding.

I looked up at her and waited for something to happen. "Well, did it work?"

She looked back and shrugged. "Only time will tell."

My dad slid his chair back and headed to the kitchen, rummaging around in the cabinets as the glasses clinked together. I waited silently, wondering what he was searching so hard for. After a few minutes, he emerged from the kitchen with three tall glasses and a bottle of champagne. His smile was from ear to ear, and he seemed so young and full of hope. I smiled back, as did Lady Cambridge, and he popped the top off and started to pour our glasses to the brim.

"What are we celebrating?" I asked, as he handed me a

glass of bubbling liquid, tickling my nose.

"We're going to go home," he said excitedly.

I snorted. "Let's not get ahead of ourselves."

He shook his head. "Nonsense. It's going to work."

I stared back at him and waited with my eyebrows raised.

He cleared his throat and raised his glass, waiting for us to mimic him. "Here's to going home. It may not be today or tomorrow, but it's going to be soon. My brother will find us here. I know it."

I half smiled as I set the Jasper stone down on the table and let my nerves calm before we clinked glasses. Lady Cambridge had the same smile as I did—we both had our doubts but neither of us wanted to break the happy moment. We nodded and sipped the bubbling liquid until my face felt a rush of heat and my cheeks were like a warm summer day. Lady Cambridge gasped as she set her empty glass down on the table and stared at the Jasper stone. She seemed to stop breathing, locked in a trance.

"What is it?" I asked.

"Where did you get this?"

She looked back at me and grabbed the stone before pushing it into my face, a little more aggressively than needed for a stupid gem.

"Ezra gave it to me." I pushed her arm back, giving me distance to breathe. "What's going on?"

"This 'stupid gem' is what started Ragnar's madness into power. This 'stupid gem' is what tore my family apart. This is what Ragnar needed to destroy our world as we know it. It's the final piece of magic that he sent my Izzy to search for once it had gone missing. If he has the other half, then we still have an opportunity to kill him."

I cleared my throat and let my brain process her words. We didn't have a second half... Our second half was Ember entirely. She was created from the magic of the Jasper stone. Could we still destroy him without it?

"Oxana made Ember, her daughter, from the other half."

Lady Cambridge gasped. "Oh my, well, that is going to be a bit more difficult then." She paced back and forth. "Damn it, Oxana," she whispered under her breath.

I watched her mind race and figured she needed to know. "Hey, we might not have the other stone, but I wanted you to know that your daughter is still alive. Margo is married and has a son that you should go back home to. We might not have the stone, but you still have something to look forward to."

She stopped pacing and smiled back at me. "Yes, your father told me. And I want nothing more than to wrap my arms around my child when we get back." She seemed to swallow her tears of happiness. "Do you know if she still wears her Labradorite pendant?"

I looked back at her confused and nodded.

"Good." She smiled and pointed back at me. "Any chance your world has heard of a magical liquid called squid ink?"

I smirked. "Luckily, I know just where to find some of that here. Back to Clara's we go."

Chapter 13

Freya Chamberlin

We walked back into the bar and a feeling of happiness rushed over me as I watched my family and friends enjoying their night and living as if in a normal mundane world without a magical mishap on the verge of destroying our world. My mom looked up from behind the bar and smiled as she waved for me to come over. I turned to Jaxon and kissed him on the cheek, my own flushing as the room became much warmer with embarrassment. He winked and walked to the kitchen before disappearing.

I made my way to the bar and hugged my mom from behind. "I love you, Mom." She froze, inhaled heavily, and turned around, embracing me in a hug that was long overdue.

"Oh, Freya, I love you too." She smiled back at me, and in this moment, the world seemed right.

The door opened as Aisling, Declan, and Ezra walked in.

Aisling's face seemed as if she was ready to scream. I walked to the end of the bar, meeting her and pulling her to the side for more privacy. She leaned over across the bar and grabbed my arm. "Girl, it's been a night, let me tell you..."

She filled me in on the night's recent events but seemed to be hiding something more.

"Have you seen Ember recently?" she asked, concerned.

I thought about my blurred memories of grief the last few weeks and shook my head. "I honestly can't recall. My mind has been a little busy."

Jaxon interrupted our conversation with concerned eyes. "Hey, I actually saw her this morning."

I turned back and stared at him in disbelief. "You did?"

He nodded. "Yeah, she was looking for something, but now that I think about it, it was sort of weird. She seemed distracted."

"Ragnar," Aisling answered. "He must've gotten to her." She shook her head. "We need to get her a bracelet like this," she said, as she handed me one. "It will keep him out of your pretty little head too."

The smell was pungent. I laughed in disgust and set it down on the counter. "Geez, Ais, didn't they have any better scents at the store?"

"Handmade and home grown. Wear it so your tongue doesn't end up down my throat too."

I stopped laughing and looked back at her with caution. "Do I even want to know?"

She shook her head. "Let me just say... Haven has a hell of a persistent boyfriend under mind control. But if that tongue comes anywhere near me again, I will be cutting it out."

My eyes widened in shock. "Ezra? No." I blurted out in laughter, then her eyes darted back to me, daggers glaring as she nodded. "Oh. My. God. How could you leave that part out?"

She clicked her tongue. "Girl, I'm serious. Put that damn bracelet on."

Jaxon grabbed his woven leather and wrapped it around his wrist, securing it quickly.

I nodded. "Okay, I will. Thanks, Ais."

She smiled as she walked toward Eric and Aunt Lynn with more bracelets in hand.

At least that might give us some sort of advantage.

The room seemed relaxed with everyone laughing, and the bar felt like home. That is if 'home' without my sister and dad was even an option anymore. But it was a breath of fresh air. Aisling and Declan were across the room shooting darts. Aisling, of course, was beating him as he pouted like a child. Her champion smile was one for the books. She knew she could bring him to his knees with or without the darts.

The night was peaceful, and nothing could stop tonight from being a normal family gathering with the locals. I looked at the clock and realized hours had passed and it was almost closing time. I started to help my mom clean the countertop and get the place back in order. Aisling and Declan each gave me a hug before bringing Aunt Lynn and Eric home. Eric had drunk a little too much bourbon, and I laughed as I watched him let his guard down and tumble while trying to stand straight. It was an unusual situation to see him in. Vulnerable and open. He was laughing and smiling and holding back tears all at once. A whirlwind of emotions as he nodded towards me on his way out. He needed a good night's sleep and an IV of electrolytes in the morning or even some healing tea would do the trick for the hangover he was going to have. I smiled and waved them off.

So much for soul saving in the morning.

The locals took their last beer and emptied it before heading for the door and walking home. Jaxon went to the office and started to close out the books, leaving only my mom and I to close up behind the bar. I walked over and turned off the light of the open sign, closed the blinds, and just as I was about to turn the lock on the door, the handle twisted and the door creaked open, making me jump back.

"Sorry, we're closed," I said, opening the door fully to let down the customer gently.

I gasped when I was mere inches away with the scarred faced man standing in front of me, smirking. I swallowed hard and quickly looked down at my wrist and flinched as I realized I never put the bracelet on. "Shit."

Everything happened so quickly that before I could even warn Jaxon or my mom, my vision became dark, and when the light finally came back, I was no longer in the bar.

The car ride was peaceful. I looked over at Jaxon and felt the rush of happiness and was excited for our bright future ahead of us. Our new plan to get ahead in life was dangling out in front of me, just waiting for me to grab it. I stared back in the rearview mirror and watched the winding road follow us home. I had finally decided to let go of the pain and hurt of Alex abandoning me and knew it was time for a fresh start.

My parents' divorce didn't matter anymore.

Jaxon was with me.

Life was normal.

We had our whole lives ahead of us.

And for once... I was happy.

My brain started to fog as I tried to process what was happening.

I looked down at my Mark and realized it was no longer there. I lifted my hand off the steering wheel and tried to feel the rush of magic flow through my fingertips.

But nothing happened.

Jaxon looked back at me and grabbed my hand, squeezing it tight between his fingers.

"What's wrong?" His eyes glistened. "You know we're going to get through this. Don't even worry about anything."

I nodded, confusion filling my head. I looked around the leather seats of the Camaro and then out of the windshield, watching as our familiar homes passed us in Crystal Rock.

"How did we get here?" I asked. But never heard an answer.

The stop sign ahead of us was approaching quickly. My body went into a full panic mode as I finally remembered this scene all too well.

"Oh no, not again."

I looked over to Jaxon, panic filling me, making me feel uneasy. His eyes seemed lost and began to glow an eerie green as Jaxon's body disappeared and left me alone in the Camaro heading for the oncoming headlights of the semi-truck. I braced myself as the truck driver inched closer to my driver side. I threw my hands up, ready to try and defend myself, anxiety creeping over me and my PTSD reliving itself.

"Stop!" I yelled. "This isn't real," I whispered and looked back at the passenger seat where Jaxon had been seconds ago, only to see Ragnar sitting there instead —smirking.

"You're good." His voice sent shivers through me. "Not many could resist my mind games. But, you child... You continue to surprise me."

I turned to my left and waited for the impact to come. But instead, time stood still. The hum of the Camaro silenced, the truck was stuck in mid motion, and the world had an eerie glow to it, no breeze, no warmth from the sun. Nothing seemed natural.

I took my foot off the brake, and the Camaro stayed in place.

I slowly moved my foot to the gas pedal and pressed it slowly to try and get the fuck out of here, but nothing happened.

I turned toward Ragnar and snarled, "What do you want?"

He laughed in a menacing way that made any form of confidence I had a second ago dissolve. "I, myself, don't want anything in particular."

"Then, get out of my head."

"I can't do that, either." He smirked and cracked his neck, inhaling sharply. I watched cautiously as his eyes pierced into mine with an unnatural seasick green.

I grabbed the steering wheel and looked away, feeling

nauseous the more I stared back at him. "Then, what do you want?" I asked through gritted teeth.

He waved his hand, and the car disappeared from under us as I watched whatever world we were in transform. He and I were left standing in the middle of the road. My eyes bulged as we were standing in front of my home, but no one was in sight.

Whatever world we were in... it wasn't ours at all.

I was deeply trapped inside Ragnar's very own mind game. He was playing with me.

"We want the same thing. Maybe for different reasons, but ultimately, we want the same thing." He pointed to my home and smiled. "We both want your father and sister back." The lights turned on inside my home, and I saw two silhouettes behind a closed curtain, laughing and cheers being exchanged with glasses. I studied their shadows carefully when I recognized my dad's height with a young girl standing next to him.

"Why are you showing me this?"

He snorted. "What? You didn't want to know that your sister and father were safe and alive?"

"Haven?" I gasped before running toward the door which seemed to continuously become further and further away as I tried to reach the porch. It was an endless game of running that would never lead me to my destination. When my lungs were finally emptied and my legs became wobbly, I stopped and dropped to the ground, trying to catch my breath. "Where are they?"

"See, that's just it. I can't seem to figure it out, but I can see them too. I have searched countless hours the last few weeks trying to find them, and every glimpse I get of them

brings me back here, yet when I search your home, I see no sign of them."

"You've been in my home?" My stomach grew sicker as his presence in my safe space made me want to vomit.

His smirk grew. "And you had no idea. Sound asleep with your boyfriend." He clicked his tongue and waved his finger in disgust. "But still, your sister and father are nowhere to be seen."

I looked up, tears filling. "That's because they're not here."

His scarred face glared back at me as his face distorted in a way that terrified me. He had the look of pure evil sent from the gates of Hell, trying to drag me down with him. He grabbed my arm and squeezed it hard while pulling me to my feet, shaking me angrily.

"Stop playing games with me, child. I need my stone back, and they have it. I can sense it with them. And I will burn this entire world down and walk out of the flames without you and your loved ones if I don't get it."

My entire body shook with adrenaline and fear equally. "But I don't have it."

"They do," he screamed in my face, splattering spit into the atmosphere. "I want it!"

"Well, they're not here." I tried to pry his hand off my arm. His tight squeezing began to make my arm tingle as the blood tried to force its way back to my fingertips. When he wouldn't release me, rage filled me, and I could feel the rush of magic growing inside me for the first time in weeks. Shocked to feel anything, I grasped at the little tingling of magic as it began to fade. I quickly thought of all the horrible things that Ragnar had caused that started with Isadora, and

I could feel the anger coming back, along with the tingling of hope. I had some sort of magic in his head, and I wasn't going to waste it.

"Ignis," I screamed, letting the rage release from me as fire ignited along my arm. The rush of power made me feel briefly invincible. I grabbed his face and let the fire spread across his body. His scar ignited like an exploding volcano. My flames were cool to my touch, but I could feel the heat bursting onto him, and it made me smile.

He quickly released me. Fear crossed his face as he tried to extinguish the flames.

"Get out of my head," I yelled, pushing harder against him as his face sizzled.

"Okay, okay," he yelled, throwing his hands up into a plea of surrender.

I held my hands between us, anger fuming through me. "Send me home."

"I just wanted to help you. They have something I need, and you want them back. It could be a win for both of us."

I breathed heavily as I watched his face turn from fear to promising my most desired wish. Did he know how to get them home? Did he have that kind of power to bring them safely back to me?

I inhaled sharply and shook my head. "I'll find them myself." I blew out a breath. "Get me home, now." I brought the flame back to my palms, threatening the return of torture.

He exhaled heavily. "Fine, but when you can't reach them, do me a favor and send me my daughter, Isadora. With her, I can get everything back myself."

"Isadora?" I questioned before my body jolted, and the bar came back into view.

Jaxon stood in front of me, waving his hand in front of my face. "Hey, Freya... Hello?"

I grabbed his hand, breathing heavily, and looked around at my surroundings. The bar was locked down, and it was only him and I left. "Where is everyone?"

"Everyone left, your mom is home with Clara, and I just finished the papers in the back. What just happened?" His eyes were filled with worry as he grabbed my face and turned it back and forth, looking for the damage that was surely to be seen while in such a trance.

I glanced down at my palms as I whispered, "Ignis." But nothing happened.

He stepped back in confusion and waited silently.

"Ragnar," I whispered back, answering him. "It's nothing..." I pulled his hands away from me and marched to the bar and grabbed the bracelet Aisling had left me, quickly tightening it around my wrist. I lifted my arm up and showed him that Ragnar's mind tricks would be no more.

His shoulders lowered as he looked around the empty bar. "He never came in here."

I nodded. "He must've been close enough to get in my head."

Jaxon's brows furrowed as he walked in front of me. "What did he want?"

I pursed my lips. "Nothing that I would give him."

"Wouldn't or can't?" he asked while grabbing my hands and pulling me into his arms.

"Babe... I had my magic in his head. I lit him on fire, and he was actually hurt by it."

He pulled away from me and studied my face. "Wait, what? Explain what the hell just happened."

I nodded as I threw my hands up in defense to try and settle him. "He said he could get my dad and Haven back, but he wants the Jasper stone in place of it."

"I thought you had hope of finding them yourself?"

"I do." I huffed. "Or I did. I don't know? I mean, what if he can bring them back? What if we can't but he can?"

Jaxon looked back at me and shook his head. "He can't be trusted." He grimaced. "Plus, we don't have that stone."

I nodded, pulling myself closer to him and trying to hold both myself and the world together for one more night.

Our silence had me debating if he was thinking through the scenarios too. If Ragnar had a way to get them back... did we trust him? Or did we try to use Isadora and get them back? Did she even know how to get them back? What did Ragnar want with her? My head started to pound as the thoughts became overwhelming.

I squirmed in his arms and walked back to the bar, jumping up and sitting on the ledge. "I mean, I did have hope... I, I do. I just want a failsafe, just in case Eric's theory is wrong. I don't want to throw his offer off the table." I inhaled heavily. "I want them back so badly that I would do anything to see them again."

Jaxon huffed. "Be careful. There are a lot of consequences when teaming up with an evil villain like that, and we are currently in the middle of living one of those nightmares that came from his descendant."

"I know... I'll stay away from him. Nothing good will come from that man." I looked back at Jaxon and waited for reassurance because deep down, if Ragnar could help, or Isadora could just by giving him a worthless stone, then it would be worth having my family whole again. I knew I had to let it go for now, but the idea was not fully off the table. I set the idea secretly teetering on the ledge in my head and closed its door for now.

He nodded. "I think that's a good idea."

Chapter 14

Aisling Meadows

The sun began to peek through the blinds. I sat up and groaned as I tried to maneuver out of Declan's death grip. He was still sound asleep and snoring lightly. I smiled as I watched him sleep peacefully and was happy that he had some sort of quiet in his mind. I walked down the stairs and headed toward the kitchen. If I wasn't going to be able to sleep any more, then the least I could do was make some coffee and get my day started.

I knew Freya would be wide awake by now doing the same as me. When she told me that Haven and her dad were possibly closer to us than we thought, I knew it gave her a whole new hope. Of course, we couldn't tell Alex about it yet. As much as Alex had started to come around to me, a part of me still didn't like her for abandoning my best friend. I knew her reasonings were good, but two years of pain and sadness bottled up in *my* Freya made it hard to forgive and forget everything she did overnight.

I grabbed my phone and decided to send a quick text.

Aisling: Hey girl, you awake?

I waited for ten seconds before realizing that maybe she was finally sleeping sound and I may have been the one to just wake her up. I glanced back at the text and debated on deleting it before I saw the message get read, then she started to type back. I exhaled, relief washing over me.

Freya: I'm awake. Honestly, Jaxon is next to me snoring so I haven't slept much at all, but I know he needs the peace too.

I laughed as I filled the coffee pot with the dark brew grounds and a dash of cinnamon for sweetness.

Aisling: Declan too. LOL. Maybe they are more than just Anchors. They are too in sync.

Freya: LOL, right?!?! What are you doing?

Aisling: Thinking about root beer floats. Is it too early for ice cream? :)

Freya: It is NEVER too early for ice cream. Where do you want to meet?

Aisling: I'm on my way. Just bring out the warm blankets.

Freya: Already on it :)

I pressed the go button on the coffee and let it brew inside the home, filling the sleeping, snoring Declan with a sweetness to wake up to. I opened the freezer and grabbed the ice cream and root beer from the fridge and headed for the door.

"Excuse me, where do you think you're going this early?" Aunt Lynn asked, as she stepped in front of me, blocking my way to freedom and the cold morning air. I fumbled with the soda, and she caught it before it fizzled inside the bottle.

"I... Ugh... I'm just going to Freya's. Neither of us could sleep."

Aunt Lynn looked me up and down with her eyebrows raised. "You sure you're not going on another Ragnar suicide mission?"

I laughed and grabbed the soda back from her. "You think I'd be sharing root beer floats with that asshole?"

She smiled. "I would hope not." She released the bottle but continued to block the doorway. "Do not try anything extra without help from others. Please." She crossed her arms and pleaded with her innocent eyes. "Ais, you are the light of my life. If anything happens to you when I'm only a defenseless mundane, then I could never forgive myself. And your parents would never forgive me, either."

I exhaled and shook my head.

"Speaking of your parents, they are almost done with their work tour and should be heading back home in December. I've been debating and letting them in on our secret... What do you think?"

My eyes bulged as I thought of my mom watching a flame grow from my palm, and my dad would probably be terrified and then excited about it as he would try to replicate the flame. I smiled when I thought about them being in on the secret and that way they could keep an eye out for danger.

"I think... that would actually be kind of awesome. How would you explain your relationship to us?"

She shook her head. "Nothing would change. I'm a distant relative, and they wouldn't need to know more unless Eric would ever want to tell them." She shrugged. "I couldn't hold it against him. They are his family."

I smirked. "But you raised us. You did the hard part." I winked at her and kissed her cheek.

"Now back to not doing anything stupid." She crossed her arms and stood with a stern look.

I scoffed. "First of all, you are not defenseless, and secondly, nothing would be your fault, but thirdly, I am truly going to Freya's. Neither of us can sleep. You are more than welcome to come with me if you can't sleep, either."

I heard a throat clear behind me, making me jump again.

"She's only not sleeping because I'm not letting her."

The ice cream dropped from my grasp as Eric reached and caught it before it hit the ground and splattered the walls.

I turned around and watched Aunt Lynn's face turn ten shades of red.

"Oh... Sure, you can't sleep, but for other reasons." I turned back at Eric, who was smirking and balancing the tub of ice cream over my hand with one finger. I smirked at him before turning back to Aunt Lynn. "You could have at least picked someone better looking."

"Hey, now. We come from the same bloodline." Eric laughed.

"Luckily for me, that bloodline is long diluted and has been manipulated by many others over the centuries."

His smirk dissolved as he turned the tub of ice cream away from me and let it go, just out of my reach and ready to crash onto the floor.

"Levis," I whispered and smiled when the tub floated in midair without spilling a drop.

His eyes approved as he grabbed the tub back from me. "Someone's been practicing."

"I took Latin in school, thanks to Aunt Lynn."

I watched as Eric's face saddened.

A pit in my stomach grew as I felt his pain of the last thousand years, regret painting his entire being. "Hey, look. I'm sorry. I just... I'm just giving you a hard time. If Aunt Lynn wants you around, then you can stay. But if you break her heart again, I will kill you myself. Blood or not."

He smirked. "I wouldn't dare make that mistake again."

"Good." I nodded.

"Good." He smiled.

I turned and watched Aunt Lynn smile back at both of us.

"You said you're going to Freya's?" Eric asked.

I nodded.

"I'll walk you there."

"I'm okay, it's only a block away."

He tucked the ice cream under his arm and held it sternly. "I wasn't giving you a choice. Your aunt would kill me if anything bad happened to you."

I looked back at her as she nodded.

"Fine." I walked up to Aunt Lynn and kissed her on the cheek before she finally let me pass. "Please let Declan know where I am."

"Will do." She smiled.

Eric walked up next to her and lifted her chin up, kissing her lips slowly and tucking her hair behind her ear as she blushed.

"Don't be gone too long," she whispered.

He shook his head. "Ten minutes. Don't fall asleep before I get back."

She smiled sleepily.

"Ew, okay, that's enough. Let's go great great great great great whatever you are, Eric."

We all laughed as I walked out of the house and waited for him. He met me down the driveway in the cold morning air with snowflakes starting to fall, making Crystal Rock look like a snow globe that had been shaken up. The snow began to stick, and a part of me was glad that Eric was holding the freezing ice cream while I carried the soda.

We were both silent as we made our way to Freya's.

"Hey, I never thanked you—"

Thanked me? For what?" I interrupted.

He stopped walking, "Well if you would've let me finish."

"Sorry... Continue." I waved my free hand.

"Thank you for always looking out for our girl, and thank you for always being there for my niece. You are the most devoted and loyal person I have met, and honestly, I am proud that you come from my bloodline, even if you are not."

I stood there silently at the unexpected compliment.

"You don't need to say anything. I am just happy that my only born son lived... And that your 'aunt' was able to raise him and his following generations. They were able to live the life that her and I had always dreamed of having together. She raised them all exactly how we both had wanted. I just wished that I would've known. I would've made sure your family always had everything they needed, and I would have done everything to keep you all safe."

I smiled. "Aunt Lynn did all of that for us. She was always the whispering angel on our shoulders." I looked back at him and laughed. "I guess opposites really do attract. Because she truly is a good one."

"That we can agree on." He smirked.

I looked back at Aunt Lynn's house and then back to Eric. "You truly do love her, don't you?"

He stared back at me and exhaled slowly, he nodded. "Now that is without a doubt."

My phone rang, breaking the only peaceful moment that we will ever have between us.

"It's Freya, I'm sure. Probably just wondering what's taking so long."

He nodded as I grabbed my phone and watched her name light up on the screen.

"Hey, I'm two houses down."

"Um... Be prepared," Freya whispered back into the phone. "Izzy is here right now."

"Izzy?" I asked, confused.

Eric's eyes darted toward Freya's house as he sped up his pace, dragging me along.

Chapter 15

Freya Chamberlain

"Margo told me to let it go, she swore that I was seeing things, but I know what I saw. I know this journal. It copies whatever the other journal does," Isadora said, shaking her head as if she were starting to realize she may actually be crazy.

"I know what it does. You used it on—" I shut my mouth, realizing that her mind was all boggled, and she had no idea what she did to me.

"I opened the book and saw yours and Jaxon's names written across the pages. I swear I didn't read it. It was just a quick scan. I knew I needed to get it to you. The pages were glowing pink ten minutes ago. I swear."

I stared back at her wearily, wondering why she even cared or wanted to help me with anything. She handed me the journal and stood awkwardly as I examined the pages that nearly destroyed my secrets to her.

"I'm leaving," she said, hands up as she slowly backed away. "I just hope it helps with your father and sister or whatever. I'm sorry."

I had no words, just stood in shock that she was standing in my home and neither of us were trying to destroy one another. The door opened as Eric and Aisling came marching in. Eric's face furious as he made his way to Izzy, throwing her against the wall.

"What are you doing here?" he growled. "I told you not to come near them without me."

Fear spread across her face as she looked away from Eric, trying to hide herself.

"I'm... I..."

I didn't know what to do. As much as I didn't like her, I thought we were supposed to be "nice" to her. My body unexpectedly jumped between them, pushing Eric back from her and then feeling disgusted with myself for even wanting to help her at all. I stood shocked at my own actions. "She's helping us," I said quietly.

"To hell she is," Aisling jumped in.

"No, really." I lifted the journal up and waved it back and forth. "Something was glowing with this, and she ran it over to me. And the last glowing book we found became very useful for Jaxon, so I really don't want to pass this up." I threw the journal back onto the table and stared at them all. I was trying to solve a puzzle, along with figuring out how to get my family back, continuing to set the souls free, finding out Ragnar's weakness to destroy him, and giving myself a happily ever after with Jaxon.

Was that too much to ask for?

Aisling and Eric stepped back and watched the journal with wide eyes, both in sync, pointing up at the journal. I tuned quickly and froze at the journal levitating in midair.

Then, a pink hummingbird came fluttering out of the pages and began to circle it.

I ran back over to the table and grabbed the book, laying it back down carefully as if it were a bomb waiting to detonate. The pink hummingbird fluttered back into the pages and disappeared.

"Oh my god," Izzy said, as she covered her mouth. "That's impossible."

"What is?" I asked.

"My mother used to use a hummingbird just like that when I was a child. But that's impossible. She would've been destroyed in the dagger world. Or at least, I assumed that she was gone for good."

"Lady Cambridge?" Eric asked, now inching his way closer to the journal.

Izzy nodded.

I grabbed the front cover of the journal and slowly cracked it open as Aisling, Eric, Izzy and I all leaned in too close for comfort to be standing this close to the two Immortals that we tried to kill months ago, now, here we were, working together to bring my family back and rid this world of the plague that Ragnar wanted to spread.

The book flew open on its own as the pink hummingbird came fluttering out as the pages began to turn on their own until it came to the last few pages, and I saw a new entry. I read the words a hundred times over as my eyes fluttered too quickly with excitement. The pink hummingbird made one final twirl above us before it exploded into a fountain of shimmer and disappeared.

I looked up at everyone's stunned reactions.

"It's them." My voice cracked while breaking the silence. "I need a pen. Someone get me a pen."

Aisling ran to the kitchen and came running back with a pen in hand. "Write," she demanded, as she shoved the pen into my hand. "Here, write," she frantically said as she joined me, reading over my shoulder.

I froze. "Could this be a trick?"

Eric looked back at me and shook his head. "Izzy is right, that hummingbird was something her mother used to do, and if our theory is right, then the middle just might be able to let us connect with them through this somehow." He shrugged. "I mean, magic doesn't come with a manual."

I looked back at Izzy, who was now standing further back from the rest of us as she wiped a single tear from rolling down her cheek. She seemed so small and childlike with this new form of her not being so... evil. I stepped closer toward her as Eric grabbed my arm, holding me from her. I turned quickly and glared at him.

He instantly let it go and shrugged apologetically. "Instinct."

I turned back to Izzy cautiously, and she flinched when I was mere feet from her. "I'm leaving." She wiped another tear. "I hope that helps you guys." She turned for the door and started to walk away. I grabbed her arm, and as if my hand was ice, I watched as her entire body froze into place.

Aisling rolled her eyes and walked back into the kitchen, Izzy's eyes following Aisling's steps.

"Thank you." I swallowed hard as my words escaped my throat, bringing her attention back to me.

She nodded and looked away.

"Your mother is alive?" I asked.

She turned back and grimaced. "I want to believe it."

I half smiled back at her. "If I have hope, then so should you. I may not like you, but I know the feeling of losing a mother, and honestly, I never want anyone to feel that way." Her eyes seemed to fill with hope, which made me a little uncomfortable. I cleared my throat, letting her wrist go. "Let's just get them back."

Her eyes glistened with tears building, ready to spill. "Thank you," she whispered before turning and walking out of the house, her emotions leaving her as I heard the sobs start in the distance.

Eric walked up next to me and put his arm around my shoulders, pulling me into him and shaking me excitedly. "Let's bring them home."

"Bring who home?" my mom said, as she walked down the stairs, Jaxon following behind her, both rubbing their eyes.

I grabbed the journal and shoved it into my mom's hands with a smile.

Her eyes bulged as she read the line over again and again. "They're alive?"

We all nodded before jumping with excitement.

"Seafoam green." She smiled from ear to ear. "He will be so happy with it."

Aisling walked back from the kitchen, juggling too many iced mugs for all of us and started scooping the ice cream as Eric grabbed the soda and began to pour.

"Looks like celebration root beer floats are in order," she said, handing each of us one filled to the brim and overflowing.

We clinked glasses and accepted this little win. I set the

mug down and picked the pen back up. My hand shook slightly as I debated on the best words.

Meet us at Jaxon's home as soon as you can. We're coming for you.

I stared back at the journal, which now seemed like nothing more than pieces of paper glued tight to the leather bound cover. I closed the journal and rubbed the front cover, tracing the infinity symbol carefully.

Please work.

"You know, she looks just like Lady Cambridge." Eric's voice interrupted my silent prayer. "I didn't see it before, but now I do."

I stared back at him, confused.

"Ais... She looks just like Izzy's mother." He pointed to the corner where Aisling was talking to Jaxon and shrugged. "Whatever is going on in Izzy's head, seeing Ais and knowing that is her descendant of a child she believed was dead may have triggered something inside her to help her heart grow a few sizes." He shrugged again. "Little love, that's what her mother always called her."

Aisling walked over and snapped, "Yeah, that's what the evil bitch wouldn't stop calling me when she kidnapped me. Psycho." She clicked her tongue and glared in annoyance. "That woman is no family to me. We may share blood, but we are far from family." She lifted her shirt and shared her scar across her stomach with the others. "True 'family' would never sacrifice their loved one's life for more power." She scoffed.

I nodded and grabbed her hand, trying to calm her. "Hey, just because she helped doesn't mean we trust her."

Aisling's scowl started to fade as she exhaled slowly.

"When Haven gets back here, she can lighten that scar of yours if you would like. She did the same for Jaxon," I added.

She shook her head. "No, I like the reminder."

I nodded and released her hand.

Jaxon lifted his shirt and rubbed his matching scar. "Hey, at least we have twin scars now." He winked at her.

She looked back at Jaxon and smirked. "Mine's a little more wicked."

He grabbed her shoulder and pulled her into his chest. "Whatever you say... cousin."

They both laughed and grabbed their root beers, cheers-ing.

"Hey, guys," my mom's fragile voice chimed in, "Can I come with you today?"

I turned around and stared at her, shocked that she wanted to do anything at all. But to have her want to be out of bed today and wanting to stay busy was probably the best move yet. She seemed hesitant after asking. I walked over to her and hugged her tight. "I think it's only fair that you're there too for our family reunion."

I looked at Eric, who nodded with a smile.

My mom looked up and smiled, both of us relaxing our shoulders and letting happiness consume us with a side of hope that would hopefully turn out to be worth it today.

Chapter 16

Jaxon Oakes

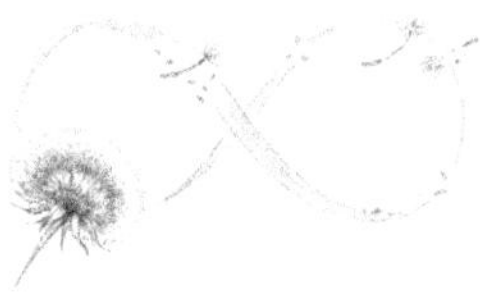

I decided to head to my parent's home, which was still known as the soul house until they were all free. After staying with Freya for the last few weeks, it was time to make my way back to my parents' for a little quality time. Honestly, as much as I didn't want to spend time apart from Freya, I knew, deep down, that it was healthy to give each other a little bit of space.

Back at her house, I watched as Alex cheered with her, and they seemed like they needed a little bit of mother-daughter time reveling in happiness. Unfortunately, going home, I knew Izzy would be there. Which was exactly why I had been staying away. The pure thought of that evil bitch in my house... near my family was what I couldn't stomach. My mother was playing house with the evil twin. But that was the new norm.

I guess.

I took the porch two stairs at a time and reached the door handle. I hesitated for a brief moment before walking inside. I inhaled slowly as I reached the living room with the souls swimming above. Watching them follow a circular pattern and dance musically in silence. I smiled and reached up toward the ceiling. A few of the souls stopped dancing and bounced their way to my palm and then trickled down my arm, circling it, tickling my skin as they made their way back up to the ceiling swimming pool.

"Pretty neat, huh?" My dad walked in behind me, putting his hand on my shoulder and watching the souls bounce. "We're going to need something magical in this room once they are all free." He chuckled. "It's just going to seem so dull without them."

I snorted. "They deserve to be free."

He slapped my back gently. "I'm glad your heart is always in the right place. You have humanity that cannot be shut off, and I am grateful that you got that from me." He smirked. "Your mom with her sister on the other hand..." He scrunched his nose before laughing.

I laughed with him. "Thanks, Dad."

We walked into the kitchen where my mom was sitting with Izzy at the table drinking coffee. My mom had a map laid out in front of her. I walked over and studied the map. My brows furrowed as I realized it was a map of Crystal Rock, but it seemed old. The paper was frayed along the edges and seemed discolored, as if coffee had been spilled across the entire map.

"JFK?" I asked, as I realized the open field in the raised area.

My mom nodded. "Yes, and here is the cave. Izzy was just telling me about some memories that seem to keep popping up."

I leaned back against the counter and poured myself a

mug of coffee, rolling my eyes at anything that came from her mouth. I looked over at Izzy, who quickly looked away from me.

"I know you don't like me—"

"I don't trust you. There's a fucking difference. I don't know you enough to decide if I like you."

She stood from the table and seemed to want to run away. "I don't trust myself, either, but I can tell you one thing. Staying here the past few weeks has brought back memories that I had thought I had long forgotten. Mags has reminded me of so many good memories, and it made me realize that my head has been twisted over the years."

I scoffed and stared at her in annoyance. I didn't agree with her staying close to my parents at all, but my mom had this tight grip on her wellbeing. It was disgusting to me. After all of the horror stories that I heard, my mom just let her walk right back in her life as if she didn't try to kill her as a teen and hadn't been hiding from her for a thousand years. I turned and glared out of the kitchen window where I had first seen Isadora walk up to our house and stir up a tornado inside me, making this house, my house, spin. Now, she was making my head spin. I dumped my coffee and steadied my adrenaline building inside of me. "I should leave." I set the mug down and turned back to face them.

"No, please don't," my mom pleaded, as she reached me by the sink. "Please stay for a little while. I've missed you."

"Mom, I can't be around her. She just pisses me off. Jim wouldn't be missing if it wasn't for her. Haven would still be here. My girlfriend is broken because of her. I just can't sit around a fucking table and play nice with the bitch that ruined everything."

Izzy's eyes bulged. "Me?" she asked innocently. "Freya? What did I do? I don't understand."

"Of course you don't. Your mind is worthless." I punched the cabinet and walked toward the front door.

"Wait," Izzy yelled from the kitchen. "Please, let me fix whatever I have done. Please, give me a chance."

"You've done enough damage," I yelled and pushed the front door open to walk down the stairs. Unsure of where I wanted to go at the moment, I knew I needed to get the hell away from her before I took a boulder and crushed her pretty little skull with it.

I stopped walking and debated on doing just that, then I heard the front door open. I pushed myself forward, further away from the bullshit.

"Hey, JFK." Her high pitched voice sent rage through my body.

I turned quickly and watched as Izzy ran closer toward me, both of my parents watching from the front porch.

I couldn't do it. If she took one more step toward me... I was going to snap.

She inched closer.

And there it was. She was too close to me. I couldn't hold back any longer. She needed to take a step back and wouldn't budge. So, I shoved her away. Her eyes widened as did mine but she insisted on coming back. I shook my head in anger and wanted to resist but she didn't seem to understand that I needed her as far away from me as possible. I swallowed hard before I shoved her again, only this time she fell onto the ground. I hovered over her and without thinking I leaned down and grabbed her by the throat, trying to keep my anger at bay. "I don't want anything to do with you."

She squirmed underneath me, seeming so tiny now that her magic was gone. A powerless human being who deserved to die a thousand years ago from a plague.

Izzy pleaded, tears pooling from her eyes. "J-F-K. Please." She struggled to get the words out. "Take me." She choked on her breath. "Or show me."

I could feel my hands tightening around her neck, and my own rage did not want me to let her go. But I looked up at my mom being held back by my dad and her pleading eyes made me release her neck. I stood up and exhaled heavily, trying to calm my own anger.

I knew it was a bad idea to come home.

I huffed and started to walk in any direction away from her with the cold air starting to freeze my lungs.

"Please, take me to JFK," Izzy pleaded, as she turned over on all fours and tried to stand, still gasping for a full breath.

"No," I spat.

"Please." She stood and ran to me.

Her touch felt like acid on my skin as I pulled away from her. "I said no. If I take you back to JFK, then I'm killing you there."

"Jaxon!" my mom yelled and ran down by us. "Shame on you."

"Shame on me? Shame on her. We're only in this mess because of her and her psychotic father. Her stupid pull for power brought us here. Nothing else." I shrugged my mom's hands off me. "Why the hell would I take her back to where this nightmare began?"

Silence grew louder as Izzy kept her head down and my mom's pleading eyes bore into my soul. My dad paced back and forth with his arms crossed.

Of course, he was still trying to keep the peace, as usual. Just once, just fucking once, I wanted him to jump between what was right and wrong and choose with me.

"I'm leav—"

"I'm being pulled to your field, that JFK place. I can't explain it, but I need to go there. I know you don't trust me, but something is screaming at me to go there."

I froze and glared back at her, not expecting that. I studied her face as she hugged herself and seemed broken.

Good.

"I would go alone, but without magic, I'm afraid of what I might find." She shrugged and kept her eyes staring off in the distance.

I inhaled slowly and debated. "It's probably Ragnar—"

"It's not."

"And how do you know that?"

She lifted her face and looked back at me. "When it's him... it's dark. My brain gets the chills, a sickness runs in my veins, his presence in my life or my head is evil. I can feel it now. And whatever *this* is, is the exact opposite." She shrugged innocently. "I just need to see it for myself. Your mom pulled out the map to try and see if Callum could do a mirage spell. We just wanted to see if we could get a quick glimpse of the field without actually going there and putting ourselves in danger. But Callum couldn't get it to work. I need to go there and see for myself."

My body rocked angrily as she spoke. Today was not turning out how I expected. I walked back a few steps and took a seat on the porch. I laid my head between my legs and cupped my hands behind my neck. We hadn't been to JFK since Jim and Haven disappeared. The wreckage that was left there was surely going to be a devastating sight to see. And the thought of Ragnar possibly being there, plotting against us, or us walking into a trap was a little messed up.

A mirage spell?

I thought about the grimoire and didn't recall such a spell in it. I had studied that book cover to cover since I got it. And I didn't remember anything like it.

"What's needed for the mirage spell?"

Izzy looked up and wiped her tears as my mom gazed back at me with hopeful eyes.

"You." She smiled as she waved for me to follow her into our home.

We walked into the kitchen with the aged map laid flat on the table. My dad had candles holding each corner to keep it in place. But the closer I looked, I realized they had been trying a spell on the map and not just staring at it. There were herbs placed at each corner in a small pile.

My mom handed me a small needle. "A drop of blood in each pile, then place your palm over the field. The Himalayan salt and sage leaves will move there if it works."

I looked back at her hesitantly with the needle in my hand. "What do you think is there exactly?" I asked my mom, ignoring Izzy altogether.

"I'm wondering if it's Jim and Haven somehow, stuck in

a portal. Or maybe my father. I don't know. I want to believe it's something good."

I nodded and quickly poked my index finger, squeezing it and placing a single drop in each corner. Instantly the salt and sage started to twirl.

"Now place your hand over the field to reveal what needs to be found."

I moved my hand without hesitation and willed every piece of salt and sage to work its magic and show me what was needed. Everyone surrounded me and watched patiently. The salt and sage began to rise as if it was a projection screen ready to show a movie. I raised my hand higher to give the piles of salt more room to show. A perfect rectangle was made and began to glow. My brows furrowed as I watched the field come into view, only to gasp as the tree that should have been covered in frost and snow was in a bright, warm area of wildflowers surrounding it and glowing.

My hand shook as the glow became brighter and brighter before I pulled my hand away, in shock, gasping for breath, trying to wrap my head around the beautiful site.

"Impossible," I said.

My parents and Izzy all asked in unison. "What is it?"

I stepped back and looked at each one, confused. "You didn't see it?"

My mom shook her head. "Baby, it was a blank canvas of salt."

My brows furrowed. "Blood magic is weird. I think I like my earth magic better." I laughed as I shook my head.

"Me too, bud. Me too," my dad chimed in and laughed. "What did you see?"

I paced back and forth and debated on what my own eyes had seen. "I mean, it doesn't make any sense. Truly impossible. Well, I mean... We're witches. At this point, anything is possible, right?" I jumped up onto the counter and sat down, crossing my ankles and swinging them nervously as my head spun. "It's twenty-two degrees out today, right?"

My mom looked out of the window and nodded. "I mean, it snowed last night, and it's sticking. So, I'd say it's pretty cold today... Why? What's going on?"

As much as I wanted to share the information with my parents. I did not want to share it with Isadora.

"The wildflowers," Izzy's voice cracked.

I turned my head quickly and stared back at her. "You saw it too?"

She nodded quietly. "It's definitely not Ragnar, but whatever that was... I don't know."

My parents just stared between the two of us and waited.

"There was a circle of wildflowers surrounding my tree. I mean... The lone tree in the middle of the field. It looked so bright and..."

"Beautiful. Whatever magic that was is definitely from something good. The leaves were so full of color and life," Izzy chimed in.

I turned toward her and nodded in agreement.

"Freya," I whispered and swallowed hard as realization hit. Of course it would be her magic, it had to be. It was a breathtaking sight and only someone as pure as her could hold magic like that inside of her.

Izzy's eyes studied me as she nodded.

"We need to go check it out." I swallowed hard before I spoke again. "Izzy... You can come with us." I inhaled slowly, regretting my decision already. "But you do anything questionable at all, and I will take this dagger and shove it into that black heart of yours." I pulled the Hildisvini blade from my back pocket and waved it in front of her. No longer full of magic or a prison world, it was still a sharp enough blade to kill someone with.

Izzy gasped and grabbed her chest, shaking her head. "I won't." Her eyes widened with fear. "I want to live."

"Good," I said, as I put the blade away.

Chapter 17

Haven Vine

The sun started to come up, only I had not closed my eyes through the entire short night. I was too excited and filled with hope that today could be a good day. I sat up and laid the journal down on the bed that I had held on to all night long. I waited for a glow of anything to come through. When I finally sat up and set the journal down in front of me. I twirled Freya's moonstone earrings and willed the book to respond. The earrings made me feel a little closer to home, wherever home was. I stood up and grabbed the Jasper stone and rubbed it between my fingers.

Ugh, I miss you, Ezra.

"This stupid stone has done nothing for us." I lifted it into the air and examined the small dragon fossil that remained and laughed quietly. "All this fighting over a stupid, worthless piece of Jasper." I felt anger for the first time in a while begin to consume me as I wanted to chuck the stupid stone out of the window and be done with it, but then the journal began to glow pink and the little hummingbird made its way out of the pages and began to flutter above it.

I dove across the bed, tossing the stone onto the pillow and ripped the journal open, not caring about anything else, and let my excitement take over.

I turned the pages and followed the hummingbird passing through each page like a ghostly being before it finally stopped and hovered over the last page where new handwriting was waiting to be read.

I jumped up with the journal and carefully held it in my arms to not disturb the writing as if it were to disappear or detonate if I moved wrong.

Meet us at Jaxon's home as soon as you can.
We are coming for you.

My entire body jolted with excitement as I ran down the stairs to the kitchen and screamed in excitement. "They got our note, they know we're alive, they're coming for us," I squealed, as my dad and Lady Cambridge jumped out of their chairs to read the entry as I set the journal down carefully in front of them.

"Could it be a trick?" Lady Cambridge asked and stepped back.

"No one else knows about this journal besides Freya and—" *Isadora,* "Shit," I paced back and forth. "It could be Isadora if she won in the fight, and no one is left of ours, it's possible."

My dad slammed the journal shut. "No, we are not

doing this." He walked to the window. "We finally have hope of going home, and we need to believe it. I know they're still alive. Haven, you know it too. We would not be here if our Anchors were dead."

He was right. I nodded and flipped the journal back open to the writing and smiled. "It's them."

"Let's get over there and wait," he said, and Lady Cambridge nodded.

"Is it okay for me to say that I'm nervous to go back home?" Lady Cambridge asked.

I looked at her and smiled. "To be fair, home looks a little different than what you are used to."

"Just the word *home* sounds good enough for me." She smiled.

I thought of the time spent here and smiled. At least, I was able to make up some time with my long lost dad. We celebrated Thanksgiving and Christmas together before entering into the new year. He surely made every day we spent here memorable. Even though I knew that he was hurting just as much as I was. But somehow, he kept his composure and made each day as special as he could. The amount of time we lost in our world was long gone, so the only thing we could do was make the best of forever together again.

The days spent in the street in front of his home and practicing magic, or better yet, perfecting his magic had been fun too. I felt a tear roll down my cheek as a smile spread across my face. He had truly improved his skills, and I was happy that he was excited to continue to learn. His eyes had bulged when I grew a dandelion in my palm and held it out for him to try and recreate. But instead, when his hand touched the flower, it wilted and became a wish and began to wisp away into the air and multiplied, twirling around us before dancing away peacefully.

As if my dad read my mind, he said, "We have had fun here. I mean... I know it wasn't under the ideal circumstances, but hey... These last few weeks, months, whatever it's been, have been wonderful for me."

I turned and smiled at him. "Selfishly, I've had fun with you, Dad."

Lady Cambridge cleared her throat. "You two are wonderful people. The bond between a father and daughter is so special. I'm sad that my girls never got to experience that. Watching you two work together has been an eye opener." She smiled and walked toward the coffee pot for a refill. "I know what we have to do to kill Ragnar too."

My eyes bulged. "Well?"

"With Ragnar having his mind games, I cannot say. If he decides to get into your pretty little head, then all is lost... You will just have to trust me."

I opened my mouth, ready to argue, but my dad stopped me.

"You are trusted," he said and nodded back to me, waiting for me to agree.

I nodded while checking my pocket and realized I left the Jasper stone upstairs. "Shoot. I'll be right back."

My dad nodded and watched me disappear onto the second floor of his home. I walked back to Freya's bedroom that I had been occupying for as long as we'd been here. I opened the door and walked over to the calendar and crossed off another day before standing back and examining the amount of sunrises and sunsets we've had here, and it was almost three months' worth of time. I shook my head in disbelief and prayed that when we made it back home today that we would not be in some new timeline universe where our loved ones were long gone or that Ezra hadn't left Crystal Rock yet. I silently prayed that he had waited a little while longer for me.

My dad and I had made so many memories over the months that a part of me deep down, behind the sadness and guilt of leaving everyone behind, unsure if they even made it out unscathed, a selfish part of me was truly happy to have had this time with my dad to make up for lost time. Plus, his cooking was phenomenal, and I truly needed to teach Aunt Clara how to perfect the egg for the top of the burgers once we got back home.

I set the pen down and smiled, exhaling slowly, ready for our next adventure to start and to finally be able to close this chapter in this world. The unknown future was scary to think about. So, instead, it was time to just let it go and breathe and, lastly, get the heck out of this place. I closed my eyes and turned around slowly, twirling Freya's moonstone earrings. I just needed the Jasper stone and we would be on our way. Lady Cambridge already had the squid ink from this world, and that was all that was left. I smiled before opening my eyes.

But then a chill ran down my spine, and my entire body froze as I realized I was not alone...

Chapter 18

Freya Chamberlain

We made our way to Jaxon's home, but surprisingly, no one was there.

"Hmm. That's weird. He said he was coming home," I said, as I walked up to his room and noticed everything was left untouched. Worry grew inside me as I thought of the worst case scenario. Just as the impending doom began to hit me, my phone buzzed.

> Jaxon: We are heading to JFK. Good luck today. I love you.

I took a deep breath and relaxed. Why he was going there was another story, but at least I knew he was safe. It was time to get my family back. I inhaled slowly and let my mind focus on the moment instead of the future.

We've got this.

> Freya: Good luck to you too… With whatever you are doing????
>
> Jaxon: All good things.

Freya: Better be!

Jaxon: Don't worry that pretty little head of yours. I'll be back before you are :)

Freya: If all goes well, then we will be back in no time at all, grilling at Swig & Jig together.

Jaxon: Sounds perfect to me. And hey, Clara is on her way to you. I filled her in about Haven and Jim.

I smiled and then worry grew over me, wondering what the heck he was doing. The fear of losing him again was too much to take. I needed him to know that I needed him around and that every minute we had together was another minute I never thought I'd have back.

Freya: Hey… I love you very much. Just in case I haven't said that enough lately.

Jaxon: …

He began to type and then stopped. I waited for his reply, and when nothing more came, I decided to put my phone away and head back downstairs. It was time to bring my family home. I ran down the stairs and met Eric and my mom in the living room under the souls. Luckily, they had started to deplete with setting them free, which was a great feeling.

"Let's get them home and then we will set the rest of these souls free the rest of the week," Eric said.

A knock on the front door made me run to it with

excitement. I opened the door with Eric following behind me.

"Hey, Aunt Clara. You are just in time."

She walked in with the brightest smile I had seen in weeks. "Oh, child, come here." She grabbed me and pulled me in tight for a hug. "Where is your mother?"

She squeezed me so tight that I struggled with my words. "Living. Room."

She released me and walked fast over to my mom. "Oh, Alexandra, this is the best day yet," she said as she made her way into the soul room.

Eric put his hand on my shoulder as I exhaled slowly. "Ready, kiddo?" he asked and looked back at my mom and Aunt Clara in the living room. My mom was fidgeting with her fingernails but nodded.

I smiled. "Beyond ready." We walked back into the living room with them. "Mom? Are you okay?"

She looked back to me and inhaled slowly, then exhaled. "Yes, I'm very ready." She smiled and grabbed my hand.

My phone buzzed again. I quickly grabbed it and read Jaxon's text.

Jaxon: You are NOT going to believe this.

Photo loading...

Believe what?

It was too late. Eric grabbed my arm and we were all warped into another world. The middle was waiting for us. I gasped when we reached the other world and quickly tried to fumble with my phone, but as soon as I tried to get the phone screen to light up, nothing happened. I stood in Jaxon's home with wonder about what I wouldn't believe. At this point, being a witch, I would believe just about anything. You could tell me that dragons existed today, and I surely would just nod and accept it.

All of a sudden, I felt a rush, and a heavy weight came with us this time. It was the first time we had more than just us, and it seemed to take a toll on Eric. He stumbled for a second and then straightened back up. He shook his head and nodded to me reassuringly.

"I think I'm going to be sick," my mom said, as she ran for the kitchen, Aunt Clara trailing behind her.

Eric smirked as he followed behind them.

I remembered feeling the nausea the first time we traveled too. It was a feeling that your body was still lagging behind in the normal world while your mind was here. It just didn't sync up right away. It was definitely something to vomit over. I put my phone in my back pocket and met them in the kitchen.

My mom was bent over the sink with Eric holding a cold rag across the nape of her neck. He seemed so caring that it made me want to laugh. She spent the last eighteen years running from him, and now, here he was, taking care of her and keeping her safe.

How ironic.

"What are you smirking at?" He turned as I jumped up onto the counter and crossed my legs, swinging them back and forth.

"Oh, nothing."

Aunt Clara was searching through the cabinets, pulling ingredients that she was famous for.

"Overload tea?" I asked, as she stopped searching and turned toward me.

"It also helps with nausea. Great for pregnancy, vertigo, hangovers, and literally everything else." She smiled. "I've been trying to get it on shelves everywhere for too long now."

"Big pharma." Eric scrunched his nose. "Good luck, but hey, I'll take a cup of that while we wait."

I laughed and walked outside to the front porch, looking up and down the empty road and praying to see my dad and Haven coming toward us. I inhaled heavily and held my breath, waiting to see anyone show up in the distance. When the empty roads sizzled in the sunlight and stayed motionless, I exhaled.

"Ugh." I groaned.

I heard the door open behind me, then Eric stood next to me along the railing, searching the street himself. "Give them time. Remember time works differently here."

I looked up at him and huffed. "I know. I just feel like everytime something happens, we get so close to winning, and something always gets in the middle of it. Our plans never fully work."

He laughed. "Actually, you guys trapped her and I in the cave months back. Definitely didn't see that happening that day."

I smirked. "Well, that was one hell of a fight."

"You're telling me, kid." He motioned his hands to his neck and imitated a quick snap. "Powerful hands you had with the help of those souls."

I smiled.

"Speaking of souls, how about we send some of them

home while we wait for the others. Clara and Alexandra can wait right here while we talk to the souls. It'll keep that mind of yours calm."

I nodded and looked to both ends of the road one last time before walking back inside. I headed for the living room with the souls swarming above me and reached for a bouncing flicker of light and let it dance down my forearm where my Mark used to be.

"This one." I enclosed the soul and waited as Eric walked back into the room.

"Leila." He smiled. "You're going to like her." He shook his head and inhaled slowly. "Alright, hold on."

He grabbed my arm, and the room disappeared as a lady appeared in front of me with long wavy dark hair that was covering half her face. She looked up at me, her winged eyeliner peaked at the corners of her ocean blue eyes making them stand out, stunningly with bright red, plump lips and her tanned skin. Her dress was long and silver with sequins filling every inch of it. Red heels that were surely not meant for long walks and practicality. She looked like she was dressed for a gala. I stood in disbelief as I realized, though different... her features looked a lot like Aunt Lynn. She could have easily been her sister, even down to her small frame. I looked back at Eric with wide eyes as I real-ized his type never really changed, he had only been looking for women similar to Aunt Lynn over the years.

Her stare became a glare as she looked over at Eric, her sweet smile turning to rage as she rushed at him, punching him across the jaw. "You!" she screamed. "You left me at the ball." She retracted her fist and punched him again. "Standing there, waiting for you to come back, and instead your wretched woman back stabbed me, literally, with that stupid dagger."

Eric threw his hands up after the second punched and guarded his face from her blows. "Hey, hey, I had no intentions of harming you."

"No, but your precious Anchor did."

"She's the jealous type." He grabbed her wrists and pinned her against the wall, facing away from him. He leaned into her ear and growled.

"You don't say," she sneered, as she kicked back into him and made him fall to the ground, groaning in pain. "I never liked blondes, anyway." She smiled and walked over to me, circling, making me feel slightly uncomfortable.

"I had nothing to do with any of it," I said quickly and raised my hands in surrender.

She laughed and grabbed my forearm, studied the blank canvas, and looked back up to me, eyebrows raised. "Where'd your Mark go?"

"Squid ink." I pulled my arm back and shrugged.

Leila yanked my arm back and tapped it hard.

"Ouch." I slapped her hand. "Excuse you."

She began to laugh. "Oh, darling. Eric failed to mention that magic does not simply disappear." She released my arm. "Come."

Eric sat up and shook his head. "The squid ink got Izzy too."

Lelia stopped in her tracks bond turned back around to face him. "And you didn't think to track it down?"

Eric stared back at her, confused.

"Men, such stupid creatures." She huffed as she walked to the lone table with too many objects spread across it.

I chuckled as I walked with her, slight hope that maybe she knew something to help me.

"Palm," she requested, as she grabbed the pocketknife sitting open on the table.

She blew at the flameless wick of a candle sitting in front of her, and I watched in amusement as the wick lit itself and the fire danced as a woman in a dress appeared in the flame.

My eyes grew as the beauty was mesmerizing.

"Such a young witch." She clicked her tongue and grabbed my palm. She laid it parallel to the flame but high enough that it didn't burn. She took the knife and made a small cut, making me want to retract my hand, but she held it firmly in place so that I had no choice but to embrace it.

I stared at it and watched as the blood began to boil but still felt cool to the touch.

"I don't under—"

"Shh..." she whispered, as she leaned in closer and studied the bubbling blood. Then, before I could freak out, she swiped her finger into my blood and licked it. My eyes bulged in disgust. "I'm right." She smiled and licked her lips. "Your magic isn't far from you, my dear. You need to retrace your steps. If it was truly gone, then it would have never boiled."

"So, the licking part wasn't necessary?" I scrunched my nose and swallowed hard.

She smiled. "That part was just for me to see what kind of magic you have. Syphon, and a very powerful one at that."

Eric walked over to us. "She's a weird one, but gorgeous

as hell, and she makes one hell of a brandy old fashioned." He smirked. "Her magic... Is it damaged?"

Leila smiled and walked closer to Eric. He stiffened as she touched his arm and rubbed it gently, avoiding his question. "We did have fun, didn't we?"

He nodded. "We did."

"Isadora." She shook her head. "She truly was one jealous bitch."

Eric laughed. "You have no idea."

"Well, I think I have some idea." She traced her body with her palms. "Dead and all."

Eric nodded. "We're here to right these wrongs. Freya is helping me release everyone to be with their descendants."

Leila shook her head. "I have none left." She looked back at me and smiled. "I liked when you took the souls from the dagger. You have a strength to you that I admire. If you wouldn't mind... I would love to give you my magic before I go."

I shook my head, feeling undeserving of any gifts. "I don't even have magic."

She smiled. "No, but you will. You are going to want me to help you in the future." She winked.

I looked at Eric who nodded. "She's a brilliant witch. It wouldn't be wrong to have her on your side."

"But how?"

"Save me for one of the last ones." Leila walked over and smiled, kissing my forehead. "I will help you unlock the best part of your powers when you're ready."

She stepped back and walked away as the room began

to dissolve, then we were standing back in the soul living room with my mom and Aunt Clara.

"What did she mean?" I asked Eric, still trying to understand what the hell any of that was about.

Eric smiled. "She's very in tune with her magic. She's a mix between old and new magic. She uses elemental mostly, but she loves the Pagan magic... She loves spells, hexes and potions. She can unlock your innermost power if you let her search you."

I swallowed hard. "Has she..."

"Unlocked mine?" He smirked. "Let's just say that the dance we were heading to was to celebrate her helping me with my mind manipulation powers."

I gasped. "She did that for you?"

He nodded.

"But I thought you created the middle with it."

"I did. She just helped me unlock how to manipulate others. Compulsion at its finest." He shrugged. "I don't use it often because I don't find it fair to twist people's minds." He swallowed hard. "I am not Ragnar. And that's exactly why I don't use it."

I stepped back and watched as Eric's jaw tightened and flexed, his emerald eyes became distant. "What did Ragnar do to you?"

He scoffed. "To me? Nothing."

"Liar."

My mom stood up and circled Eric, carefully placing her hand on his arm, closing her eyes and breathing in slowly as Eric exhaled heavily.

"Damn it, Alexandra." He released my mom's hand and straightened his suit. "Okay." He inhaled slowly and then spoke softly. "He murdered my parents before he was sent to the dagger world. He ruined the entire village with his power before he was finally gone."

I gasped, and without processing his emotions, I grabbed him, hugging him tight. His body tensed and then released as he wrapped his arms around me. "Your father doesn't know how it happened. He was hiding Margo, and when he tried to come back, I stopped him from going any further. Ragnar destroyed what we knew as Crystal Rock before he was locked away."

"I'm so sorry," I whispered.

"I will not let him do it again." Eric released my grip and grabbed my arms, placing me sternly in front of him. "You and your family are safe. I need you to trust that." His eyes glistened. "I will stand at the front of any battle before I let him get anywhere near any of you. Do you understand?"

"You are not sacrificing yourself for anyone. You have spent your whole life being stuck and never living it. When is it your turn to live?" I asked.

He laughed. "I have lived a thousand years. I have lived."

"No, you've babysat others. That's not living."

He crossed his arms and clicked his tongue. "Freya Alexandra Chamberlain, I am tired. If I can protect you, your sister, your father, your mother, Aisling, Lynn, and every one of their Anchors, then I will say I lived a successful life no matter how long it's lived."

I shook my head. "It's not going to come to that." I crossed my arms, mimicking him. "Let's just reunite our family first and then kick Ragnar's ass."

He laughed as Aunt Clara and my mom stayed silent with all of their eyes on me.

"End of discussion. On to the next soul," I said, as I reached up and plucked the next dancing soul from above. "We'll be back." I smiled and nodded to my mom.

Eric grabbed my arm, and just like that, the room disappeared and a tall dark haired man appeared in front of us.

"About damn time, Eric." His husky voice was intimidating. I stepped back and hid behind Eric who put his arms up in surrender and kept me behind him.

"Long story, Bane."

"Well, it seems like all I have these days is time." He stepped back and crossed his arms while leaning against the wall. "Explain."

Eric cleared his throat and turned around to face me. "He's harmless."

I looked up at Eric and back toward Bane and shivered. He was gigantic. His muscles ripping through his white shirt that was surely a size too small for him. I swallowed before stepping out from behind Eric and joined his side.

"Oh, the pretty little lady that helped us escape. Pardon me. I'm Bane." He reached his hand across and flashed his charming smile. "You, little one, have a lot of pow—"

"Bane, don't." Eric shook his head.

Bane looked back at me and studied me. "What the hell happened? She had so much power, I could feel it."

"*Had* is the key word," Eric snapped.

I huffed and stepped between the two. "Geez, let's not pretend that I don't exist because my magic is missing."

Bane laughed and grabbed my hand to spin me around,

then dipped me back, making me giggle as I felt a full rush of trust run through me. This man was nothing more than a gentle giant, which made me realize that he died for some reason, and I needed to know exactly what this big old teddy bear did to deserve this.

He lifted me back up, and I turned, face red with anger as I slapped Eric across the chest. "What the hell did Bane do to deserve this? You stupid, power hungry asshole."

Eric threw his arms up and looked back to Bane with pleading eyes.

They both laughed as Bane came up from behind me and pulled me tight against his big burly body. Pinning my arms across my chest, restraining me from another blow.

"Okay, okay." He laughed. "Eric had nothing to do with this one. He's my friend." He released me and let me process. "Isadora Cambridge…" He inhaled deeply and let his eyelashes flutter. "Ah, she took my breath away with her beauty and then literally stabbed me in the back. She gave me my final breath." He laughed. "Ah, to die for love is such a tragic way to go, but that woman had my heart in her hands, quite literally, and I was nothing more than a mere puppet to her games." His eyes glistened while he was in la-la land, as I scrunched my nose with his bad judgment. "Had I known that Ragnar was the man she was trying to release from that dagger, I would've gone nowhere near her. But love is blind. She had me in a daze until it was too late. Eric, here, tried to warn me to stay away from her, but I was under her spell, not a literal one or anything. Well, at least I hope not."

Eric laughed and shook his head. "Damn, Bane, I've

missed you and your stories." He exhaled heavily. "We're setting every soul free. That's why we're here."

Bane nodded as he seemed to be fully aware of the process. "I'm ready. All the souls are." He smiled. "I hope you made things right with my sister, Leila. I know she's been hanging around with me in the dagger world for a while now, and she really missed you too."

My eyes bulged. "That's your sister?"

He smiled and nodded. "Of course, don't we look like twins?" He stood tall and sucked in his belly and flexed his muscles as he winked.

I laughed and smiled.

Eric nodded. "She was one of our last stops. She wants to wait a little while longer, but she will meet you soon enough."

Bane nodded. "At least I was never lonely here. I feel bad for that Nicolai lady. She was so lonely for so long and just wanted her children back with her."

"Nicolai?" Eric asked. "Nicolai who?"

Bane shook his head. "Hm, I guess I never asked her last name. She just seemed so lonely... but man, she was one hell of a fighter. Strong woman, she almost broke my jaw when I saw her on the river bathing. I didn't mean to stare, but she was such a beauty, and I had never seen her before. Long blonde hair, braided to the middle of her back, and she was surrounded by these pink hummingbirds circling her. It was a sight to see. After she got out of the water, we talked for a while before she disappeared for long periods of time until I'd meet her back at the river bathing again." He smiled. "She was my entertainment while I was here. If you see her again, please tell her thank you."

Eric nodded and looked back at me, ready for the bittersweet goodbye. He grabbed Bane's hand and shook it sternly. "You will always be my closest friend."

Bane nodded and smiled. "You already know that I'm going to be hanging around and keeping you out of trouble." He winked as he nodded and closed his eyes. "I'm ready."

I grabbed their hands and watched as Bane's body began to glow before it shimmered and disappeared.

I exhaled happily. "He seemed nice."

Eric sniffled and turned away from me. "There's a lot of nice ones here." He turned back around. "Alright, those were the ones that I needed to make my own peace with. The rest we should be able to do in groups now."

I laughed. "You mean to tell me we could've done this all in one quick swoop?"

He looked back at me and smirked. "Groups are less draining than all at once, little niece." He cleared his throat and grabbed my arm, bringing us back to the middle where my mom and Aunt Clara waited.

"Anything yet?" he asked them.

They both shook their heads as they paced near the window.

I looked up and saw two souls bouncing opposite of the rest of them. They seemed to be dancing together and intertwining with one another. I reached up for them as Eric's hand slapped it away. I looked back at him, annoyed.

"Not those two yet."

I crossed my arms and waited.

"Just not yet... I'm hoping your father can help me with them."

I shrugged and let it go for now, but made a mental note that I would be following him along with that journey whether he liked it or not.

"Are we sure they're even here? What if we made a mistake?" my mom asked quietly while biting her nails.

"Did you guys break that lamp?" I asked, confused.

My mom's brows furrowed as she turned around and stared at it, then shook her head.

I had never seen her this nervous before. The last time would've been at their court hearing for the divorce to be finalized. A pit in my stomach grew as I realized that even then she was nervous and knew she had to get far away from us to keep us safe. Eric must've noticed my mind wandering, and he quickly changed the subject.

"Alright, group one it is. We will be done with this way sooner than I meant for us to be." He winked and grabbed my arm and a handful of souls as we were transported into their safe space to release them.

Hours passed, or so it seemed. With the time running so rapidly here, it was hard to tell how long we had actually been here, and still there was no sign of Haven or my dad. My heart began to pound rapidly as anxiety started to creep inside of me.

"Ready for group twelve?" Eric asked, as my mind raced.

I shook my head. With each trip back and forth, the pit in my stomach grew with worry.

My mom looked back at me and waited for me to break my silence. I knew I should feel good for helping set free souls that had been trapped for centuries, but I just couldn't hold myself together any longer. I just needed my dad and sister back.

I collapsed to the ground and just started to bawl. "I. Just. Need. Them. Back." My lungs began to burn as a fire inside of me grew with rage and anger. I could no longer hold it all inside. "All these families reuniting," I sobbed. "All but mine."

Eric seemed to be conflicted with his own emotions, unsure if he should comfort me or break something nearby. I knew he was holding back too, and his hope was deflating just as quickly as mine was.

"They're not here. We made a mistake," I yelled between sobs. "We need to go back home. I need to try the journal again. Maybe it was an old entry. Maybe our world was behind, and it was only just catching up with us."

My mom dropped to her knees next to me, shushing me and holding me close, letting the distance between us over the years completely break down. Every missing moment I had with her seemed to feel whole again. She was my only family left, and we needed each other more now than ever. I held on to her and sobbed like a child. She continued to rock with me and just let my emotions flow.

When the last tear finally dried on my cheeks, the room was silent, and it was time to go home. Eric turned and looked back at me, confused.

"What?" I whispered through a hoarse voice.

"Shush," he said, as he lifted his finger into the air and listened carefully.

Then, I heard it too.

The screams.

I jumped up and ran out the front door, running as fast as my legs could to the sound as Eric, my mom, and Aunt Clara trailed behind me. We ran straight into the direction of my home, and something inside me said to be ready. Something was about to happen, and it couldn't be anything good with the way the screams were hauntingly echoing down the road.

"Haven!" I screamed, as I saw my house in view and saw the shadowy figure in my bedroom window.

Chapter 19

Haven Vine

I could feel his presence here with me. A sickening feeling of death crept behind me, and I knew that I was in trouble, up here alone. I quickly turned and saw him standing there, his scar so prominent across his face as he smirked back at me. I gasped and felt my entire body freeze.

"Ragnar."

His smirk grew as he walked closer to me. My body seemed to be in more shock than my mind because every inch of me said to fight him, but I felt a fear for the first time in a long time that we were never going to make it back home after all. This man was here to ruin any last hope I had.

"You are not the twin I want, are you?" he asked. His voice sent shivers down my spine.

I was always the wrong twin. I shook my head slowly, feeling worthless in my own time of death, knowing that I was not the powerful twin yet again. So, I would die here in a world that wasn't mine because I wasn't worthy of my own power. My healing powers would not kill this man. My brain clicked on as I realized I still had Freya's syphoning. Whatever had happened in our world when we connected our hands and transferred to each other seemed to have stayed with me here, and for that, I was truly grateful, except that I hadn't mastered any of her syphoning yet nor had my dad.

"What do you want?" I demanded, trying to speak loud enough to get the others to hear me.

He laughed. "Oh, please. Your father and that wretched wife of mine are already taken care of downstairs. No one is coming for you. The others gave up on you, so no one is coming to save you."

"Fine," I spat. "Then, what do you want with *me*?"

He laughed again. "*You*? Nothing. But I do want that." He pointed to my hand as the Jasper stone glowed from my palm. My own eyes bulged as I saw the tiny dragon fossil inside of it begin to flap the half of the wing it had and fire escaped from its mouth. Then, it dawned on me.

I was syphoning magic from it. *I* was triggering it.

Ragnar's eyes grew with suspicion. "Well, damn, maybe you are the twin I want after all." He charged toward me, grabbing my neck and pushing me back against the wall. Breaking the desk that I had been writing at for the last few months, he slammed my head back against it while he struggled to pull the stone from my grasp.

I squeezed the Jasper stone tighter as I let the vines grow from my other. I extended my palm up and wrapped the vines around his neck, squeezing with every bit of strength that I had in me. But as soon as I felt like he was loosening his grip, my mind became fuzzy, and it was as if I had no control over my own body anymore. I slowly released the vines as I watched his smirk grow.

"Good girl," he whispered. "Now, give me that stone and I'll let your pathetic father live."

Without hesitation, I added, "and your wife."

He scoffed. "She is no wife to me, that betrayal cut deeper than anything should." He traced his scar on his face and spat on the floor next to me.

I grimaced at his germs spreading through the air and held my breath to keep any of his sickness from crawling inside of me. I shuddered in his presence and just wanted him gone. I felt the Jasper stone begin to flow willingly into me and panicked before I realized I truly was syphoning its power. I tried to stay calm and quickly remove it from the stone before handing it over.

I could feel his control over my actions, but I knew I had enough control to beat him at his own game.

"Lady Cambridge and my father need to stay safe. Understood?" I bargained, trying to waste time to get the rest of the power he was seeking from the stupid fossil.

He groaned. "Fine, just give it to me. And when you get back home, tell Isadora I'm coming for her next."

"I thought you said no one was coming for me?" I bit my tongue as soon as the words came out.

Ragnar glared at me and stripped the stone from my grasp just in time for me to finish syphoning the power that it contained, and whatever it was holding was something I had never felt before. Everything inside me ignited as the power was too strong for just me to hold on to. My head began to spin, drunk from the Jasper stone, and my chest began to burn. I felt as if I could breathe fire and kill this man standing in front of me. The thought became desirable as he stood in front of me.

So, with the thought... I screamed as loud as I could, letting the burning from my chest escape my throat, and literal fire began to ignite and burned the man's face as he released me and tried to block the damage. He turned and began to run away from me, then jumped down the stairs two at a time and ran through the front door. I tried to follow him, screaming as the fire continued to grow. And before I could catch my own breath, he disappeared into thin air on the road. But before he was gone, I swear I saw a mirage of Ember standing next to him before they both disappeared. I gasped and dropped to the road on all fours, trying to inhale and let my lungs fill with the cool air.

As soon as I finally sucked in some air, it was completely pushed back out of me with the impact of someone crushing my lungs as I fell over.

I opened my eyes and tried to let the head rush of power settle as I focused on my surroundings. And there, squeezing me tightly, was me... only it wasn't me at all.

It was my sister, my twin.

It was Freya.

My eyes began to fill with tears as I finally saw who was running up behind her. I swallowed hard and let the disbelief wash over me as our mom and Aunt Clara crushed us with an embrace as Eric ran up behind them nervously.

"Where's Jim?" he panicked. "Where's my brother?"

Our long overdue hug ended with my remembrance of Ragnar's words about my dad and Lady Cambridge being 'taken care of' just minutes ago. I pulled away from them and ran for the house. Without hesitation I nearly tore the door off its hinges as I ran inside and lost my breath as I got into the living room and found my dad and Lady Cambridge sitting opposite of each other on the couch, both with their eyes closed but their chests rising and falling. I stumbled back as my own relief was released. Eric met me in the living room and checked my dad's pulse as Freya ran in behind him.

Freya's relief was written across her face as she saw her dad alive. She reached out and caressed his cheek and let the happy tears flow. "He's here. He's really here?" Freya asked.

Eric reassured her that he was alive, and she nodded with a smile from ear to ear before walking back to me.

She grabbed me and examined my body with worry. "You screamed. What happened?" she asked me, grabbing my hand and pulling me back into her arms.

"I'm okay." I released her and looked back at her cautiously. "Is this real?"

She pinched my arm, and the feeling of reality set in.

"It really is you." I grabbed her arm and pinched her back, making her wince.

"Very real." She smiled as I squealed with excitement.

We both stepped back as our mom walked in and slowly sat down next to our dad as she leaned into him and gently woke him. His eyes slowly opened as his sight readjusted to the light of the room.

"Alexandra?" It was the hoarseness in his voice that had all of our emotions ready to break. He swallowed hard as she nodded and pulled her into his arms, swearing to himself that he would never let her go again.

Aunt Clara was the one to break the silence.

"Time sure moves differently here, doesn't it?" She pointed to the window. "How is the sun rising already?" She shrugged as if nothing magic intimidated her anymore in her life. "And who the heck is that?"

Lady Cambridge stirred in her sleep.

"Ragnar's wife," I answered.

The amount of gasps that were heard around the room were deafening. "Can she be tru—"

My father interrupted Aunt Clara. "She is going to help us kill him, for good this time."

I watched as Freya stepped closer to examine the woman who had birthed the other set of red moon twins. I knew she was thinking what I was. How could anyone love a child as evil as Isadora? She looked back at me and smirked.

"What?" I asked her innocently. "Crazy, right?"

"Is it weird that she kind of looks like Aisling?" She laughed as she looked back at the woman.

"It is in her blood. Genetics are wild. The sequences between chromosomes are undeniable with their bloodlines for sure."

Freya laughed. "Speaking of look-alikes, did you know that Eric dated a girl who looked like she could've been related to Aunt Lynn? I mean, before she was killed by the dagger, but still. Kind of sick, right?"

Eric huffed and rolled his eyes.

I laughed as I watched their annoyance with each other become one of my favorite duos as of late.

Lady Cambridge began to stir as she opened her eyes. She jumped off the couch and backed into a corner as she was greeted by too many unfamiliar eyes. "Where is he? Ragnar. Where did he go?"

"Ragnar was here?" Freya jumped as her eyes scanned the room.

"He's gone," I whispered.

"What did he want?" Lady Cambridge squealed, as she inched her way closer toward me. She looked upon my empty hand, and her eyes widened. "No, not the stone. You didn't give it to him, did you?"

I nodded with a smirk. "But not before I syphoned from it. Thanks to Freya's magic coursing through my veins."

Lady Cambridge seemed to hyperventilate as she processed.

I walked closer to her and sat her down. "Hey, calm down. He got nothing. But whatever magic was in that Jasper stone is coursing inside me now, and it is wild, let me tell you. I swear I breathed fire with it."

Lady Cambridge laughed nervously. She seemed to be in shock but somehow still trying to function. "Well, of course, it's dragon's magic." She laughed again, only this time excitedly. "He got nothing." She covered her mouth to try and contain her giggles. "You are a genius, Haven."

I smiled when her emotions seemed to settle, and I knew I did the right thing. Or at least, I hoped. "So, this dragon's thing... Am I going to grow wings or anything?" I asked nervously.

"Oh, no, dear. Well, I mean, I do not know fully. Have any of you met a friend of mine, Oxana, by chance? She is the keeper of the other half of that stone. It seemed fitting at the time to give her the other half that night, seeing as she has dragon's blood running through her own veins."

We all stepped back, except for Eric who seemed unamused.

"You knew about this?" Freya asked. "And didn't mention it to us weeks ago?"

Eric laughed. "Oxana is not a dragon anymore. She had some powerful fire magic back in the day but she lost her dragon magic the day..." He froze and seemed deep in a memory that he was not sharing. He looked back up and glared. "She's not a dragon anymore, she's never shifted since. I was a child, it was never real." He seemed torn between his own thoughts, or maybe he was trying to not relive his past. It was hard to tell with him.

Lady Cambridge huffed. "Oh, child. You truly don't remember? Adulthood has ripped that imagination from you."

Eric's laugh stopped as his stern gaze shot daggers back at her. "My childhood ended when my first blade ripped through the flesh of another man's chest to survive when I was seven. To protect *your* daughter and *your* people."

"My people? Our villages joined forces to conquer the lands."

Eric huffed. "We never wanted to join your husband's anything. We were fond of you, not him. The same feelings still stand today. Glad to see you survived. You've missed a thousand years of a bratty daughter being a jealous bitch full of anger issues."

I stood in shock as I watched the sentimental moment disappear as Eric turned and walked out of the house, slamming the door behind him. I watched as my dad stood and followed him, trying to calm him down.

"Well, it's nice to meet you, Lady Cambridge," my mom said, as she gently curtsied toward her.

She laughed. "Oh, darling, please... Call me Nicolai. Lady Cambridge was long gone, straight down another life path and onto peace. If I am going to adjust to modern living, then Nicolai sounds much more like the nineteenth century." She blushed.

"Twentieth," I corrected her, and we all laughed quietly as I watched Nicolai shrink into the couch, defeated for the night.

She half smiled and nodded.

"So," I turned to Freya. "What's the plan to bring us home?"

"Home," she whispered, as her mind wandered into disbelief. "We're going home, all of us." She smiled and nodded while holding back happy tears.

Chapter 20

Jaxon Oakes

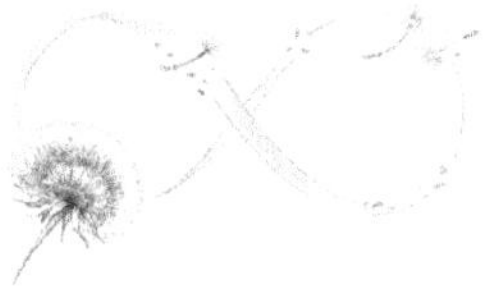

I couldn't believe my own eyes as we pulled up to JFK. I could see the tree glowing from a distance. Without hesitation, I jumped out of the car and ran for the lone tree, not knowing if it was a trap or if there was something worse lurking behind it. At this point, whatever *this* was, was something meant to be found. I could feel it pulling me in.

Whatever it was... It wanted *me* to find it.

My rapid breathing made me slow a few feet before the tree. I tried to catch my breath while standing in amazement at the tree surrounded by bright and beautiful wildflowers of all colors, and then the leaves themselves were glowing with an array of bright colors as if it were a sea of rippling rainbows. There was no possibility for them to grow naturally during any Wisconsin winter. I rubbed my eyes, trying to clear the mirage that was surely being played in my head. A mind game.

Wait...

"Ragnar," I whispered, defeated. I glanced down and saw my bracelet still wrapped around my wrist and looked behind me as Izzy came walking up with my mom, just as amused as I was. "Please tell me you're seeing this?"

She nodded with her jaw dropped.

"Is this him? Ragnar?"

Izzy shook her head and dropped to her knees and began to hug the ground. "Jaxon, you need to get Freya here, now." She sat up and cheered like a child, jumping up and down. "It's hers." She ran over and grabbed my arms. My body tensed with her closeness and then released as her pure excitement traveled to me. I tried to understand.

"Izzy, calm down." I grabbed her and made her freeze. "What is this?"

My mom put her hand on my shoulder. "Son, this is Freya's magic."

I looked back at the wildflowers as they began to sway and dance happily on their own. I grabbed my phone and called Freya.

The hours felt like days as I waited for her to get back to me. Izzy was pacing back and forth in front of me, the air around us felt like spring as long as we were standing inside the wildflowers circle. The minute we stepped back, the winter air would send a chill down our spine and our breath would become visible in the cold again. I took my jacket off and sat down in the warmth of spring and just waited for any response from Freya. I knew she was on a mission to reunite her family, and I knew the possibility of gaining her dad, sister, and magic back in one day was nearly impossible. There was a catch. There was always a catch.

I knew two things for sure. If she didn't find her family, then at least finding her magic would be a win for today.

And the other would be to find them all in one day would be epic but to come with what price? Either way... Something good was found today, and unfortunately I had *that* woman to thank for this win. I watched as Izzy continued to pace.

"Any chance you could stop?" I asked, making her freeze in place. She sat down quietly, seeming to not make a peep or the earth would shatter.

I watched as my mom walked back into the warmth, shivering from the winter air. "They still are not back. Your father said the souls have been depleting. I'm betting they are multitasking."

I nodded as my mom sat down next to me, leaning her head on my shoulder. I wrapped my arm around her and pulled her in closer to get her warmth back into her limbs.

"Having a son was the best part of my life," my mom said, as she looked back up to me and smiled. "Always a momma's boy."

I smirked and nodded. "Yeah, okay, Mom." I pulled her back in and rubbed her arms, helping with her circulation.

Izzy cleared her throat, bringing my attention back to her. I watched as she sat uncomfortably staring back at us. She quickly turned away and looked off into the distance. My mom grabbed her Labradorite pendant and began to spin it. The stone caught a glimpse of the sun overhead and shimmered, blinding me for a moment. I gently moved the pendant out of the sun's path and let my eyes refocus.

"Geez, Mom." I laughed as she placed it back under her shirt.

"Sorry." She smiled.

Izzy was staring back at us again, her jaw dropped. "You still have that?"

My mom nodded. "Of course. It was our mother's. It was all I had left after she..."

"Damn it, Mags. She left all of us that day. I not only lost my sister, I lost my mother and father all in the same day." She grabbed her head as if memories were beginning to twist and turn in her mind again. "I lost everyone." She grabbed her stomach and then her heart as she began to have a psychotic break. "My magic, my child, my family, my power..." She started to pound into the ground, and any human strength would have barely broken the surface, but after one, two, three hits the entire ground we were sitting on began to crack and shudder.

I stood quickly, helping my mom up and placing her behind me protectively. With no longer having magic or an Anchor, in my eyes, she was fragile. I needed to protect her from anything or anyone that could harm her.

"Izzy, you need to calm down," I pleaded gently, shocked that any strength could come from her tiny body that was supposed to be magicless.

She ignored me and pounded the ground harder, sending a row of wildflowers vibrating ferociously.

"Isadora!" I yelled louder, and when she didn't respond, I began pulling my earth magic in and sending her out of the wildflower circle, back into the brutal winter air.

She flew across the barrier and landed on her ass as she slid away. She sat up angrily and wiped the snow off her legs. "What the hell, Jax?" she asked, confused as she walked back into the circle.

I hovered my palm over the earth and aimed the other

at her. "Stay back," I warned, as I pulled more energy from the field and levitated the loose, jagged gravel, ready to send them through her and be done. My mom's hand gently steadied mine. The adrenaline was making them shake more than I had even noticed. I looked back at her pleading eyes and lowered my hands, the loose gravel falling back to the ground like a puzzle.

Izzy walked cautiously back to us. "I'm sorry..." She inhaled heavily without looking at us. "It's just that I never thought I'd see that again." She lifted her hands in a pleading motion. "My magic can weaken Ragnar."

I huffed and shook my head.

"This is not only Freya's." She inhaled heavily and waved her hands trying to bring my attention back to her. "Just listen to me... I know you don't trust me. I don't trust myself with power again, but I know what I have to do. Two birds with one stone for this deal." She exhaled and looked up at my mom, but I swore she began to smirk, making my blood boil. "Let me syphon everything from him and then—"

"Absolutely not," I yelled.

She was mad, and there was no way in hell she would get any of her power back. She had destroyed my mom's life, Freya's life, taken Jim and Haven away from us. She tried to ruin my life by paying a semi-truck driver to crash into me and Freya years ago. She started all of this. She deserved nothing more than her own hell she'd been living in her head. She was plotting something against us, and there wasn't a chance in hell I'd let her get any further with it.

"I think it's best if you go back to the house now. I will

wait here for Freya." I inhaled sharply. "Mom, get her out of here... please." I gritted my teeth as I watched Izzy's face change into confusion and then sink into sadness.

I watched her hang her head low. It must've been hard to have her power within reach and not be able to grab it. That was almost a sweeter revenge than anything else.

"You didn't let me finish." Izzy swallowed hard as she looked back up at us.

"Just go," I yelled, making my mom jump. She rubbed my arm quickly before she walked toward Izzy, grabbing her arm and dragging her away from any form of potential magic. She nodded as she turned back and watched me as she left.

An hour passed before I saw headlights approaching the field. I sat up quickly with guarded intentions, then exhaled slowly as I recognized the Jeep's lights. I smiled as I saw Freya open the driver's side. But then I froze as I watched the passenger door open, and Haven stepped out of the Jeep. I jumped up and ran to both of them. Freya ran into my arms, kissing me excitedly.

"They're home," she squealed. "Both of them."

Haven slowed as she met us in the field full of snow. She blushed as I set Freya down and pulled her in for a hug. Her tense body relaxed as she sunk herself into me and let the weight of the world finally leave her shoulders.

She sniffled and then laughed. "I thought Ezra might be here too." She stepped back and shrugged.

"He's with Aisling and Declan. I didn't..." I felt her emotions whirl as she looked around the field. "I wasn't sure if you guys would be back, and I didn't want—"

"To give him false hope." She half smiled. "I get it." She wiped her nose, and her tiny body began to shiver.

"Come on, let's get to the warmth."

Haven and Freya looked past me, confused but intrigued by the warm glow coming from the wildflowers behind us.

"You're not going to believe it," I said, as I grabbed both of their hands and pulled them into the forcefield of magic and under the tree.

Freya wisped her fingers along the colorful wildflowers and smiled when they shimmered brighter with each touch.

"Is this mine?" she whispered, as she dropped to her knees and started to have tears stream down her cheeks.

I nodded, smiling back at her. Haven gasped and joined her on the ground in excitement. Only this time, they were of happiness, and we finally not only had her family whole, but her magic could help her feel whole again too. Even though, to me, she was perfect with or without it.

Chapter 21

Aisling Meadows

"Would you two knock it off?" I yelled at Declan and Ezra, as we walked up to Jaxon's house after Aunt Lynn had called and told me she was checking in on the Oakes and making sure Isadora hadn't poisoned them yet.

I didn't like the idea of her being near that psycho by herself so I figured myself and my bodyguards could help protect her until Eric was back from his soul trip. I bit my lip as I realized I had not mentioned the side adventure to Ezra, only to protect his fragile heart. If I gave him false hope again, then he really might leave town this time. I had begged him enough to wait. Anchor or not, he was lost without Haven.

I opened the door and froze in the doorway, letting the guys bump into me and stopping everyone in their tracks.

"Jim?" I yelled, as I ran for him, pushing everyone out of the way. I jumped into his arms, squeezing the life out of him, then out of anger for him being gone for so long and breaking my best friend's heart, again. I jumped off him and pushed him against the wall. "You leave us again and we're going to have a problem. Understood?"

He laughed and pulled me back into a hug.

"I never intend to."

I let my shoulders relax as I enjoyed his hug. I breathed him in and tried to memorize his patchouli and whiskey scent so that my father, by friendship, would never be able to escape my memories again.

"We've missed you. And the bar misses your cooking. Or maybe it's me. But still. Glad to have you back." I stepped back and smiled. Alexandra nodded and smiled as she became glued back to Jim's hip and grabbed his arm protectively.

It was the first time that I watched them and actually smiled at their interactions. She stared up at him with so much worry and happiness that I finally understood her. She did everything she could, no matter how hard the situations were, to protect him. She protected his life because she loved him so much. She hurt just as much, if not more, while she was on the run away from her husband, children, and town, all to keep everyone safe. I grabbed her arm and squeezed it gently while smiling.

"You did good," I whispered in her ear and made my way toward the kitchen.

"Haven?" Ezra asked. Making me stop in my tracks. I turned around and scanned the room.

Just as a glass shattered in the kitchen, I ran in there in hopes of finding her. "Haven?"

But the lady standing there was not Haven at all.

Confused, I stepped back and lifted my palms letting the green orb of energy grow. My jaw dropped as the lady turned, and I felt as if I was staring at myself in the mirror, only an aged me. "What the fuc—"

"Wait, wait, wait," Jim yelled, as he ran in between the two of us before I fried her with my magic. "Ais, meet Nicolai Cambridge, Isadora's mother."

I leaned back in disgust. "And she's here, why?" I crossed my arms and stared back at my great great great ancestor and felt the bile growing in the back of my throat as my own bloodline was tainted. I was nothing like any of them. I wanted to rid her and Isadora of this world and start fresh with just me. I wanted to raise kids of my own and do better. I wanted my kids to be legends remembered for good and not connected to the hateful, jealous, murderous family I actually came from.

Jim smirked. "Well, she's going to help us kill Ragnar."

My lips smacked before I could hold my emotions in. "Right." I laughed. "And Isadora is going to join forces of good and help too, right?"

Jim shrugged. "Hey, kid, I only just got back home. But I know Nicolai is a lady of her word. She sacrificed everything to make sure our world stayed standing a thousand years ago. If it weren't for her..." Jim swallowed hard. "Ragnar had chaos magic. He would have burned our world from the inside out. He was undeniably the most powerful man on earth. His mind games along with his powers were deadly to all humans and supernaturals. He wanted to rid the world of everyone and start over with only the purest families he was rounding up."

I stepped back and uncrossed my arms. I studied Nicolai, and a part of me was happy that this woman may actually be a badass and I shared her blood. "Well, maybe she and I have more in common than I thought." I turned toward Jim and nodded. "Nicolai, I'm Aisling. I'm a descendant of yours... I guess."

Nicolai smiled and stepped forward, examining me from top to bottom as she circled me. Then, she smiled with a slight laugh. "I knew the minute I saw you." She grazed my long blonde hair and let it fall gently back onto my chest. "Mini me with Isadora's attitude for sure, but the sweetness of my Mags is buried behind those eyes of yours." She smirked and walked back toward the unfilled coffee mugs. "Well then, I think you and I should have a chat about what is going to be needed of us to destroy Ragnar."

"Us?" I asked.

Jim shrugged. "At least she will let *you* know. She hasn't told Haven or I a thing." He rubbed my shoulder as he turned to walk back into the living area. "Good luck, Ais."

Nicolai smiled and waved her hand to the open chair across from her. I inched my way closer and sat silently, studying her face and thinking about how DNA was weird. Her high cheekbones matched mine, and her eyes I could've sworn were my very own staring back at me. Her wrinkles were the only thing that really stood apart between us. I smiled as I realized this would be me in thirty years or a thousand if I had to be cursed with immortality too.

I hope not.

Her words seemed to flow as she discussed what she was supposed to do centuries ago, hoping that it would still be successful with our bloodline. Just as she was getting to her strategy, the front door creaked open, making us both stand, watching as Margo made her way inside. Isadora followed behind her, seeming defeated as she made her way up the stairs. I turned and watched as Nicolai saw her daughters for the first time in a thousand years within grasp of embracing. Her eyes welled with tears as she was frozen in her stance. Margo was the first to notice her and gasped as she was stopped in her tracks.

"Mother?" Margo whispered but stayed cautiously back, waiting for reality to slap her in the face.

Isadora made her way to the door and looked past Margo, staring at the woman standing beside me, and froze. Pure happiness flooded her before her face turned into a distorted grimace with excruciating pain as she grabbed the side of the doorway and used it to hold herself up.

It was only then that I noticed the blood slowly trickling from the side of her mouth as she grabbed her chest and dropped to her knees as Ragnar appeared behind her.

"Worthless daughter. When I tell you to get your magic back, you do it. I guess I'll have to do it myself." Ragnar pulled the knife from her back and wiped the blade on his shoulder, letting the blood pool onto the floorboards as his scarred face looked up toward Nicolai and smirked. "Nicolai and my dearest Margo. It's time you come with me. A family reunion is long overdue."

Nicolai dropped to her knees, shaking uncontrollably as she stared back at her daughters. Shock took over her body as her happy reunion that she wanted with her daughters was cut short by the man who had been holding her captive for far too long.

I let the rage grow inside of me, seeing Ragnar finally in

arm's length without being able to get into my head. The rage should've been for Isadora, but honestly, the bitch got what she deserved. She would have minutes left before she finally bled to death. I watched as she laid on the floor with pleading eyes for anyone to save her.

I stood in front of Nicolai and lifted my palms, as did Declan and Ezra, and we blocked her from her psychotic husband. I let the green orbs flicker into my palms, and the electric current ran through my veins as every bit of me wanted to send him straight to the hell he deserved. Ragnar's eyes moved from his wife to me, and he stared at me, confused, but when I met his gaze, his eyes were locked on my palms of magic. I tried to hold my anger steady and inhaled deeply. Just as I was feeling enough of a charge to release, Margo walked in front of Ragnar almost without any hesitation. For someone who was terrified of the man, she was sure not taking her time or negotiating with him to leave. I looked down and realized she did not have a bracelet on.

Damn it.

Callum bowed toward Ragnar, which was odd, considering that his wife had just walked over to our enemy and he seemed as if he didn't care at all.

"You should *all* be bowing to me right now," Ragnar snarled. "When I tell your worthless brains to bow, you bow."

I watched as the others quickly lowered their shoulders to the man in control. Only they were protected by the bracelets I gave them, so I looked back and played the part. But as I leaned over, I grabbed Nicolai's arm and held her back from advancing from the mind control. "You're staying with me."

Nicolai's eyes were stern as she looked back at me and winked while she slowly waved her wrist near my nose, sending the smell of the pungent anti mind control herbs across my face. She walked toward Ragnar with her hands gently behind her back as she pointed at her infused bracelet.

Everyone stood defenseless with Margo and Nicolai blocking his body in the doorway. I let the charge hold in one palm and grabbed Declan's water orb from advancing, his chest rising at a fast pace showing his mind was in control of his emotions.

"Good girls," Ragnar said, as he used their bodies as shields before grabbing both of their arms and disappearing into the night with a flicker of an electrical current flashing across them before they disappeared. My jaw dropped as his speed had never been a trick he had used on us before. I ran to the door, hopping over Isadora, and looked down the road as it came up empty both ways.

Everyone became frantic in the home, and the screaming and shouting became too loud. I looked down and watched Isadora struggle to breathe as she laid in front of all of us... dying. Seemingly, I was the only one to notice her at all. Her eyes met mine, and I felt like I could see right into her soul.

Help her.

I shook my head and looked around the room. Callum was in a frenzy that Margo was gone, and Jim and Alex were trying to calm him and keep him from running off.

"We need to stay together." They were yelling, trying to get through to him.

I looked back down at Isadora as her labored breathing slowed. Her fingers trying to pry to the floorboards as if they were her last lifeline to this world without any magic or an Anchor. She had nothing... and now her mother and sister had been taken by her deranged father.

Was no one going to help her?

Her eyes stared back at me while her life began to fade faster. I waited for anyone, anyone but *me,* to do something.

Help her.

My ears began to ring to the point of bleeding.

I dropped to the ground and covered my ears, trying to lessen the deafening sound. A flash of the cave came to mind when the connection we once unwillingly shared seemed to pull me toward her. I kept my ears covered as I watched my ancestor drift into a lifeless being, but for some reason Ragnar wanted her dead, and for that reason alone, I wanted her alive.

I knew what was right and wrong. And of course, of all days... today was the day that I didn't know if I agreed with my own conscience. The ringing went silent as I made up my mind. I slowly uncovered my ears to hear the bickering once again, and I didn't know which sound I would've rather listened to.

"Ugh, fine." I slid down to Izzy and grabbed her arms, dragging her fully into the house. "Someone get the healing tea brewing." When no one was quick to move, a switch snapped inside me. "Damn it, someone get me the fucking healing tea! And now!" My anger brewed inside me. "And someone get Haven here before I light the entire soul house on fire with all of you in it."

I knew I didn't mean what I said, but it was exactly what needed to be said to get the entire house out of shock and moving in ways that were helpful instead of bickering and panicking.

"Damn it, Izzy, you better hold on." I grabbed her chest and applied pressure, using my magic to try and help cauterize the bloody wound, hoping that it would do some sort of help considering that I didn't pay much attention to Aunt Lynn when she tried and showed me pre-med 101. But it was something I remembered having done when I cut my leg open at age five and my parents had to rush me to the ER, only the doctor on call was too busy to take us back. I vaguely remembered Clara being at the hospital that same day and applying so much pressure with her own palms and the tingling sensation of her closing the wound enough that I didn't need stitches that day. Had I known she was a witch back then, I would've known what she was actually doing as she gave me a sweet drink in a sippy cup.

Izzy's eyes stared back at me confused as she watched me carefully, her breathing more even. The tea came as Declan knelt down and held the mug of steam next to her and directed the straw into her mouth. I looked back at him, and his eyes seemed distant as if he was not on the same page as me.

"Ragnar wanted her dead. That means we want her alive. Got it?" I snapped at his silent debate between good and evil.

His eyes met mine in shock as his jaw dropped. "I didn't say any—"

"I know what you're thinking."

Declan's jaw closed as he smiled and shook his head. "Damn it, woman. You are something that's for sure." His smile widened as I raised my eyebrows. "Amazing, actually."

I smiled and focused on the wound. Isadora's eyes closed, but her pulse felt stronger and her breathing was even as Haven ran in the door with Jaxon and Freya.

Unfortunately, this was going to be a tough story to have to tell them. I watched as Jaxon scanned the room, and when his eyes met mine, I shook my head. I could see his shoulders lower, and he just knew what had happened. He grabbed his dad and sat him down on the couch while Alex explained everything to him. I watched as his fists clenched, and I swore I could feel the entire ground below the house rattle as he processed it.

Chapter 22

Haven Vine

Isadora's wound was healed after a little more TLC was given. It was a strange sight to see after the last time I saw her when she was trying to kill all of us and we wanted her dead. Now, here I was, helping save her from her eternal damnation that was truly well deserved. She laid sleeping on the couch under the souls as Callum sat beside her with Jaxon next to him. Jaxon's fists had been clenched since the moment he heard about his mom and rightfully so. It was as if the universe did not want all of us together ever again. I knew Jaxon was only here, instead of on a revenge mission to save his mom, to make sure that his dad stayed safe.

Callum hadn't said a word, but instead sat next to Isadora, waiting for her to open her eyes to see what she knew about Margo's whereabouts. And of course, we all wanted to know if she knew Ragnar's next move.

I stood and walked to the kitchen to wash my hands. I tried scrubbing the blood from my palms and scraping under my fingernails as best as I could, but it seemed that there would always be blood where I didn't want it. I felt as if a part of me was born to be a healer, to save people, but I also didn't want to be the one to play with lifelines that were not mine to choose. Everyone had their own path, and it definitely was not my job to save the villain. But again, who got to choose who the villains were? Versus the heroes? I closed my eyes and let the water run, trying to wash away the problems of today. Our other world was so quiet, and a part of me for a moment missed the silence, but then I thought of Ezra, and my heart leaped. I missed him. I jumped as a hand grazed my back, and I quickly turned around with bubbles up to my arms splashing onto the floor and across the man's chest as he stood in front of me.

"Haven." Ezra's voice cracked.

I stood in shock as tears spilled down my cheeks. I had been waiting too long to see him again and planning this very moment in my head for months. I had imagined meeting him along the river at sunset or in the pottery shop with Aunt Clara or even sitting at my dad's house, sipping coffee with my mom and sister with a map laid across the table, another plan to get us back. But instead, as soon as we arrived back home, he was away with Aisling and Declan. Then of course, we ended up with a phone call at JFK to get back to Jaxon's house as soon as possible and all of my plans disappeared. I was thrown into trying to save our enemy... or frenemy? I didn't know where to put her yet.

"Ezra." My soapy arms flew around his neck as I jumped into his arms. It was nothing like I had planned, but it was everything that I needed. The feeling of his broad shoulders gripping onto me as if he was never going to let me go again made me finally feel safe and at *home.* He set me on the counter and grabbed my face, studying me, waiting for me to disappear again as if it were another dream only to be woken up into another nightmare.

"You're here." It wasn't a question.

I smiled as I stared back at him, and he definitely felt real. I nodded and inhaled his scent and then exhaled with relief as he let his head fall into my chest and buried his emotions into me, only coming back up to kiss me fiercely as every spark inside of me ignited. Being back in Crystal Rock finally felt like home. I wrapped my legs around his waist and pulled him tighter against me.

"I've missed you," I said between gasps of air, kissing him.

"Are you kidding me? Life sucked without you here." He stopped kissing me and caressed my hair as he studied my face again. "You are never leaving my sight again."

I laughed. "I mean, that's a little obsessive."

He laughed and shrugged innocently.

"But maybe for a little while." I smirked.

"Oh my god, you two. Get a room," Aisling said, as she walked into the kitchen. "She's not even home for an hour, and you're already shoving your tongue down her throat. Let the girl breathe some earth air for a minute." She laughed and shuddered. "So gross."

I jumped down from the counter and grabbed her, pulling her into a heavy embrace. "Thank you for keeping him here," I whispered, as she let her shoulders relax.

She whispered, "I knew you'd want him to stay." She squeezed me tighter. "I don't know how much longer he was going to last as the third wheel."

We all laughed as Ezra unlatched Aisling's grip on me and lifted me back onto the counter. "I love you."

"I love you," I said back to him and watched as his smile finally met his eyes.

"So, what are we going to do?" I asked once everyone made their way back into the living area. I sat on the stairs with Ezra, no one else seemed to want to sit while being on edge. Everyone paced on their own paths in the living room while I just needed the closeness while I had it. "Nicolai had a plan to kill him."

"Did she tell you how?" Eric stopped pacing, and his eyes met mine with hope.

Hope that I didn't have to give him. I shook my head and slunk back into Ezra's arms.

Aisling stood and walked into the center of the room. "She started to tell me. Right before Ragnar invaded." She nodded to herself, as if she was trying to process the puzzle pieces she had been given. "I think I need her awake." She pointed to Izzy and frowned. "I need to talk to her. We share the same blood with her mother, plus her being a twin—"

"Twin! That's it," Freya interrupted and ran over to Izzy. "We can track Margo. They share the same DNA being twins." She grabbed Isadora's hand and poked her finger with the pocketknife she had kept in her pocket.

"Ow," Izzy slurred, as she opened her eyes. She jerked her hand back and clenched her fist. "What the hell was that for?" she asked groggily.

"Oh, shush, it's just a little blood," Freya said and walked over to the dining room table, unraveling the map that seemed to have seen better days. I jumped up and met her over there. Freya looked back up at me as she held the pocketknife over the map and let the blood drip onto the center. She lifted her palms over the map and froze. She looked down at her hands and then put them behind her back, embarrassed.

I grabbed her hand and leveled it with mine while I whispered incantations to search the map. We knew where her magic was, the problem was, we knew it was not just her magic hiding in the wildflowers. It seemed the only way to give it back to her was to give both witches their magic back. The only good thing was that we found where it was hiding, instead of it being gone forever, which at least gave us more hope than we ever could have imagined.

The blood droplets on the map began to spiral together and then began to drift toward the river. I could feel my stomach tighten as the droplets began to follow the river, and all I could think of was that he had drowned her, and we would find her floating.

"A boat?" Freya asked.

I turned toward her and nodded, hoping that she was right. Then, within a matter of seconds, they came to the edge of Crystal Rock and drifted off the map completely. "Shit. We need a bigger map."

Freya turned around and searched behind her, throwing the maps onto the ground. It wasn't until Isadora laid another map out in front of me of all of Wisconsin and its surrounding borders that the blood began to follow its path to Iowa and then circled the map before stopping. No longer on the water, but a place that was just across the bridge. I tried to visualize the area and couldn't think of anything in that specific location that was familiar to me. I looked back at Isadora, standing in front of me, weak but healing quickly. Her shaking fingers laid across the map as she pursed her lips and shook her head.

Freya turned back around with a map and froze as she realized we had an extra set of hands to help. I looked behind her and watched as everyone crowded in the doorway, watching us nervously.

"The casino," Isadora whispered with a raspy voice. She reached for the chair and tried to steady herself. "Oxana."

Eric stepped up and helped her into the seat. "You're not going to be any help like this. You need rest."

"I'm fine." She laughed nervously and then winced as her wound was still internally sewing itself back together. "Is there any of those pain meds here that I could maybe take? Then, we can go save my mother and sister."

Eric laughed. "You are worthless without magic."

Isadora grimaced and sunk lower into her chair. "It's strange... For the first time in as long as I can remember, my head is quiet."

I looked at Freya, confused, then back at Isadora.

Izzy exhaled and seemed relieved. "I can't hear his voice anymore."

My eyes grew wide as I walked over to her and checked her pupils. "Isadora?" I lifted her chin up as she half smiled. "Who's voice?"

She blinked a few times and looked around the room. "My father's voice. It's gone."

Eric spun her chair around to face him. "You mean to tell me that asshole has been in your head the last thousand years? And you didn't think to tell me?" He pounded down hard on the table, vibrating the blood on the map. "I've spent a thousand years dealing with your father's shit, and you didn't think for a second that it'd be nice to let me know?" He hit the table again, and Isadora flinched and covered her face, seeming like a child who had never been able to grow up.

It was Aisling that met my side, both her and I moved between Eric and Isadora as Freya watched carefully. Then, we stood to protect the fragile, broken girl that was being manipulated her whole life. Aisling ripped her bracelet off her wrist and kneeled down by Isadora and tied it across her wrist while I put my hands up, trying to keep Eric away, and waited for him to calm down.

He turned around and punched a hole in the wall, then another hole and another. Finally, my dad grabbed him and pinned him against it. Eric tried to push him off, but my dad turned him around and had him in a headlock as he pushed him back against the doorway.

"Calm down, brother."

"How do I stay calm? I've been babysitting for Ragnar's mind games, a sociopath for the last thousand years. And all those souls... All those people... All those witches deserved to live. Ragnar killed them all. Ragnar put every crazy idea in her head. He tried to kill my niece and Jaxon with the semi. Your daughter, Jim. He broke Izzy. Hell, he tried to break all of us." Eric pushed my dad back against the wall and released himself. "I'm going to fucking kill him." He punched another hole as the blood trickled down his fist. He pushed the back door open and began to walk toward the gate.

I looked at Ezra with hope that he would stop him from going alone, but instead, Ezra shrugged and let him go.

"Freya, you need to do something." I turned around and pleaded.

She was already ahead of me and ran out the door. Jaxon tried to chase after her, but our dad grabbed his arm and stopped him from following after her.

I grabbed the chair and sat down, inhaling heavily as I stared across the table at Isadora, and for the first time, I actually felt sad for her. She had not looked up since Eric went on his temper tantrum and now seemed so young and scared.

"Izzy," I whispered, hoping to break her silent stare from the table. "Izzy," I said again before she finally met my gaze. "Your magic is at JFK too... Do you know how to get it back?"

The room gasped as everyone processed what we had truly found on our quick departure after coming back home.

Aisling stood and looked between the two of us. "You're sure it's—"

I silently nodded, waiting for Izzy to answer me.

She looked up slowly and nodded. "Yes, I think so."

"She can't have it back," my mom interrupted. "Are you kidding me? Do you know what hell she has put us all through?"

"We can't risk it," Jaxon agreed.

"She's had her chance," Declan joined.

Aunt Clara stayed quiet, which was always her way of trying to stay neutral unless a vision showed her otherwise. I looked at her and waited for something. Any form of advice. Any sort of backup. She shrugged her shoulders.

"Ezra?" I turned and waited.

He stood in the doorway and looked down at Isadora and then back at me. "I'm sorry, Haven. I have to agree with all of them. She killed my parents."

Declan nodded.

"Did she, though?" I stood up and pointed at her. "This tiny human being? Sure, maybe she was a powerful Immortal at one time, but what if her thoughts had never been hers to act on? What if Ragnar was the one who held her strings and led her to every wrong-doing just like Eric said? What if—"

"We can't bank on 'what ifs' right now. We've all already lost too much," Jaxon chimed in, shoving out of my dad's grip on him before he walked out of the door after Freya and Eric.

The room became quiet, and everyone seemed to be having their own internal dialogue, debating on what *should* be done.

"I don't want it back," Isadora said under her breath, bringing my gaze back to her. "I don't know if it was just my magic letting him reach me or if the blade to the back finally severed the link from him. But either way, I don't want to take the chance again. I can finally hear myself think. I can't risk letting him back in."

"The bracelet will help," Aisling reassured her.

Isadora lifted her wrist and examined the twisted leather. She sniffed it and immediately retracted her head before laughing. "This smells familiar." But then she stared at it with deep thought.

"My Aunt Lynn gave me the recipe for a mind block spell. So far, it's worked against your father for me." She glared at Ezra for a minute and then back at Isadora.

She sniffed it again. "My mother used to have something like this... She tried to give me—" She froze. "She tried to give me a necklace with this exact scent centuries ago, the day... oh my god... It was the same day I killed my sister." Tears fell from her eyes. "My mother tried to protect me. She tried to protect my sister." She sobbed uncontrollably, too many emotions flooding her brain as it rerouted too many memories at once. I watched as the big bad Immortal became nothing more than a powerless child built from trauma and chaos. "The cave... She tried."

Aisling's eyes widened as she walked over and bent down in front of Izzy. "Hey, which cave exactly?"

Izzy's sobs slowed as she looked back at Aisling. She wiped her tears and swallowed hard. "It doesn't have a name, but I know where it is. It's the one near your field."

Aisling's eyes grew wide as she ran out of the door after Freya and Jaxon. My mom followed behind her as the screen door closed.

I watched through the screen as Jaxon and Aisling stood at the end of the driveway and watched carefully after Freya and Eric, then my mom walked past them and out of sight.

Chapter 23

Freya Chamberlain

Eric was halfway down the road already without slowing. "Hey, wait for me." I sped up and reached him, pulling his arm and stopping him. Eric flinched as he turned around. I stared back at him, trying to catch my breath until my mom's silhouette creeped up next to me and made me jump.

"Eric, you're not going alone." My mom grabbed his shoulder, and instantly, he stopped fidgeting. "Don't make me use this on you. Your brother just came home, and he can't lose you now. He needs you... *We* need you."

Eric gazed back at my mom, and you could see his rage growing behind his emerald eyes. At the mention of my dad, his eyes softened. He nodded, and she slowly released his arm. 'Damn it, Alex. You promised you would never do that to me again."

"Yeah, well, you were going on a suicide mission for no reason."

He shook his head. "Ragnar took Margo and Nicolai. I

made a promise a thousand years ago that I would keep the twins safe. And as of right now, I don't know if Margo is."

"Ragnar must need her for something. If he's keeping her alive," I added.

"We don't know that," Eric yelled, as he turned to face me. "We don't know shit."

The silence grew as the three of us stood in the middle of the road, headed toward a sure death if we went at it alone.

"We just need to make a plan." I said, breaking the silence.

"Oh, right, because all of our other plans have worked, so well," Eric spat.

A twinge of pain shot through me as I remembered the thyme spell and inhaled heavily, giving myself a minute to breathe instead of spitting venom back at him.

"I need to do this alone," Eric said, turning toward my mom and pleading. "You need to take the girls and my brother far away from here. I made a promise to always protect you, and whether you believe it or not, my 'chasing you' was my only way to keep you far enough away from Izzy back then. Had I known it was Ragnar all along, then my entire life would have been lived differently."

My mom nodded as I watched her wander into the past. "I don't hate you," my mom whispered. She looked back at Eric and shook her head. "I understand why you did it. I ran from my family to keep them safe too." She rubbed her arms in the cold air, and I watched as she shuddered before looking back at me with sad eyes, then back to Eric. "We're not that different, and if you think for a second that taking him on alone is the answer, then you are not as clever as I thought you were."

He inhaled heavily.

"I forgive you," she said, and Eric seemed to relax with relief as if they were the words he needed to hear for far too long. "I forgive you." She reached for his shoulder and patted it. "No persuasion used, just peace."

Eric opened his mouth to argue, but then came up short and exhaled. "Fine. Back to the soul house to come up with another extraordinary plan."

We walked back together, and I laughed silently as I watched Eric and my mom make small talk about nothing important. It was such a natural conversation that my laugh became louder as they both turned back at me and wondered what the hell was so funny.

I stopped walking and bent over and tried to catch my breath, going through a rollercoaster of emotions. "I'm sorry. It's just that a few months ago, we wanted to kill you, and a few months before that, my mom was not 'mom' to me, and yet here we are, one big happy family and working together."

Eric raised his eyebrow and smirked. "So, that's funny to you?"

I sucked in the cold air and tried to contain my laughter while I nodded. I began to feel a little insecure as I watched them stare at me crazily before my mom joined me and laughed too.

"I guess I'm glad you didn't kill him after all. He's kind of been helpful... Kind of." She smirked and linked arms with me.

Eric rolled his eyes and kept walking, "Yeah, well, I'm

still debating on keeping you two alive or running off with my brother alone."

Me and my mom stopped laughing and looked at each other.

"Kidding." He turned around and smiled. "Can we just have that family dinner for Christmas when all of this has been taken care of?"

I nodded with a smile. "At least one of these holidays, it will be sure to work out."

He smirked as we walked into the house. Everyone seemed to be in a frenzy of ideas as they all gathered around the table, plotting pros and cons and advantage points. I looked around the room and didn't see Ais or Isadora. I turned and saw them in the living room at opposite ends of the couch, but talking softly.

"Eric, get over here," my dad yelled, as we met them in the kitchen.

I peeked my head around the doorway to the living room and waited to make eye contact with Ais. I hesitated to leave them alone together until she looked up at me and waved me off. I nodded and brought my attention back to the others in the kitchen. Jaxon laid his arm across my shoulders and pulled me in against him.

"What are you guys thinking about doing now?" Eric rolled his eyes as he stood next to my dad. For the first time, I looked at them, like really looked at them both together, and I noticed their similar features. I stared and saw their high cheekbones and strong jawlines match up. The dark hair was similar in color, but my dad's had more of a wave to it, or he just didn't style it the same as Eric with it slicked back. My dad's hazel eyes shimmered with hope as Eric's emerald ones watched his brother with admiration. My dad brought his arm around Eric and laughed as they pointed to the map, and I could see them both reminiscing on a thousand years ago, which was still hard to wrap my head around, but at the same time, it seemed familiar to have a sibling found after being lost. All of a sudden, it was an empty hole that seemed to fill.

"You okay?" Jaxon whispered, as he leaned closer to my ear and kissed my cheek softly.

I nodded and blinked the tear away that was trying to form. "Yeah, actually. I am." I looked up at him and reassured him.

"Can we talk for a minute?"

I stared back at him, confused, but nodded as he pulled my hand and brought me upstairs into his room. He closed the door behind him and walked over to me.

"I heard Ais and Izzy talking while you were grabbing Eric. I don't know how I feel about this, but I need you to know what they are plotting by themselves."

"Ais and Izzy? Since when are they friends?"

Jaxon frowned. "Ais thinks we should get Izzy's magic back. She thinks that she's on our side."

I stood and debated as to what our actual options were. If she had her magic back and decided to go rogue on us, then we would be at a disadvantage. But if we needed her and she was powerless... then what?

Ragnar wanted her dead for a reason.

"Freya, we can't let her get it back. We can't. We saw what happened last time."

Ragnar wanted her dead for a reason.

"Babe, are you hearing me?"

Ragnar wanted her dead for a reason.

He looked at me and grabbed my hands. "Babe?"

"He wanted her dead for a reason," I said louder than I meant to, and Jaxon stepped back, shocked.

He shook his head. "I don't give a damn what Ragnar wanted. Isadora has tried to kill all of us, and because of her... you and your mom went into a spiral of depression for weeks, and I'm not letting that happen again. You barely were holding on, and I can't lose you again."

He looked down at the ground and continued to shake his head. "I can't."

I walked to him and grabbed his face, making his eyes reach mine. "I am not going anywhere."

"You don't know that."

"I know I have Haven as an Anchor, and she's one determined lady."

He shook his head again. "If Izzy betrays us..."

I covered his mouth, not wanting to hear my own thoughts coming from his lips. "I know."

He nodded. "So, what now?" His chest shook as he exhaled, trying to hold his rage inside. "I don't like this one bit."

I nodded. "Me neither. But I do think we have a better advantage with her than without." I swallowed hard. "I think I have an idea."

He looked back at me and waited.

"I think we need to link her to one of us Anchors and not tell her which set. I think she would take our lives a little more seriously."

He huffed and laughed. "She doesn't care about any of us."

I raised my eyebrows. "No, but she cares about herself."

His thoughts finally connected with mine as he began to smirk.

"You think you can link to one of us?" I asked. He seemed deep in thought. "I mean, she will want to protect everyone like her life depends on it..." I smirked. "Well, it actually will."

He smiled for a second and then frowned. "Damn it, I wish I could ask my mom. She would know."

"What about your dad?"

He shrugged. "I mean, I can ask him, but I doubt it." He lifted my chin and let his lips reach mine.

"What else is in that head of yours?" he whispered, as he pulled back.

I smiled. "I have a few more ideas. But I think it's best if I keep them to myself right now."

He furrowed his brows and bit his lower lip. "Do those plans involve me with a shirt on or off?"

I laughed. "My head is running on overload right now. I think some of my thoughts need to stay PG right now."

He laughed as he pulled me in closer, and the smell of sandalwood and lavender mixed in my nose as I let the calming scent take over for a little while.

"We need to get your mom back," I whispered, not wanting to ruin the moment but knowing that it was the elephant in the room.

He was quiet for a minute and then looked back at me. "Your Aunt Lynn Anchored herself to Eric and Izzy. Do you think there is a limit on how many people can share a bond like that?"

I shrugged. "I'm thinking we should link her to me and Haven."

He laughed. "Absolutely not."

"I would rather have her linked to me than anyone else." I swallowed. "I can't lose anyone else."

He huffed. "So, you can do some suicide mission *again* and sacrifice yourself *again*. I think not. And Haven is too much like you. We can't have the two of you sacrificing any more than you already have." He pulled me in closer. "Just let me do the linking. It's best if I'm the only one that knows who it is anyway."

I shook my head, but he squeezed me a little too tight.

"No way," I said, but as I thought about it... I knew he was right. If Ragnar got in any one of our heads and warned her, then she would have no motivation to keep the rest of us alive. I laughed nervously. "Fine... Just let me breathe."

"Oops, sorry." He laughed and released me, kissing my forehead. "I need to go look through my mom's grimoire and talk to Lynn."

Chapter 24

Jaxon Oakes

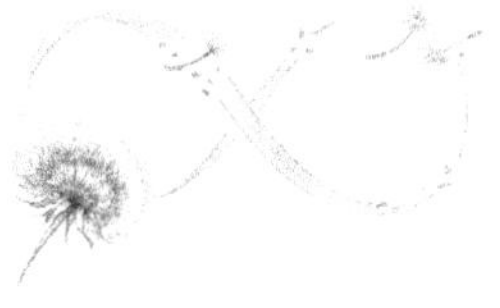

She was out of her mind if she thought I was going to let her link that bitch to her at all. Knowing Izzy, she would get her magic back and then syphon from both the twins. I wasn't going to take any chances. I needed to talk to Lynn. She had done this exact spell before with Izzy and Eric. I just needed to be sure if there were any side effects of having a third person added to an Anchor bond.

Lynn was seated on the front porch swing with Eric's arm around her, swinging back and forth. They both turned toward me as the door creaked open.

"Hey, uh... Lynn, can I borrow you for a bit?" I asked.

Eric's gaze was burning into me as he raised an eyebrow. "Damn, can I just get one free second with my lady? Haven't I lost enough time with her?"

Lynn laughed and nudged him. "Oh, shush. Come home tonight, and we can have a whole date night."

I shrugged and waited. "I kind of need to ask you some important questions."

She nodded and pointed to the open chair next to the swing, and I walked over and joined them.

Eric stood and stretched. "I should head back inside anyway."

"Nah, you can stay," I assured him.

Lynn grabbed his hand and rubbed his fingers, interlocking his palm to hers, pleading eyes staring back at him.

He grimaced. "Alright." He sat back down and wrapped his arm back around her shoulders, pulling her in tight for warmth.

"I'll be right back." I ran inside and grabbed a blanket before running back out and laying it on Lynn's lap.

She smiled. "Thank you."

I nodded. "When you linked yourself to the Anchors, were there any side effects that I should be aware of?"

She frowned and seemed to be at a loss for words. "Can I ask who you're trying to link?"

I inhaled slowly, counting the seconds before all hell would surely break loose.

"We think Izzy might need her magic back, and she will need an Anchor to have it. Plus we could use the leverage of another powerful witch. So, we wanted to link her to a set of Anchors... She will have to try to keep us alive if she wants to stay alive herself."

When the silence became deafening, I looked up at the two of them and waited for answers. They were staring at each other and seemed to be having their own internal conversation.

"Come on, say something."

Lynn turned to me. "You have your mother's grimoire and her magic. You can do a hell of a lot more than you think." She smiled. "The only side effect is..." She inhaled and exhaled slowly, her gaze never leaving Eric's. "You feel connected in a way that pulls you to them. Keeping you close enough that you don't *want* to be another city away. You will feel lost or broken without them near you. A constant pull in the direction you wish was opposite."

Eric's eyes saddened as his jaw dropped. He slouched lower into his seat and shook his head. "You never told me that."

Lynn shrugged. "I could handle that kind of hurt alone."

"Lynn." He grabbed her face and grazed her cheek softly. "I'm so sorry. I hurt you even when I wasn't aware that you were nearby." He pulled her into his chest and kissed her head. "Centuries you followed me and stayed hidden. So close, but just out of reach."

She shrugged again. "I thought you loved her..."

He scoffed. "She had taken everything from me... I was trying to protect my brother and Mags from her wrath." He shook his head. "And after all this time, I realize it wasn't even her. It was her father all along, toying in her head." He inhaled slowly. "He knew anytime I had a glimpse of a smile and he would tear it away from me, all the innocent souls. And then you..." He looked away and then turned back to Lynn and held her chin, "You had to watch me do so many terrible things."

She closed her eyes and tried to turn away. "I also watched you try and clean up every mess she caused. I watched you become a father to Declan, and I watched you slowly heal a piece of you that was taken from... Taken away by me... I also ruined a part of you for my own selfish reasons. I had many times that you were alone and grieving that I could have come to you, but I chose not to because of my own disgust with myself and what I had done to you too. I had taken your child away from you and raised them as if they were my own while you fell apart." She stared back at him with saddened eyes as he wiped her tears away. "I guess we have both done things we regret."

He grimaced and nodded. He lifted her chin gently and kissed her lips.

"Truce?"

She sniffled and nodded. "Truce."

I cleared my throat, feeling as though maybe they needed more time to catch up from their distance. "We can talk later." I stood and turned toward the house.

"No, no, no. Sit," Lynn said, as she grabbed my arm and pulled me back down. "I want to help any way I can. I may have given Aisling my magic, but one thing I will always know how to do is spells. And that is only something you can learn with years of practice." She smiled.

I nodded and began to explore our options.

"Who will you link her to?" she asked.

I shook my head. "That's for me to know."

She frowned.

Eric stood and shook his head. "Link her back to me and Jim. Our immortality will surely have a better hold on her that way."

I laughed. "Oh yeah, because that worked out so well the first time."

Lynn chuckled and covered her mouth when Eric's eyes glared back at me.

"I'm just saying, I don't think that's the best idea." I

shrugged. "Besides, whomever I decide on will be known only by me." I cleared my throat. "I can't have her knowing who she doesn't need around."

Eric inhaled deeply and held his breath before nodding. "You're right."

I smirked. "I'm sorry, what was that?"

"Don't be a dick." He rolled his eyes. "She's going to be drawn to whomever you link anyway. So, I guess we will see who she decides to hang around more." He laughed. "Noble boyfriend of my niece. I hope you're ready for her to be attached to your hip."

I swallowed hard and sat back, annoyed.

Was it that obvious?

He smirked. "Predictable."

"I have a plan." I nodded. "Just don't ask about it again. If Ragnar gets in any of our heads and figures it out, then that set of Anchors will be his true target."

He nodded.

Lynn cleared her throat. "Well, why don't you give Jaxon and I some time to discuss this plan further?" She stood and kissed him. He nodded and paced back and forth while she tugged on my arm and brought me with her into the house, closing the bedroom door behind her.

"What should I do? I didn't realize how obvious my choice was."

She paced back and forth before finally freezing. "You *know* who you have to link Izzy to." She half smiled. "I know you don't want to, but you do know, don't you?"

I inhaled and released the last breath of air I had before my decision was going to torment me from the inside until Ragnar was in his grave.

I nodded. "Yes, I know. I just hoped that you had a different option."

Her eyes met mine with sympathy. "Our loved ones are our most sacred. I know you want to be the hero and link her to you and Declan. But we both know that Ragnar will be after the twins."

I nodded again.

"I promise they will be okay."

"Lynn... please... Don't make promises that you can't keep. Hell, you don't even have magic anymore to ensure anyone will live."

She stepped back and nodded apologetically. "But I still have faith in the living." She smiled. "Freya is strong, and linking Izzy to her and Haven, it will give all three of them an immortal chance against Ragnar. Jim and Eric have immortality to help, but the other sets of Anchors won't be the true target. And as much as I don't like Izzy... I don't hate her, either. She was a manipulated child, and she deserves her chance at revenge just as much as any of you."

I nodded.

"Plus, my sweet Aisling has had some form of undeniable power ever since her and Ezra were bonded as Anchors. I believe she may have to play a bigger role in all of this as well, and I hope that you will keep her close to you just in case."

I inhaled deeply. "Seems as though I am the protector after all."

She smiled. "You are the one with the biggest heart, that is undeniable."

I smirked. "Alright, alright. Tell me what the hell I have to do to save the world today."

Chapter 25

Aisling Meadows

I knew I couldn't tell all of them because I couldn't have everyone tagging along and triggering suspicions for Ragnar, in case he had little minions working for him. I needed to go to the cave and see what that Cambridge lady was saying. She seemed adamant about checking the fine print.

"What're you thinking about?" Declan whispered in my ear, pulling me back to reality.

I shook my head and smiled.

"Liar." He smirked. "But I won't pry."

I nodded and kissed his cheek before standing up and walking over to Haven.

"Hey, would you mind walking with me for a minute?"

She looked back at me with worry.

Ezra stood and glared at me.

"I'll bring her back in a minute. Calm down, ya brute."

He rolled his eyes and laughed.

We walked into the hallway and opened the attached

garage door and stepped out into it. I closed the door behind us and waited for her attention.

"What's going on?" she asked, looking around the empty garage.

"Izzy's mom mentioned a cave right before she was taken. She said that we could find the answers in a cave. The only cave I can think of is—"

"The one they were sealed in." She began to pace back and forth and shook her head. "We've been in that cave plenty of times, and I've never seen any writing on the walls or anything."

I bit my lower lip out of an anxious habit. "I know. That's exactly why I haven't said anything more. She was ripped away basically mid-sentence."

Haven stopped and turned quickly. "What if it's glamoured?" She smiled as the wheels began to turn inside of her head. She straightened her glasses and started to pace again.

"I mean, that's possible. Or we might have the wrong cave."

She swallowed and inhaled heavily. She fidgeted with her fingers and then looked back at me. "Can I tell you something that I'm pretty freaked out about?"

I stared back at her confused and nodded.

"I have had this burning in my chest ever since I stole the Jasper's powers before Ragnar took the empty stone. The problem is... it's literally burning. I feel like I could blow fire, and I really want to go somewhere open to release whatever is stuck inside me. I'm trying to figure out the best way to not alarm anyone, and I don't want Freya to try and help me right now without her magic." She exhaled heavily as if the weight of her world just lightened.

"Oh my god, Haven. What can I do to help?"

She bit her lower lip and closed her eyes. "Let's go check out the cave, but I want to try and syphon this magic out of me and contain it somehow while we're there."

I stared back at her worriedly. "Why don't we tell the others? Maybe Eric or Aunt Lynn—"

"No," She shook her head. "I just want to do this myself without an audience. I'm nervous that I may turn into a full blown dragon and kill someone."

My jaw dropped as I stared back at her. "But what if you kill—" *Me*, I wanted to say. But instead, I shut my mouth when I saw her eyes begin to fill with tears. "Okay, sure, yes." I swallowed hard. "Just you and me." I nodded, and she smiled.

"Thank you."

"Don't thank me yet. I don't know what the hell we're supposed to do with a supernatural creature that has been long extinct." I shrugged.

She laughed. "I feel like it may be nothing, but a part of me just wants to be sure."

I nodded. "Let's sneak out the back right now."

She looked back at me and closed the distance between us. "Thank you... Maybe not for this, but for keeping Ezra close."

I hugged her tight bond let the embrace seal our silent deal of friendship and understanding.

We took one last look at the house as we jumped in my car and kept the headlights off until we were further and then made our way to the cave. There were no hiccups or interruptions, which made me scan the area again just to be sure that we were not being brought to danger. When we saw the entrance to the cave, we ran for it.

The cave was quiet.

"Ignis," I whispered, afraid to speak too loud in case the cave shattered into a million pieces with us inside.

The flame grew and lit up the entire cave, making my nerves settle a little more.

I heard Haven exhale too when we reached the center of the cave and saw we were truly alone.

"Well, that was scary." She laughed nervously.

I nodded and began to scan the walls.

The loose gravel behind us began to shift, and we both froze, extinguishing the flame and turning around. We waited in the dark silently.

Neither of us were breathing as we saw a flashlight heading our way.

Haven's gasp escaped before I could grab her mouth and silence her. But then she laughed.

"You are never going to let me leave your sight again... are you, Ezra?" She laughed again as Ezra came into view.

He held his hands up in surrender. "To be fair... I love you, and I'm linked to her." He shrugged his broad shoulders and stood a distance from us.

"Well, come on over." I laughed as I finally exhaled. "You know we have phones. A simple text or call would have been less scary.".

"Yeah, well. You two ran off so fast, I knew it was some secret mission I'm sure you would have kept from me. You women always think you can do it all. But you don't have to do it alone."

I looked at Haven, who grimaced back at me.

"Well, to be fair…" Haven began.

"We just wanted to check out a lead that Izzy's mother mentioned. I just didn't want to get anyone's hopes up until we knew for sure. That's all."

Haven fidgeted next to me. I watched as she grabbed her necklace and began to twirl it the same way Freya always did. I laughed to myself as I watched our cover story break. She couldn't keep a secret from him.

"I think I consumed some dragon magic from that Jasper stone you gave me, and now I'm afraid that the rattling in my chest is going to make me implode or start flying in the sky," she blurted out and then grabbed her mouth.

Ezra stepped back and then leaned over himself and grabbed his knees before laughing so loud that the entire cave rumbled. Haven and I looked back at one another and waited for him to catch his breath.

"Something funny?" I interrupted. "That's exactly why *we* left you home."

He stopped laughing and stood up, shaking his head and looked at Haven. "Babe, I wish you would've told me. That stone has been with me a long time. I can help you."

Haven gasped and then ran and jumped into his arms.

"You are not a dragon." He cupped her face and kissed her forehead. "But that rattling inside your chest is magic that doesn't want to be contained in a healer. Your magic is trying to push it out to heal you. If anyone else were to consume it, it would make their powers magnify." He lifted her chin and peered into her eyes. "I can hold it until we get the Jasper stone back. I've held it before. It's just not meant for long term use inside of us."

I watched as Haven stared back at him, confused.

"It was a long time ago. I was only a child, but I haven't done it since."

"Are you sure you can hold it?" I asked nervously.

He set Haven down and walked back toward me as she followed.

"Ember was made out of the other half. The magic that stone holds is strong, but as a protector, I was made for just that. And now that I have my Anchor, I can hold it for a lot longer." He grabbed my forearm and traced the triangles. He looked at Haven and raised his eyebrows. "Or she and I can split it and hold it?"

I felt my Mark begin to tingle. I pulled my arm away from him and rubbed it. I looked back up at Haven and watched her desperation grow as she rubbed her own chest. I turned back to Ezra and nodded. "What do we have to do?"

He smiled.

"Are you sure we won't turn into dragons?" I asked nervously.

He nodded as we all laughed.

"We will be able to hold it for a little while, but we really need to get that stone back to contain it for good."

"Shouldn't magic be free? I feel like magic is an energy that wants to fly high, and really, if it's not being held by a witch... shouldn't it be free?" Haven asked.

Ezra looked between the two of us and shrugged. "It's really not my choice. My mother and father protected the stone for years for a reason. They did not want it in any

Immortals' hands, and I'm assuming Ragnar is the worst one yet."

The three of us stood in a triangle and agreed.

"So, how do we do this?" Haven asked nervously.

Ezra swallowed hard. "You're not going to like this..." He stared back at Haven and then me and shook his head.

"Damn it, do you have to sleep with her or something?" Haven asked.

Ezra laughed as he grabbed her hand and rubbed it reassuringly. "I meant that you're not going to like how it feels to take it from you." He smirked. "I'm not touching any other woman. It's always you."

We both exhaled in relief.

"Ais, give me your hand. Haven, I need you to stay as still as you can. I'm not going to lie to you... it feels like it's being ripped from your chest. You will lose your breath for a minute, but I will try and take it as fast as possible. And then, Ais... It's going to fill your lungs. It should feel like an icy winter's night. There should be no fire."

I nodded, nervously.

He looked back at me and then to Haven. He leaned in and kissed her lips. "Just take a deep breath."

I could feel his hand shake slightly in mine, and I knew that he was trying to seem strong about this situation, but then I felt his worry as he closed his eyes.

"Hold on," I whispered. "Just give me a second."

He released my hand and nodded.

"This will work," I said reassuringly. Whether I was reassuring him or myself, I didn't know. "Okay, we are going to do this quick, and as soon as it's over, we are going to search this cave high and low until we know how to defeat Ragnar. Deal?" The three of us nodded and got back into our triangle stance.

We joined our hands, and the grip felt much tighter this time. Ezra was no longer shaking. He seemed to have needed an extra minute himself.

"Ez... You've got this," I reassured him.

He turned back toward me and nodded with a more confident smile.

He began to whisper an incantation that did not seem to be Latin. I listened carefully to his words and began to feel my lungs fill with the icy air he was describing. Haven's hand tightened around mine as she began to crush my fingers. I looked at her and watched as sweat began to form on her forehead, and I could tell she was trying to stay silent and not let Ezra know her pain. I squeezed her hand back and tried to balance out her grasp. I rubbed her hand with my thumb and waited until my lungs felt completely iced over.

Haven exhaled as she opened her eyes slowly. She released our hands and nodded excitedly. "It's gone. The burning is gone."

Ezra looked at me cautiously. "I'm good. Are you?"

I smiled and nodded.

"Let's not tell anyone about the dragon idea... please," Haven asked nervously.

We all laughed, then Ezra picked Haven up and kissed her. Haven laughed more and smiled. She whispered the words 'thank you' as Ezra spun her around. I nodded and began to search the cave.

The icy lungs felt weird, but mostly, they felt as if the Wisconsin winters took my breath away.

"Ignis," I said, as I walked to the walls and stepped back in shock as the flame was ten times higher than it ever had been before. "Whoa."

Ezra put Haven down. "Enhanced powers for the time being."

"You don't say." I stared at the flame and smiled at the power I felt within me.

We searched the cave for nearly an hour, as we tried to pull out any loose stones and knocked on the wall in search of anything hollow.

"That's it. We've searched every inch, and nothing is coming up. Freya and Declan have called me twice, and I'm pretty sure that Declan is already on his way to us."

"Where is the next closest cave?" Ezra asked.

"There's another one about a mile north," Haven answered.

I shook my head. "It has to be here. It's too much of a coincidence."

"We've searched the entire place... plus, don't you think that Eric or Izzy would have found something while being trapped in here? They had months to search the damn place."

I stood and stared at the walls, and something inside me screamed that we were right where we were supposed to be.

"No, it has to be here." I shook my head.

"Ais, there's nothing," he said. "Let's go check out the other one. Call Declan and let him know he can meet us."

I turned and punched the stone wall, regretting it instantly as I felt my bones crush in my knuckles.

Haven looked back at me and grabbed my hand

without hesitation as she began to whisper and let her vines wrap around my mangled knuckles. I could feel her healing powers giving me relief almost instantly. I was truly grateful for her silent remedy at my own stupidity.

Magic was the one thing that we didn't have before. And it was the one thing the Immortals didn't have when they were trapped here, either.

I looked down at my free palm, and my eyes widened. I pulled my healing hand away from Haven and stared at the vine that was unraveling from my fingertips, the bruising still there, but the pain was manageable. "Hey, do you still have that hagstone?" I asked Haven, as I flexed my fingers.

She looked back at me, confused, but then smiled as she looked around the cave. She reached under her shirt and pulled the small stone with the hole in it wrapped with twine and began to look through it at the empty walls.

"Lady Cambridge was definitely clever," She said, as she ran to the north wall and began to point as she held up her hagstone. "There."

I grabbed the stone, and my jaw dropped. I pulled my phone out and snapped a picture through the hole and stared in awe at our accomplishment for today. We had exactly what we needed to kill Ragnar, and now all we needed to do was find a new magical sword or have Jaxon try and forge one.

Chapter 26

Freya Chamberlain

"I don't understand why we have to have Anchors anyway? Can't we just be witches and live a non-normal magical life?" I asked Eric while we sat there waiting for Aisling to come back from the cave.

I didn't like that they had run off without us, but without my magic, I understood the added danger I could put them in. I tapped my foot and sat annoyed while waiting for the world to come back together. At least, my own world.

He cleared his throat and looked back at me. "Anchors were created to balance the magical world. Not one person should carry so much power that they can destroy our very world. Ragnar chose chaos magic when he sacrificed his mother. He tapped into the dark and dangerous magic that he had through killing his most beloved family member. In his mind, he believed he was doing something for the greater good of power. But in reality, he destroyed himself along with his family, both his family name and his married one. The Anchors were a way of having the power of one divided into two souls so that if one became evil or attempted a sacrifice, then the other would consume their whole magic if they were worthy of it or they both would lose it. Izzy and Mags were the first born set of Anchor twins. They were both meant to be good. It wasn't until their father manipulated Izzy that she turned. After Oxana completed the immortality spell on your father and I, I ended up with an Anchor as well, only it was an unplanned Anchor. I guess mother nature was displeased with the unnatural spell and punished us with another to be paired with. A friend, a stranger, or a loved one. We get paired with each other for a reason. Whether that means we have the same intentions, or maybe it is to balance out our goods and evils, we are all born with the choice to be good, but we all have evil buried deep inside of us. So, who knows... Maybe our Anchor is meant to keep us grounded enough to keep us on the right track." He shrugged.

I smirked. "A simple answer would have worked, but I think those were the most words I've ever heard you say in one sitting."

Eric grinned and shook his head. "Whatever. A second lifeline is never a bad thing."

I agreed.

"You and Haven were born Anchors, just like Izzy and Mags... That hasn't happened in over a thousand years. I'm hoping that means something good. I've searched the earth for anything similar to them, with nothing but time on my hands I have located almost every family known to have any magic at all. Whether I met their bloodlines in the dagger world or on earth, I've met them all, and none are like you and your sister, besides Izzy and Mags. So, we restore nature's balance or defeat Ragnar and hopefully reset all of our strengths." He shrugged. "You two being born has to be for something."

"Let's hope so." I half smiled, feeling the weight of the world of doomsday coming back on my shoulders. "So, we've agreed. Isado— Izzy, gets her magic back, but she will be Anchored to one of us pairs?"

He nodded.

I swallowed hard. "Who do you think Ragnar will try and kill first? I mean, if you had to guess."

His jaw tightened as he contemplated. "If it were me... I'd kill all of your loved ones first and have you watch, then when you felt defeated and had nothing left to lose, I would let you try and fight me to your fullest potential before ending your life too."

My eyes widened.

"See, that's the evil part in me... in all of us. We all have it, but I would never hurt you. That's just a villain's mindset."

I swallowed hard and closed my eyes, trying to imagine my own strategy as a villain, but I knew that I could never hurt someone to that extent. I could never take someone's life, someone most loved and held dear. I could never inflict that sort of pain on anyone after living my life without Jaxon and knowing the amount of pain it caused me to never see him again. And knowing that abandonment I felt from my mother. And watching my father destroy himself in alcohol while losing her. The amount of pain Ragnar thought he could cause me had already happened. Only I was lucky enough to have them all back. Magic saved everyone I loved once. Ragnar had nothing on me. I'd felt the pain he could enforce on me, and even though they took time, I survived each one. Maybe not gracefully, but I did it.

Only this time, magic could save them again...

I opened my eyes and stared at Eric.

"I have an idea."

His eyes narrowed as he questioned my silence.

I shook my head. "Not here. Too many ears."

He looked around and nodded.

I smiled as I let my mind wander with so many outcomes that could occur as a new plan exploded inside of me.

I looked around and watched as each member seemed to be plotting revenge, and I knew that I had the answer within me.

"We need to go get my magic back."

My mom stood and nodded excitedly. My dad and her joined me in the hallway. Jaxon stood and shook his head to Callum as he tried to rise from the couch. His dad nodded and sat back down.

"Stay with the remaining souls," he whispered to him.

Callum's face said it all, and Jaxon was trying to give him a job to keep him busy. I knew his dad's mind was wandering far too wide for him to focus on any new mission right now. Callum sat silently and rubbed his temples as he waited for his wife to come back home.

My phone pinged as soon as I had my mind set. I answered quickly.

"Hey, Ais, we're going to JFK." I froze as her voice was a higher octave as her words came through excitedly.

"What? Slow down... Hold on, you found it?" I pressed the speaker button and let the others listen in.

"Yes, Nicolai carved it into the walls," Aisling said.

"Are you serious? This whole time it was right in front of us?"

"Well, technically, we needed a hagstone to uncover the glamour, but essentially, it's all here," Haven spoke through the speaker.

"Perfect. Meet us at JFK. I'm going to get my magic back tonight."

"Even better," Aisling answered excitedly and hung up the phone.

Jaxon drove my dad's car, and I sat in the passenger seat, nervous as I prayed that it would work. If it was my magic and it ran scared, then hopefully it would willingly come back to me like a lost puppy. It was meant to be mine. It needed to be mine. My parents, Izzy, and Eric followed behind us, and every time I checked the side mirror, I saw them all trying to talk over one another. *Or were they yelling?* I turned around and watched carefully as my dad was sternly pointing to Eric, and I could confirm that he was yelling. My mom was in the backseat, shaking her head and yelling back. And Eric was driving, clenching the steering wheel tighter. Izzy sat silently and stared out of the window.

"What the hell is going on with them?" I asked Jaxon and turned back to face the winding roads.

Jaxon stared in the rearview mirror as his brows narrowed. He shrugged.

"I'm sure they'll fill us in later." He grabbed my hand

and kissed the back of it. "You need to breathe. You need to focus on this task right now."

I inhaled heavily and nodded before exhaling.

"We're going to get your mom back," I whispered, trying to not shatter his heart.

He turned to me and smirked. "What did I just say?" He smiled. "Focus on your magic, not my mom right now. I know we will get her back."

I half smiled, wanting to believe him and myself. But a pit in my stomach had my nerves starting to quiver.

"Hey, look at me," he said, as he made the turn for the bluffs and began to incline where our ears began to pop. "Count to ten. Deep breathing."

"How are you always so calm?" I asked, annoyed and thankful.

"I guess I get it from my dad. He always goes with the flow. Even tonight, he didn't argue about staying back. He knew he would put us all in danger with a different mission in mind. He just knows how to handle his emotions."

"Like father, like son." I smiled and squeezed his hand. "Ten, nine, eight." I inhaled heavily and closed my eyes.

I opened my eyes and looked back in the side mirror and watched as the four of them, silent and staring out opposite windows. I froze when I saw Izzy's hand reaching forward and holding Eric's shoulder. He leaned back and grabbed her hand and rubbed it gently. I blinked and tried to clear my sight. I looked back and confirmed it to be true.

I grabbed my phone and texted Aunt Lynn.

Freya: Please tell me what Eric's plan is...

She began to type and then deleted her message.

I closed my phone and glared in the side mirror as JFK came into view. Whatever he was planning was not anything good, and now I knew everyone knew but me.

Chapter 27

Haven Vine

I saw the headlights approach and jumped up. Ezra and Aisling followed my stance and watched cautiously. We exhaled with relief as everyone we knew jumped out of the two cars and started to walk toward us.

We stood under the bright glowing leaves of the tree, the purples and blues and green tints mixed with gold were mesmerizing. Sitting in the warm air, we watched as the snow outside of our globe began to fall. I shivered at the thought of winter never ending in Wisconsin.

"Well, here goes nothing," Ezra said.

"You really think this will work?" Aisling asked me.

I looked at Freya as she walked closer and then back at Aisling and nodded.

At least I hope so.

I watched as Izzy followed silently behind them. She seemed hesitant with every step she took, battling with good and evil about getting her magic back. I thought we all were truly anxious about her having any form of power again. But Freya was right... There was a reason Ragnar wanted her dead and powerless. There was something about her that needed to help us go up against him. Or maybe we were wrong... Maybe she was playing all of us.

My stomach tightened as she came closer. I waited for a smirk from her, but she remained timid. I broke my gaze from her when Jaxon joined us in the warmth and opened his grimoire. Slicing his finger and scanning the pages, he smiled when he landed on a page and nodded. "Found it." He cleared his throat. "Ais, your Aunt is a brilliant woman. She told me what we need to do."

Aisling smiled. "She's literally the best."

Jaxon nodded. "Agreed."

Freya walked in and seemed excited, but then I watched as she fidgeted with her new tourmaline necklace and her breathing was a little too uneven.

I pulled her near me and whispered, "Hey, it's going to work."

She stopped fidgeting and pulled me tighter and lowered her voice. "I know. I just don't know how much time we have after this part..."

"After?"

She squeezed me a little tighter. "I have a bad feeling that Eric is hiding something dangerous."

I pulled back and questioned her.

She shook her head.

"Like against us?"

She shook her head again. "I think it's more of a suicide mission."

I gasped.

She covered my mouth and shook her head as Eric walked up behind us. "Don't say anything."

I nodded and watched as Eric walked past us and stood next to Izzy. He seemed to be in deep thought.

"We will call Lynn after this," I whispered.

Freya nodded and seemed content with that.

The warmth in the dome was so nice that I wished all of our winters could stay like this. As beautiful as the snow could be, the cold was never my friend.

"Freya, I need you in the middle by our tree. Izzy, you need to stand with her, back to back against the trunk. I need each of you to place a hand on the bark and your other hand must touch one another." Jaxon looked at the sky and pointed. "Babe, you need to be facing north, and, Izzy, south." They shuffled around the tree as told. "Everyone else, we need to surround them in a circle, interlocking arms and facing away from them. It may get bright, and we don't need anyone blinded by this transfer," Jaxon spoke confidently.

Everyone turned around quickly.

Jaxon walked over by me and whispered, "just do the best you can, you might feel this too."

I looked back at him with questions but he shook his head and inhaled deeply. Making my pulse start to race at the unknown.

"Are we sure about this?" Izzy spoke softly.

I turned my attention away from Jaxon and watched as Eric broke the circle and walked up to her. "If you betray us... I will kill you myself and make sure you never meet Valhalla."

Izzy swallowed hard and nodded. "I'm not—"

"Leave her alone." Aisling spoke up for her and walked between them. She grabbed Izzy's arms and straightened her up. "Are you with us?" she asked her and studied her.

Izzy nodded. "I'm more afraid of the control my father might get back over me with it."

Aisling reached into her pocket and pulled out a leather string with a stone attached to it and gently put it over Izzy's head, securing my very own hagstone along her chest. "Your mother wanted you to have something like this a thousand years ago. She has always tried to protect you... My blood runs in your veins." Aisling shrugged. "Call it a change of heart, but I believe you are one of us too."

Izzy's shoulders relaxed as she wiped her tears and swallowed hard. "Thank you."

"But Eric is right... If you betray us, Valhalla will be forever out of the question for you."

Eric smirked and raised his eyebrow as he touched Aisling's shoulder.

Izzy nodded and closed her eyes. "If he gets back into my head... Eric, you must kill me. Valhalla or not. I will not live another day being controlled. Do you understand me?"

Eric's smirk disappeared as he nodded. I watched as the soft side of him came back. He stared at her as if they were old friends again. "Let's hope it doesn't come to that."

I turned back around and squeezed my dad and Ezra's arms. There seemed to be a silence in the dome of wild-flowers as the tree's bright and colorful leaves billowed down around each of us. The glow the tree had was beyond any sight I had ever seen. It was breathtaking to say the least.

"I just need everyone to focus on containing the magic

in our circle. If anyone unlocks their arms, this magic will flee. Whatever you do... Don't let go of one another."

I turned and watched everyone nod in sync.

Jaxon walked up to Freya and kissed her gently. "Breathe," he whispered. She obeyed and inhaled deeply and released it.

He hovered his palm over the ground and began to whisper incantations as the ground began to rumble. I turned away and watched the outer circle as the snow began to cover the field outside of us. A shiver ran through me as the winter's cold air seemed to force its way into my chest. All of a sudden, the field disappeared, and I felt Freya's syphoning being pulled away from me. I could feel my vines trying to hold on to the power and then they slowly began to let it slip through their grasp.

Then, the pain began to course through my chest as if I was being ripped from our universe back to the middle. I squeezed Ezra's arm tighter, like he was going to become ash if I released him. He looked back at me worriedly as my body began to tremble. I could feel the magic in the center of the tree trying to find its way, and I could feel my Anchor's pain as it tried to find its way back home. The magic coursed between the three of us as it began to split between Izzy's and Freya's syphoning. It coursed through me first as if I was the sorting hat it needed to decipher where to go. I watched with trembling hands as the others looked over at me nervously.

Jaxon's palm reached my shoulder, and instantly, the trembling stopped. But then I lost my grip with the others and lost control of my stance. "No... No!" I yelled before blacking out and waited for the ground to break beneath me.

"She's fine, keep going," Ezra yelled, as he held me against his chest and his palm hovered over my dad's as he protected our circle bond with his very own shield, holding us together without me needing to help at all. "I've got you."

I felt like a ground wire as the transfer of power flowed to each one of them. I could feel *all* the magic, both equally, as powerful coursing through me. It was so strong that shock consumed me as I realized I had only had a small taste of Freya's magic while being in the middle. Her power was far beyond mine, as was Izzy's. The good and evil intentions fluttered through my mind as I looked back at them both, touching the tree as power coursed into them. I watched as the bright light began to glow in both of their eyes. The purity of them seemed to outweigh the evil that was trying to join them on their own little internal battle for power. I watched as Izzy would clench and tremble as she fought back any dark stem that would try to take over, and eventually, every dark intention of magic seemed to disappear as only the bright light stayed flowing between them.

I felt the magic coursing through us begin to settle as it leveled out between the two of them and completely left me. My very own vines began to extend from my palms without warning and wrapped around the two of them, slowing the flow and recharging all of us as if they borrowed their very own magic to bring me back to health. I stood carefully, Ezra cautiously releasing me.

"I'm okay," I said, standing as I walked back toward the

tree. Jaxon walked with me, still whispering incantations as my vines retracted and came back to me. Both the witches fell to the ground and trembled. "It's done," I said quietly, as if I were to break the circle with one word spoken too loud.

Everyone turned back around slowly and released the circle as Izzy and Freya breathed heavily, standing and finding their balance again.

"Well?" Eric broke the silence.

Freya placed her palm out in front of her as did Izzy, and in synchronization, they whispered, "Ignis."

The wildflowers exploded into a million pieces around us, and the colorful leaves of the tree began to fall and disappear into branches as the dead of winter came back upon us, the dome holding us together in the warmth shattering as their palms both ignited with flames higher than ever before. Izzy and Freya looked at one another and smiled excitedly. Both nodded and hovered their other palm over the very ground we stood on. "Orbis Terrarum."

The ground began to shake, and Eric smirked with excitement.

They extinguished the flames, and both turned and embraced one another, which seemed to be an odd sight to all of us.

Freya let her go and ran to me, hugging me tight. "Are you okay?"

I nodded and smiled. "One last test," I said, as I released her and held my hand out to her. "Syphon from me."

Izzy's smile vanished as she looked away.

"Are you sure?" Freya asked.

I nodded. "I trust you."

Freya slowly brought her hand to mine, and our Marks began to glow as I began to feel the slight pull from deep inside me. She released it quickly. "It works... that's enough."

I laughed. "You really think I'd let you take it all?"

She smiled.

Izzy sat down under the tree and stared at her palms.

I walked over next to her and offered my arm to her. "Go ahead."

She shook her head.

I sat down next to her as everyone watched cautiously.

"Izzy, do it. We need to make sure you can syphon too."

She shook her head again.

"I can heal myself. I'm the best witch to go up against."

Eric walked over and sat down next to her. "Here, try me."

She swallowed hard and looked away.

Eric pulled her chin back toward him and stared into her soul. "I know what you're thinking about... When you syphoned against Mags... That's not going to happen again."

She began to sob as he pulled her in for a hug.

"Give us a minute," he said to all of us.

None of us questioned their alliance as we began to walk back to the parked cars.

Ezra put his arm around my shoulders as we walked. I turned and watched the two ex-villains bond as friends again. A feeling of peace traveled through the field as Eric held his arm out for her, and she slowly reached for it, pulling back once. Eric grabbed it and placed it on him without giving her a choice. I watched as his new Norse Mark began to glow, and she quickly released it. She shook her palm and stared back at him in shock and then smiled before jumping in his arms and hugging him tight. His laugh echoed through the bluffs as he set her back down and kissed her forehead.

"Welcome back, old friend," he said.

I smiled and felt a feeling of happiness consume me as a happy ending for everyone seemed to inch its way closer for all of us.

Chapter 28

Freya Chamberlain

We were just about to leave JFK when a figure appeared in front of us, blocking my Jeep's door. I jumped back and ignited my palms in defense.

"Oh my god, Ember! You can't just pop up like that," I screamed.

"Sorry." She tried to smile. "It's bad... Ragnar has his wife and Jaxon's mom, and he's holding them hostage. Worse... he's at the casino and has both of my moms locked in the office. I just barely made it out of there before he began to go mad. He tried to use the other Jasper stone half, and when nothing happened... Well... He's coming for you. All of you."

"When?" Jaxon demanded.

"I don't know." Ember fidgeted with her fingers and began to look around the field cautiously.

"Did he hurt my mom? Did he hurt any of them?" Jaxon asked.

I grabbed his hand and tried to calm his anger as I could feel the field begin to rumble.

Ember shook her head. "No, he seems to want her for something. He kept talking about finally having his family together and how he was going to rid the world of all others. He wanted a pure line of witches to restart."

"Pure? There's nothing pure about him," I huffed.

"He wants to take their blood and create new witches out of mundanes with their power. He thinks he can control who has magic in this world." Ember shook her head. "I left as soon as I could... If he knows that I'm actually made from a part of that stone... he will kill me."

She began to sob and shake. I let go of Jaxon's hand and pulled her in tight and tried to keep her calm, but she continued to cry.

"I left my mothers. I left them like a coward for my own safety." She continued to cry.

"We will get them back. We will get everyone back," I said reassuringly.

"He's crazy. We cannot let him get control of Crystal Rock. He has plans to destroy these lands. He wants to let the river flow through all of these fields and bluffs and bury his past to start fresh. He wants to kill everyone that is undeserving of power."

And with that... Ember collapsed in my arms and seemed completely defeated. Eric made his way to us and quickly slung her over his shoulder as if she was weightless.

"What the hell was all that about?" he asked.

"She's terrified," I said.

"Does Ragnar have Oxana?" he asked.

I nodded.

"Damn it." Eric shook his head angrily and slicked his hair back with his free hand.

Aisling began to whisper to Jaxon, just beyond my hearing. I turned around and glared as their secrets began to bloom, and I wasn't a part of it. He shook his head when he saw me as if not to worry. I rolled my eyes at them both.

Izzy walked over as Aisling whispered to her.

"Yeah, it's in Door County," Izzy answered.

Aisling smiled."Can we borrow it?"

Izzy shrugged and nodded. "Of course." Her eyebrows raised as she waited for an answer as to why.

I turned to Jaxon and nodded. "Hey, do you think Ember can help us? We need something from your past and it might be out of our time limit to reach it."

Eric looked back at Jaxon and patted Ember's backside. "She's not going to do much good right now."

"Give her some healing tea and then she can teleport us to Door County. There's a sword sitting there that we need."

Eric's brows furrowed. "Door County?"

"Izzy mentioned to Ais something about a dragon sword that she hid there," Jaxon said.

Eric turned to Izzy and smirked. "You kept that?"

Izzy blushed. "Well, technically, I hid it away. Why do we need it?"

Aisling walked over to her and whispered.

Izzy's eyes bulged as she looked back at Aisling. "Are you kidding me?"

Aisling smiled. "It was all on the cave walls. Your mother was one step ahead all along."

She smiled. "Okay... Well, let's just start driving now, and Ember can track us when she's awake?"

Aisling studied her and then agreed.

I didn't like the idea of splitting up again, no good movie ever had a happy ending where the characters went in every direction.

I gritted my teeth as Jaxon and Aisling divided everyone into separate missions.

Eric, my dad, Haven, and I paired together to finish the last of the soul freeing while my mom would watch Ember sleep on the couch. I hoped that Ember would wake up sooner than later and help us make the five and a half hour trip to Door County a thirty second one. Now we just had to pray that she would help us bring them back safely. Jaxon, Aisling, Declan and Izzy were on their way to Door County for the sword. Clara, Ezra, Callum, and Aunt Lynn went back to the cave to work on the strategic planning. We all hoped that Margo was still alive with Ragnar and her mother.

"Hey, come on," Eric snapped. "You have to get your head clear."

I swallowed and snapped back to reality. Tinker jumped onto my lap, which seemed to help calm my nerves, but something about today seemed off. I just had a bad feeling, and nothing seemed to help. Tinker purred louder on my lap and even she seemed to want to hold me here.

"Leila is going to want to wander in your head, and I can't have you worrying about everyone else. I need you to be selfish for a few minutes and focus on only you right now."

"Geez, I get it," I snapped. "Let's just get this over with."

My dad walked over to me and rubbed my shoulders. "You've got this, kiddo."

I looked up at him and smiled, letting my shoulders relax. "Thanks, Dad." I leaned in and hugged him tight. "I'm glad that you're back home." Squeezing him and memorizing his scent of patchouli and whiskey, I swore with him working at the bar that scent lingered on him forever. "Promise me that you will be right here when I get back?"

He smiled. "Of course."

Tinker jumped off my lap and ran out of the back door, heading for her freedom walk in the sun before the winter air would force her back home.

Eric cleared his throat and laughed. "He's coming with us today and so is your sister."

I turned around and stared at Eric, confused. Haven's brows raised too.

Eric nodded. "Yep, they're tagging along with us. We have unfinished business to attend to while there."

My dad looked to Haven and then back at Eric and had the same dumbfounded look that I had.

Eric smirked at him. "You'll see, brother, you'll see."

Haven shrugged. "I guess I've spent plenty of time in that world. Might as well take a field trip back."

I inhaled heavily and walked to my mom, hugging her tight. I whispered, "Something may be off with Ember, so please keep an eye on her."

My mom nodded and kissed my cheek. "Don't worry about me. Good luck."

I smiled and hugged her tight. "Love you, Mom."

I watched as her shoulders relaxed, and her eyes filled with happiness. "Love you more."

"Let's not make it a competition," my dad yelled from behind us, and Haven smiled.

We laughed, and I nodded before joining them under the last remaining souls.

"Cowabunga," I said, "or whatever Callum says."

They smirked as Eric held Leila's soul in his palm before grabbing my hand as we were ripped from our world and transported back to the middle.

Leila stood in front of us, smirking. "I knew you could do it." She jumped up and down and grabbed my hand, twirling me around and examining me closely. "Oh, I knew it. I knew you were more like Eric than anyone." She leaned into me and licked my cheek. "Yep, you are so much like him." She grabbed my wrist and poked my finger with her needle and licked the drop of blood that began to pool.

I tried to pull it back, but her grip was strong. I looked at Eric and my dad as my eyes bulged in shock.

Eric laughed and shrugged. "Just go with it."

I tried to fix my expression from disgust and failed with a resting bitch face instead.

"Hi to you too," I said and waited for her shenanigans to stop.

She laughed. "I'm just excited. Today is a good day."

"Let's hope so," I said, swallowing hard as I built the courage to ask her the burning question. "What did you mean I'm more like Eric?"

She let go of my wrist and faced me. "Let me show you." She looked at Eric and my dad for approval as they nodded. My dad seemed just as nervous as myself but trusted his brother's plan. She jumped up and down, and before I could say anything, we were ripped from the soul realm and stood in the middle of a field... not just any field, but *my* field.

JFK was bright as any other sunny day. The sun beamed onto the field, and the warmth made my cheeks turn rosy as a summer day greeted us. The green grass tickled my ankles as did the flowers, as long as the eye could see. I watched as the dandelion wishes flew around us as the wind gently blew.

"How—" I swallowed and sat down slowly in disbelief. "How is this possible?"

Leila laughed and tapped my skull. "It's you, my dear. I knew you were strong, but now with your magic, you are going to be invincible. I have no doubt that you could take on Ragnar all on your own. But truly, I wish that your twin was here with us. I'll have to see inside her head when we get back to them."

"What am *I* actually doing?"

"You are able to manipulate the mind, just like your Uncle Eric can."

I looked around and panicked. "Are *we* like Ragnar?"

She shook her head reassuringly and put her hand over my mouth. "You are nothing like Ragnar. That man is nothing but pure evil. He has no sympathy bones inside of him. I've been inside his head. Years ago. And I will tell you right now... I know his weakness."

"His weakness?"

She sat down next to me and nodded. "Ragnar was not always evil. I took a head dive into him and realized that he was a normal child. He was a scared little boy. He loved his mother so dearly. She was his world. And when she abandoned his father and ran with him, he became cold. And a new fear triggered in him that one day she would abandon him so easily too." She stood up and paced. "Ragnar has a weakness of abandonment. He selfishly sacrificed his mother to keep her with him always. She whispers to him, only instead of words of wisdom and approval, she is constantly screaming back at him with hate and disapproval for the world he is trying to create. She does not want him to have any power in the world. She wants him to let her go and give her peace. His mother seems to have a way of making herself available to guide us witches when all seems lost."

"His mother is still here?"

Leila shook her head. "She is not here, here, but she is *around*, if that makes sense?" She fidgeted with her long fingers as she plucked a dandelion from the ground and began to peel the petals one by one. "I saw her one time... She came to me with a secret." She left one petal on the dandelion and handed it to me. "She made me promise to find the one who can set her free... My job is to open the mind of the ones who can do it... She made me promise to find you and your twin."

I stood up and shook my head. "She's a ghost?"

Leila raised an eyebrow and studied me. "Have you seen her?"

I frowned. "I don't know. I thought I made her up when I lost my magic. She was a sheer-like woman and talked in riddles. I never told anyone because I thought I was going crazy."

Leila smiled. "She can-not talk to many, only the ones that have the strongest minds."

I blushed.

"Again, Eric has seen her too. He was told to protect the broken one. He never elaborated more on it with me personally. But I saw her when I did a head dive to help him unlock his potential. When I asked him about her, he shrugged me off as if it was nothing. But deep down, I knew that was exactly why he stuck with Isadora through all those years. He had made a promise to not only his mother, but her late grandmother that he would. Eric is a man of his word, and that was something that he knew he needed to hold up on his end." She sighed. "I truly thought that he and I may have had something more... But he never let go of Aislynn. That was his one true love through it all. I hope that after all this is over, you help him find happiness again. He truly deserves to live a life and not always be a babysitter."

I agreed. "I think he's up to something. I'm nervous that his life is going to be short lived. I can't let that happen."

We sat down in the field and stared out at the horizon in silence with the warmth of the sun soaking into our bones.

"You know that heroes sacrifice one person to save everyone else... Only true villains would sacrifice the world to save themselves. And, Freya, my darling, you are no villain. If it comes to Eric needing to sacrifice himself for the world to be better, then you must let him."

I shook my head and clenched my fists. Leila watched me and grabbed my hands, relaxing my grasp and rubbing them gently.

"Freya, you know that you made this place all on your own, and I cannot find a single fault to make me believe we are not truly here. I think you can come up with a pretty brilliant plan to ensure that that doesn't need to happen." She winked and tapped my head, then leaned into me and whispered in my ear.

I looked back at her with my eyes wide as I realized what I might have to do. "You really think I can do that?"

"I'd rather you try it my way than the plan you were strumming in that beautiful head of yours." She smiled and nodded. "I think you are stronger than you think. But come on, let's get back to the others. Time is precious."

I stood and grabbed her hand, pulling her up and hugging her tight. "Thank you," I whispered, as she patted my back.

Haven, Eric, and my dad were waiting for us when Leila showed me how to get back to the middle.

"She's a natural, just like you." She pointed to Eric and smirked. She walked over to Haven and grabbed her face, pulling her close, breathing her warmth. Making Haven's glasses fog up, she spun her around and examined her. "So crazy how much you two look alike. I have never met an identical twin in my short lived life and especially not a pair of witches." Leila smiled wide. "Let's go head diving." And without approval, they disappeared for a brief moment before returning.

I stood back in shock as I looked at Eric and my dad, waiting for them to be just amused, but Eric laughed. "What?"

"That was no time at all..." I said.

"That was about the same for you," he answered and shrugged.

My dad nodded and rubbed his head. "I just don't get it." He laughed. "I kind of miss my mundane days when all of this was hidden."

Eric smacked him on the back of the head. "You were never mundane, you idiot. You just forgot *how* to be a witch... For a long ass time."

My dad shrugged. "It's coming back to me."

"Good," Eric said. He looked at his watch and seemed nervous all of a sudden.

"What is it?" I asked.

He inhaled deeply and nodded. "It's time."

Haven hugged Leila and walked over next to me. She leaned into me and whispered, "Leila is something else... Did she help you too?"

I looked back at her. "Yes, you?"

She smiled excitedly as she lifted her palms and her healing vines glowed bright as they extended, but they were thicker than usual.

"I feel like I can heal a lot quicker now." She smiled. "What about you?"

Eric interrupted. "Alright, alright. Leila, it's time. We have one last stop in the soul world before we can close this place for a while."

Leila rolled her eyes. "I'm ready. My brother is waiting for me." She leaned into Eric and kissed his cheek.

He put his arm around her and pulled her into his embrace, kissing her lips gently. "I can never thank you enough."

She pulled back from his arms and smirked. "Just love

me in our next life." She winked at him, then kissed his lips one more time. Eric smiled and nodded silently. Then, before I knew it, she began to spin a mile a minute until she vanished into thin air and became red and gold glittering micro orbs scattering all around us.

Eric inhaled heavily and then let his shoulders relax. "Alright, last of the souls. I'll grab them. Stay put."

He disappeared, and when he came back, he held the last two in his palms, gently closed, containing the bouncing souls. He looked at my dad and then swallowed hard. "Hope you're ready for this, brother."

My dad stared back at him, confused. And when Eric opened his palms, two figures appeared in front of us. A lady, beautiful, with long dark hair, hazel eyes, and perfect skin stood next to a tall man that looked identical to my very own dad.

It was more so a feeling than a knowing, but I gasped as I realized who they were.

My dad's knees buckled as tears began to flow down his cheeks. His hazel eyes matching his very own mother's became filled with joy.

"Mother, Father," he whispered, as Eric put his arm underneath my dad and helped lift him to his feet.

"I was always hoping that it was you guys." Eric swallowed hard. "I guess I never had the strength to be sure. Just hoped that one day, I would be able to get you along to our sister in Valhalla."

"Oh, my boys," their mother cried out happily. She nodded and ran to them, squeezing them tight. "I guess you are no longer boys now, are you?" She laughed.

Haven and I stood back and watched their long overdue embrace.

"Not for a very long time," Eric replied, as he pulled his mother back and memorized her. "You look just as beautiful as I remember."

She smiled. "I've loved watching you grow over the centuries. You both were never truly alone." She looked to her husband, and he nodded.

I watched as their father swallowed just as hard and pulled them both in for a hug. "I am so sorry we were not there for you both. We should not have kept so many secrets from you. We were never sure when that bastard Ragnar was listening to us. His mind games were not to be taken lightly. Rumors had spread throughout the lands and we tried everything possible to keep everyone safe."

Eric and my dad nodded and patted him on the back as if no explanation was needed at all.

My dad spoke first. "I was never mad at either of you. I was mad at the destiny we were to fulfill. It was Mags's father. Regardless of the evil he was and is... he was still *her* family. I had always hoped that he could have a change of heart."

They both looked at one another with worry.

"Is? As in... He is still free?" Their mother looked at them both with fear. "I thought you being here with us meant that he was finally taken care of."

Eric shook his head. "We're not dead... Yet."

I tried to clear my throat as everything I had assumed was true. Eric knew that he was planning on not staying in our world, and I wanted to scream, but instead, my eyes filled with tears. Haven stood next to me as we watched in silence. I could feel tears begin to pool at the corner of my eyes, and as much as I wanted to wipe them away, I felt as if I were frozen and not supposed to be here during this intimate moment at all.

Haven turned to me and wiped her own tears. The movement caused our dad to turn around, and he shook his head and smiled with pride. "Mother, Father, on a happier note, I want you to meet my girls, my world."

He reached for us and pulled us to them, introducing us one by one. "My Anchor twins."

Our very late grandparents smiled and hugged us each one by one.

"We have watched you two grow as well. And the sacrifice your mother made was a heroic one, regardless of my Eric keeping his secrets. She still had done the right thing. Too much magic in one place could have broken Ragnar out sooner than anyone could be ready for." Their mother spun me around and smiled. "Freya Alexandra Greystone... Chamberlain was never truly your name, but it suits you now. And Haven Claire Greystone. Although, Vine has been a pretty good last name for you and your healing magic." She winked. "You two are beautiful. I always wondered what my sweetest daughter would've grown to look like, and here, standing in front of you two, I see her in you both."

Haven and I exchanged a look.

She swallowed hard. "Time is such a strange thing. Isn't it? I mean, I feel as if yesterday my boys were just children, and now, here they are and with grandchildren for us." She began to get choked up as she sniffled. "I mean, in another world, we would've all been together. In another world, we would've aged and loved and been merry, but here we are, stuck in a time warp and uniting as a family for the first time, centuries later. I do wish that you would've brought Alexandra here with you as well. Maybe in Valhalla... You be sure to tell her that she is a forever kind of love. As is your Aislynn, Eric. I am sad that I was unable to be there for you but I am also happy that I had unfinished business and could wait for you all here." She exhaled heavily and straightened her shoulders. "Now to get down to that unfinished business."

She reached her hand out for me and then Haven. We gave her our hands and stood, confused.

"Now, we don't have much magic left, but we have saved a little bit for this very day. Ragnar thought he could consume it all, but he's nothing more than a mere idiot." Our grandmother looked back at us and smiled wide. "It was nice to meet you both." She nodded as we smiled. She never released our hands as if she would crumble if she did, then turned to her sons and kissed each one on the cheek. "Jimmy and Eric, we are ready."

My dad cleared his throat and stood behind us. "No, there's just not enough time. We have so much more to talk about."

"Time is a funny thing, my son. Time is the one thing that is never on our sides. And from the vibration that is starting to rumble underneath us... I have a feeling that something is going terribly wrong back in your world."

I hadn't even noticed it until she said it. I looked down at my feet, and the pit in my stomach grew as I realized it was shaking. I looked back to Eric who was already kneeling on the floor and feeling it for himself.

"She's right. Something *is* happening."

"Haven, Freya, take this magic and hold it dear. When all seems lost... know that you are never alone. And then pass it along to your children and theirs when the time is right."

I nodded as Haven swallowed hard.

She closed her eyes as her husband joined our hands, and the magic began to flow instantly. There was no syphoning, no barrier that needed to be broken. They were willingly giving us their magic. The flow began to slow as their mother opened her eyes and smiled. "There." She patted my hand and released us. "It isn't much, but something to remember us by."

I looked at Haven and watched as her hazel eyes brightened just a touch as the gold hues stood out a little more, thanks to our grandparents.

"Thank you," I whispered, as a part of me felt wrong to take any magic at all.

"It is our honor to pass it on to our grandchildren."

"Aisling." I whispered to myself, realizing she deserved to be here too. She was Eric's very own descendant.

Eric smiled. "They already gave me this... for her." He held a small ring in the air. "It has a drop of each of their magic in it. She is covered."

I smirked. "You think your son deserves to give her that?"

He laughed. "I haven't decided that... But time will tell."

Chapter 29

Jaxon Oakes

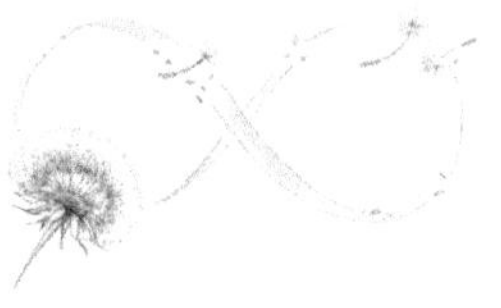

"She will text you when she's back. You can stop checking your phone," Aisling snapped and slapped my phone out of my hand.

"I told you to let me drive." I rolled my eyes.

Izzy laughed quietly in the backseat while Declan snickered with her.

"How much further?" I asked.

"Geez, what are you? Five? It's just another few blocks that way." Izzy pointed to the left and shrugged. "Lake Michigan is beautiful, though, if you've never seen it. There's something about the waves, how quickly they can change from calm to a riptide in a matter of minutes. The Mississippi River flows with strength, but Lake Michigan is not one to be reckoned with."

I couldn't stand hearing her talk. No matter what everyone else's excuse was for letting her help us, I still didn't trust the bitch. Just knowing that she didn't stop herself from trying to kill my mom centuries ago would always make me cringe at the idea of her sitting behind me.

If it wasn't for Freya and Aisling wanting to keep her alive, I would've severed her link altogether and let her Anchor bond shrivel her to pieces as age and magic sucked her dry from the inside out.

I smirked to myself and held in a laugh.

"Turn here," she interrupted my thoughts.

Aisling made a quick left turn and slowed as we approached the small towns where too many people were busy shopping the small stores and fishing the piers. The sun was setting, and it was beginning to get dark as families waited to cross the street to get to their favorite restaurants and hangouts with their jackets bundled up and hats protecting their ears from the cold. Aisling slowed the car even more and carefully waved families across. My jaw dropped when I saw the goats eating the grass on top of the roof of a restaurant.

"Whoa, where are we?" Aisling asked.

Izzy pointed to the north. "Straight ahead a few more miles to Ellison Bay, and there will be a resort where I met a friend to keep a motel room just for me. It was a safe space when I needed time to think. I found it years ago and moved the sword to it in case of ever needing a fast getaway. I stored an aluminum boat and the sword there just in case. Not that the aluminum boat would've taken me far on a day where the waves are like this." She shrugged.

I laughed as I looked to my left and watched as the waves crashed hard against the shore, the white caps merely only a foot apart. I imagined her trying to paddle a boat through the waves and laughed out loud when I thought of them consuming her.

I turned back around as she glared at me.

"Yeah, well, I have trust issues, and apparently, my schizophrenia was actually my psycho father planting ideas in my head. So, when I decided to have a getaway plan, it wasn't just for myself, it was for when I couldn't handle myself and wanted to keep Eric safe too."

I faced forward as I felt that to the core. "Wow... The bitch does have a heart after all." I smirked as I stared out of the window. Declan smacked my shoulder from behind me. I saw her sink back into her seat out of the corner of my eye and felt a little guilty.

Maybe she is more than just a villain.

"I know I'm linked to a pair of Anchors... And if you truly think I would risk even my own life to get away, you're insane. Maybe the apple doesn't fall far from the tree. Not only that, but my own sister, you know... Your mother decided to take you away from the love of your life and made you suffer for two years, so if I'm the only sick one in our family, then that's fine, but I personally never would've done anything heartbreaking enough like that to my own child."

"You have no child!" I snapped, feeling defensive of my mother, even though I knew she was wrong for what she had done to us too. I turned around as she crossed her arms and raised her eyebrow, glaring back at me.

"Don't I?" She pointed toward Aisling and smirked. "I may not have been fully in control of my thoughts, but my father was not with me the *entire* time. I had free will to do as I pleased too, and those were the days when I chose to roam on my own, far away from Eric and Crystal Rock."

I could feel my blood boiling. "I can't wait to start my own family and not *ruin* them with secrets like both you and my mom have. I can't wait to give my kids the life they deserve, full of love and family. And you know what? I will teach them magic so they know where they came from, and they will choose their own path when it comes to being a hero versus a villain. But I already know that when I raise them with Freya, they will choose to be heroes." I swallowed hard, crossed my arms, and faced the front again.

I felt Aisling's eyes staring at me from the driver's seat, and I shrugged.

"What?" I asked, annoyed.

She smiled. "Oh... Nothing."

I turned to her, "Ais, what?"

She laughed. "It's just cute listening to you planning a future with my BFF. I love it. It gives me hope for a future after all of this."

I laughed and nodded.

The car became silent as we pulled into the resort parking lot.

Izzy and Declan stepped out of the car first and began to walk up to the motel. I watched as the cold breeze along the water made Izzy shiver in her long sleeve sweater. She crossed her arms and began to rub them. I went to step out of the car, but Aisling grabbed my arm and pulled me back in.

"Hey, can you do me a favor?"

I stared back at her and nodded. "Of course."

She cleared her throat. "Remember when you duplicated the obsidian dagger? Can you do the same with this sword? Just in case she tries to pull a fast one."

I looked at her and smiled. "That's brilliant. So, you don't trust her, either?"

She smiled and shrugged. "I'm a planner. And I don't trust anyone with something as important as our only weapon to kill her father."

"I will need a few extra minutes with it. Will you stall for me?"

"Of course."

We met up with Declan and Izzy as they began to walk up to the door with #3 on it and unlocked it. We walked inside what I thought would be a ragged motel room with stained sheets, but instead, it was a spacious little home with a small kitchenette and raised ceiling with large wooden beams. I looked around in awe at the room decorated in a Viking theme with dark blue walls and pictures of longships framed on them. I looked beyond the headboard and saw a matching symbol to Jim and Eric's new Norse Mark hanging above the bed. Instead of it being a moldy old room, it was like a small personal studio, and it was actually cozy. She jumped on top of the bed and reached above the raised rafters, until we heard clinking metal above her head. She grabbed the piece and brought it down.

"A key?" I asked.

She frowned. "Unfortunately, when I was immortal, the cold didn't bother me as much, my skin healed more rapidly than it does now. But seeing as someone stripped that from me... I will have to freeze my ass off in the water."

I smirked. "Bummer."

She turned and glared at me. "Yes, it is." She grabbed the key and the blanket off the bed and walked out of the motel room, heading straight for the pier. We ran after her and watched her cautiously as she stripped naked under the pier light and dropped the blanket next to her pile of clothes. She dove over the cement wall, straight into the waters of Lake Michigan, six feet down and then another few feet as she held her breath. I watched carefully as I saw just a glimmer of her skin in the rising moon's light as she swam to the bottom.

"Be ready for that distraction," I said to Aisling, as the waves crashed loudly against the break wall.

Aisling nodded.

The winter air was beginning to get more brutal as we waited. I pulled Aisling under my arm and tried to keep her warm as seconds passed. Declan stayed by the wall watching Izzy intently and kept his water flowing freely in his palm, ready to pull her back with his water magic or if she tried to escape.

"Thanks," Aisling whispered through chattering teeth. "I don't know if it's my nerves or the cold."

I laughed. "It's probably a bit of both."

She nodded. "Here." She held out her palm, scanning our surroundings before whispering, "Ignis." A fire grew in the palm of her hand, much bigger than usual. A green glow flickered through the orange flames.

"Whoa." I backed away a little and stared at her.

"A small side effect that Ezra and I gained. No worries, it'll be back to normal when this is all over."

I nodded, unsure, but accepted the unbelievable at this point and wasn't going to complain about the instant warmth.

I looked down and saw a piece of driftwood next to us. I grabbed it and put it behind my back, ready for duplicating.

Seconds turned into nearly two minutes, or so it felt,

but Izzy had still not resurfaced. Declan ripped his shirt off and unbuttoned his pants. Just as he was getting ready to dive over the small wall that kept the waves from crashing into us, Izzy gasped for air as she reached the surface and swam for the ladder.

Declan looked back at us and nodded with approval. "She's got it." He reached over the wall by the ladder and offered his hand, lifting her and pulling her to the cement pier with us as if she weighed nothing at all.

She steadied herself and stared back at Declan's half naked body. "You wanted to join me?" She laughed through chattering teeth.

He rolled his eyes and buttoned his jeans back up as he pulled her into his bare chest to help warm her body faster.

"Here, it's still here." Izzy leaned closer into him as she yelled back to us with excitement over the waves. Declan grabbed the sword and set it down on the ground away from her and immediately wrapped her in the blanket, rubbing her arms and trying to keep her body from going into shock. He grabbed his shirt and pulled it over his head with one hand, never letting Izzy go.

"It's heavier than I remember." She shivered.

I leaned over and picked it up, studying the beauty of the blade along with the handle.

Izzy explained, "It's made from dragon's blood, very old blood. Nearly nonexistent now."

"Nearly?" Aisling asked.

Izzy smiled through chattering teeth. "Well, technically, dragons still exist just as witches do. They are just more discreet about it nowadays." She shrugged as if it was common knowledge and we were peasants who were kept away from the secrets of the world. "Oxana used to be able to spit fire. She was a whole different person back then. Now she's forgotten how to live. She has contained her true form for far too long and has probably lost it entirely."

"Oxana?" Aisling spit out and laughed nervously. "The casino lady is a dragon?" She swallowed hard. "Ember's mom?"

I watched as the two began to debate on the dragon myths, and Aisling pinched my torso as she walked over to Izzy and began the over dramatic distraction. I quickly began to chant under my breath with a piece of driftwood in the one hand and the sword in the other. Declan watched me carefully, confused but silent as he realized what I was doing. Aisling kept Izzy facing away from us and began to argue with her and I knew I needed to be quick.

I repeated the chant until the driftwood became a duplicate of the dragon's sword. Declan smirked and walked away from the two girls and walked next to me as I handed it to him. He placed the real sword behind him, hanging perfectly along his back under his shirt, placing the duplicate along the cement wall.

The arguing stopped as Izzy turned around and rolled her eyes.

Aisling winked as she walked back over to me, letting Izzy dress under the blanket.

"You know, Jaxon, your mother has had to tell you the stories of our past. Has she not?"

I shook my head. "She never really said much of anything beyond our normal life. Hell, I didn't even know that she was older than this century until a few months ago.

I didn't even know she had a sister at all. She's full of secrets. Again, why I won't be sheltering my own kids."

She shrugged and clicked her tongue. "Well then, let's head on back before the world burns." She grabbed the sword and froze for a second. She studied the blade and then looked back at me. "Hm, it's not as heavy as it was."

"Must be your fingers getting blood circulating again. All that anger and rage can do that to you..." I smirked as she turned and began to walk back to the car.

Declan nodded for me to go forward. I grabbed Ais, and we began to walk behind Izzy. Declan followed with the sword and carefully secured it behind his shirt, taking his already loosened belt and arranging it tight along his long torso, letting it hang heavily.

We were feet away from the car when Izzy screamed and got thrown against the motel, breaking the wooden door and falling back into the room.

"Give it to me!"

I ran into the room and pushed the girl off her.

I stood in shock. "Ember?" I tried to clear my vision as the darkness hid her features. She stood up and forced her way against me, trying to reach Izzy.

"Give me the sword! I know it can kill him," Ember screamed.

"She's under his mind control," Aisling yelled from behind me, as she cautiously came up next to me. "Ember, you don't want to do this. Here, give me your wrist."

Ember smirked. "I am not under his mind control at all." She smiled "You don't think we planned this from the beginning? We had two years in the dagger world together. He promised me freedom. He promised me the world."

Izzy stood up and spat. "His promises are never kept."

Ember laughed. "Maybe not for you... I am the daughter he always wanted. The daughter that he can trust and the one that he can keep with him."

"Damn it, Ember! Give me your wrist." Aisling grabbed her arm and slapped a bracelet on her.

Ember laughed louder, echoing through the parking lot. "I don't need that. He doesn't have my mind at all. I hate my confinement to these lands. I want my freedom. I want to see the world. I am sick of my mothers keeping me in one place. I am a teleporter! I can see the world, but they are so busy trying to protect me that they suffocated me." She ripped the bracelet off and threw it to the ground, making me grit my teeth. "See? No mind control. Now give me the damn blade, Jaxon. Or I will kill both you and your Anchor once and for all."

I laughed... which probably wasn't my best response because her eyes filled with rage as she charged me, disappearing and reappearing in front of me as she slit my throat with a small dagger.

I dropped to my knees in the doorway as I tried to catch my breath, only to be choking on my own blood. My eyes grew as she turned toward Declan with the same dagger.

Aisling jumped in front of her, ripping the replica sword from Izzy's death grip and aiming it straight toward Ember's face. "Take it, you deceiving bitch."

"No," Izzy screamed, as she jumped up and tried to run toward it.

"Just let it go," Aisling screamed, as the world began to darken. I watched in a blur as Ember picked up the sword and smirked before disappearing into thin air.

"Oh, Jaxon." Aisling sobbed as she knelt down by me and cradled me in her arms. "Declan, help me. I don't know what to do! Help me."

It was Izzy's hands that began to burn around my throat as Aisling cradled my head on her lap. "Let me cauterize it. We don't have time for him to die today."

I became freezing as the winter air made me shiver uncontrollably, I felt my body go into shock as the world slipped away.

Chapter 30

Freya Chamberlain

The ground that we stood on began to rumble as it became extraordinarily too warm. I looked to the others and panicked as the air became thick with smoke and beads of sweat started to fall from my forehead. "Um, guys... What the hell is happening?"

Eric looked back at me with fear. "Please tell me Jaxon linked Izzy to you two?" he yelled as the world began to disappear and we were ripped back to Crystal Rock. I looked up and tried to orient myself and panicked when I looked up and saw the roof of the soul house torn away. Instead of a clear sky, I saw a scaly dragon flying above us and flapping its wings while spitting fire, surrounding us in a circle of rubble.

We had two choices. Be trapped or be engulfed in flames.

My eyes widened as the pit in my stomach grew. I wished Ezra was with us to protect us from a fiery death. As the dragon flew closer, screeching filled the sky above us, evil lurking around it. Ragnar came walking up closer to the flames and smirked. His scar stretched with his smile as he dragged Margo and Lady Cambridge along with him. Margo tried to struggle from his grasp, pulling hard on her Labradorite necklace and whispering words of either prayers or incantations. I didn't know which, but my stomach began to cramp as I could feel the world, our world, collapsing in front of me. My throat filled with bile instead of courage as the moment happened so fast, and I wanted nothing more than Jaxon to be the white knight and come swooping in to save us. But I already knew they were hours away, and we were out of time.

"Well, looks like the twins will be no more. Time to rid the abominations of this earth and start over." He grabbed Margo's wrist and threw her to the ground, grasping her necklace and tearing it from her neck. He took the stone and threw it to the ground as the flames from the dragon grew wildly around us. No one moved. My eyes quickly scanned what was left of the room but panicked when I realized Ember was gone. My mom laid knocked out across the couch. I watched as her chest rose and fell evenly and thanked God that she would live to see another day. I looked to Haven, and her and I grimaced together as we knew our only hope depended on Jaxon linking Izzy to us. And even now, I had very little doubt that he would risk it.

"Freya?" she yelled.

I stood cowardly and frozen, staring back at her unsure what to do.

"Freya!" she yelled again, her palms raising as she let the vines grow and tried to surround us protectively.

But I couldn't move. I felt weak while standing in front

of him. I knew he couldn't get in my head, but I was stuck in my own thoughts.

Ragnar bellowed in laughter as if he knew he had finally won. He was finally ahead of us, and he had us surrounded. He crushed the Labradorite stone with his foot as his laughter echoed through the nearby bluffs. "All this time, and my magic was being contained with my other worthless daughter, the one that I ignored when she was the key all along to my chaos magic. My wife was clever in realizing my favorites." The stone shattered as a green flickering glow illuminated from the ground and began to violently shoot itself back into the true villain. He knelt over and grasped the ground as the pain was surely too much.

Lady Cambridge screamed in pain as he began to soak in the ugliness that was once contained and began to clench his fists and flex his arms as he stood.

"No!" she cried. "I failed you all." She sobbed harder and dropped her head against the concrete and lost it.

Eric tried to jump out of the flames to go after him, but he was thrown back with pure force of chaos. Then, my dad tried to do the same, only to be thrown back too.

Ragnar lifted Margo and tossed her to us through the flames. "Burn with them." His chaos magic surrounded him as he smiled with an unnatural strength. "Finally." He inhaled deeply as he felt his power grow.

I almost recognized the tar-like magic mixed with a bright green and realized that Aisling's magic always seemed similar to the green static. A minute of hope flashed across my mind as I thought of Aisling being more important that I had ever even thought. My legs finally loosened as I lifted my palms with hope, ready to fight.

But it was too late.

The flames from the dragon engulfed me, and the surface of my skin began to boil with excruciating pain. My hope became lost as did the last of my oxygen... All of Crystal Rock disappeared, and nothingness was my new home.

* * *

My body shut off, and my mind wandered, but time itself had lost all meaning.

I had nothing left as I felt my soul leave my body, and as I looked down at my own charred body below me, I realized that this was it... I was officially dead.

All of this worry and hope and fighting was all for nothing.

Ragnar had won.

He was on his way to destroy the world, our world, and there was nothing I could do about it. I spent my last few moments when I was alive as a coward. I was afraid to move, and because of that... I let the entire world down. I failed. I had been a witch for half a year, and I did more damage than good.

I looked down and watched the dragon flap its wings and land long enough for Ragnar to jump on, dragging Lady Cambridge with him, only to take out a dagger and shove it in her back. She winced and slumped over as he pushed her off the dragon. Ember joined his side with the dragon's blood sword as they flew off into the sky.

I held myself together as much as I could as I watched the hopeless scene unravel.

There was nothing more that I could do. The last drop of hope that I had left was praying that Jaxon would've linked Izzy to us, but from the looks of it, we were not going to be so lucky. My dad and Eric could come back as Immortals, and my mom would be alive as long as Aunt Clara was untouched. But Haven and I would be leaving our parents without any daughters at all.

If only I had moved, fought back, anything. But instead, I stood frozen in fear of the unexpected danger we were in. I was a coward in my last few moments of life, and now who knew what was to come of Crystal Rock and the world? Ragnar was ready to destroy everything we loved, and here I was, floating in the damn sky having to watch him.

My heart sank as the tears began to flow. I shook my head angrily as I felt as if I should have no sadness in the afterlife.

I looked around for any sign of the others, anyone surviving the fire. But the other bodies laid to rest below me. Except for one area covered in Haven's thick vines. I prayed that Margo was under that pile and would come out alive for Jaxon and Callum. I looked around for Haven and saw nothing. I shook my head as the burning on my skin began to cool, a light coming closer to me. The dark sky was illuminated, and the light seemed to come with peace. I half smiled and turned to see the bright light growing in front of me. I wiped my tears and inhaled in defeat as I closed my eyes and waited for the afterlife to consume me.

"Freya," a paper thin voice whispered. I nodded and

waited for the end. "Freya, you can open your eyes." The voice sounded familiar, but I couldn't recognize where I had heard it before. I slowly opened one eye and expected the light to blind me. But instead, in front of me, a sheer lady was floating next to me in the sky. I opened my second eye and recognized the lady that I had seen weeks ago.

"Am I dead?" I asked when I found my voice.

She smiled and shook her head. "Child, you are far from over." She reached her hand out to me and waited for me to take hers.

I slowly extended my hand as she grabbed it. She rubbed my fingers gently. "Freya, you will have a big job when you get back. My granddaughter is anchored to you and your sister. You both will be okay. But when you get back..." She swallowed hard. "I need you to kill my son. You must kill Ragnar so your world can live on and I can be free."

My jaw dropped as all the dots connected. "Why didn't you say that before? So many riddles."

She smiled shyly. "He was listening before. When he got his chaos magic back, he broke whatever bond was holding me here in this purgatory. I have unfinished business until I know he has been stopped. I am ready to be at peace, and I can only do that once I know his chaos has gone away for good." She swallowed hard and wiped a tear from falling down her sheer skin. "I have lived a thousand years waiting to be set free. Please, child. It is time."

I sniffled. "Time... That is never on our side."

She nodded. "I've seen." She pointed down to the ground that was in flames and shook her head. "Look at him. He's out of control. He's burning the homes of your city now, and next, he will be at the center of Crystal Rock, destroying it and the rest of the world very soon after. His heart cannot be changed. You must not fall for his lies."

My eyes bulged as I looked across the town and watched the dragon spew fire as Ragnar waved his hand around, in control of the creature's every move and every flame that escaped its throat. "Why is he like this?"

His mother's eyes saddened. "Some evil cannot be explained. He had everything growing up, and it was never enough. He always wanted more and was never satisfied. As much as I don't want to admit it, I believe he changed as a child. I tried to love him. I tried to be his world. But instead, he took that to his advantage and killed the only person he ever loved for more power." She pointed to herself. "He can be stopped, but I hate to admit that I wish I had done more to save him." She sniffled. "I, out of all people, know that time is not on anyone's side. If I'd had more time, I could've saved him too."

I squeezed her hand tighter. "This..." I pointed to Ragnar and his chaos and shook my head. "This is not your fault."

She shook her head. "No, maybe not fully—"

"Not at all." I grabbed her hand and pulled her into my embrace. "I will stop him. I know what we have to do. I promise I won't freeze again."

She pulled me back and examined me. "I need to tell you what the others will not."

I looked back at her and waited.

"Eric and your father will not survive this."

My brows furrowed in anger.

She shook her head. "Immortality was never meant to

be created nor was chaos magic. They were both created out of selfishness and neither was meant to live forever."

"Stop." I put my hands up and pulled away from her. "Please. Not another word."

She frowned. "Someone needed to tell you."

I looked back down at the charred bodies, and my stomach began to turn on me. I felt a pull back to the earth, and I knew it had to be our Anchor powers kicking in and helping us come back.

"Freya... A syphon must take his chaos magic out before you kill him, his heart will be guarded by the chaos protecting him. But I hope you find the loophole. There's always a loophole," she whispered, as I felt my body begin to shiver.

I looked back at her as my Mark began to glow brighter than I'd ever seen it before.

"Wait," I yelled, as I felt myself being pulled away. "Thank you."

She smiled and nodded. "You're welcome."

The light disappeared as I watched Ragnar fly over the Mississippi River. We wouldn't have long, but we needed to evacuate the town. I looked down at my body and watched as my Mark glowed even brighter through the burns. Everything went dark as I felt my soul fly back into my body, healing itself piece by piece.

Chapter 31

Aisling Meadows

My eyes burned from the tears that wouldn't stop flowing as I sat in the backseat with Jaxon's head laying in my lap. He was not only my distant cousin but he was my friend. One of my best friends. I looked down at him sleeping, recovering from the slash, and I studied his features. I ignored Declan and Izzy arguing in the front seat on how we gave Ember the fake sword all along, and she was angry that we even kept her out of the loop to begin with. I rolled my eyes and just waited for Jaxon to wake up. He had been through enough in his life. Enough pain, enough loss, enough lies. He had a lifetime of trauma and didn't deserve to have to deal with any more pain. The thought of another permanent scar on his body from evil people made me sick.

I felt his body twitch a few times, and I knew he was either in that half sleep with a deep thought or maybe he was still halfway in the Anchor world and debating on if it was worth it to come back at all. His chest had continued to rise, and his body seemed to have gone into shock moments after it happened. I grabbed his hand and began to squeeze it, trying to make the blood flow back to his not so warm fingers.

"Crank the heat up back here," I said to the front.

The two of them became silent as the bickering finally stopped, and Declan turned the knob.

"How is he?" Izzy asked nervously, as she kept facing forward.

"He's alive," I said.

Declan looked back from the driver seat and nodded in approval. He reached for his shoulder and rubbed his Mark. "These things sure do come in handy."

I nodded and fixed Jaxon's hair as he began to shift.

He slowly began to open his eyes as he groaned. His neck was crusted with dried blood, and I was sure it was painful enough that no strep throat could compare. He slowly reached for his throat as his eyes became wide open.

"Ember?" he whispered.

I half smiled. "She's one of the bad guys... Don't worry, we still have the real sword."

He swallowed hard, and I watched as his breathing became rapid. "Freya."

He wasn't asking, but I knew exactly what he meant. "We have one more hour."

I didn't dare tell him that we had been calling her nonstop with no answer for the last few hours. I knew that the panic would only piss him off more, and I didn't want that to weigh on him right now.

"Jaxon..." Izzy turned around and stared at him. "I... I'm really glad you're okay." She half smiled and patted his shoulder. "Your mother would kill me if anything happened to you."

Jaxon seemed to like the idea of Izzy being killed, but he reached his hand out to her and patted it gently. "Thank you," he said with a hoarse voice.

She nodded and turned back around.

I watched the exchange and smirked. "One big happy family." I laughed, and Declan smiled in the rearview mirror at me.

Jaxon shrugged and closed his eyes again.

I grabbed my phone and sent another text.

> Aisling: Freya, I swear to God, you better call me back. What the hell is going on there?????

A part of me knew something was wrong, but I didn't want to say it out loud. Declan and Izzy had already run through the scenarios, and it was enough torture already. I didn't have a clue what we were driving back to.

My phone started to ring, and I grabbed it, dropped it, and picked it back up, fumbling with the accept button.

"Freya? What's happened? Ember is bad bad. She has a replica sword. We have the real one." I practically yelled into the phone without hesitation.

I held my breath and pressed the speaker button as we waited for the damage.

"Guys... Don't come home... Crystal Rock—" Freya sobbed through the phone. "Crystal Rock is being burned to the ground. Ezra and Aunt Clara began evacuating people with Aunt Lynn when the fire started." She sobbed harder. "The middle of the town has been ripped open, fire and hell itself... Ragnar has his chaos magic, and it's... true chaos. He's destroying everything."

I inhaled deeply and held my breath as the car stayed silent. I looked up and made eye contact with Izzy. Jaxon sat up too quickly and groaned in pain. Izzy's jaw tightened as she reached her hand out for the phone.

"Freya, meet us at the cave," Izzy said. "Bring the others with you. Where's my sister?"

I watched as Jaxon held his breath.

"She's with us. She's untouched physically. Mentally, she's upset. Ragnar took his magic back from her necklace and then tossed her aside like a ragdoll. Haven's vines protected her during the... nevermind," Freya answered, as Jaxon's shoulders relaxed.

"And my mother?"

I looked back at Izzy and watched her hands shake.

The seconds of silence felt like minutes.

"She's... She's..."

"Dead?" Izzy's voice broke. "He killed her. Didn't he?" She sniffled. "After everything, he knew that if he took her away, then he would have finally taken everything from me."

"Iz—"

She grabbed the phone and crushed it. Letting the phone go silent indefinitely.

She threw the phone down to the ground in the front seat of the car and screamed uncontrollably. My eyes watered in shock as whatever anger and torment she held inside of her escaped and shook the entire car with even the road seeming to rumble. She screamed again as she grabbed her head and clenched her fists, trying to bury her screams between her legs.

"I never. Got to. Say goodbye." She sobbed and let her head sink down into her lap as she sobbed harder. "I have nothing left."

I did not love her, but I felt her pain. Everything she was feeling was rushing through her now. I tried to reach her shoulder for comfort, but Jaxon beat me to it.

"Hey." He rubbed her back and cleared his throat. "Izzy, you still have us."

Her sobs continued but became quieter as she lifted her hand and reached for Jaxon's. I watched carefully as the two of them connected for the first time, and began to mend a long lost family. I smiled as I knew there wasn't an ounce of hate in Jaxon's body that would let someone else suffer alone. He leaned back against me and caught me smiling.

"What?" he asked quietly.

I shook my head and smirked. "You are amazing, Jax."

Declan caught my eye in the mirror and winked at me.

I felt the tension in the car relax as we drove toward Crystal Rock with expectations being altered. I had no idea how bad things truly were going to be when we got there. We would drive straight up into the bluffs of Prairie du Chien and be able to have an advantage point high in the bluffs overlooking Crystal Rock. I inhaled heavily as my head tried to wrap around the day's events and felt a sickness as I thought of my parents. Helpless and home. I prayed that they were among the ones who were evacuated.

I promise to spend more time with them. Please keep them safe.

I looked out of the window as Jaxon laid his head back on my lap and let my mind wander. I felt helpless without a phone and not being home. I could feel my chest burning as the extra magic began to work with my emotions. The stress of the unknown was frightening.

Chapter 32

Haven Vine

There was so much yelling, so much commotion, as we made our way up the bluffs to the cave. I was thankful that my vines protected Margo. She seemed to be just out of reach of the flames, and I couldn't have been happier that something good happened. Lady Cambridge was just barely on her last breath when we were back in our bodies, and I was able to heal her. She took me by surprise when we were talking to the others on the phone, and she shook her head to have Freya keep her well-being a secret.

"Her magic has always been stronger with rage. I want her to stay mad at her father until it's over," Lady Cambridge said.

I nodded, not sure if that was a good idea, but I trusted her.

"I have to go and save Oxana. She's my longest friend, and if he has a dragon on his side, we won't have a chance to get close enough to syphon the chaos back from him."

Freya was angry about splitting up, especially after

lying to Izzy about her mother. She knew the abandonment and loss all too well, and she didn't think it was a great idea. But when I told her to let it be, she trusted me.

Aunt Clara and Ezra were not too far ahead of us with the rest of the town by the time we made it to the bluffs. I knew this was going to be too hard to explain to the mundane people, and now they were just as involved with supernaturals as we were. We didn't have a time machine that could erase their memories or a way of going back in time without another consequence. And we were not taking any more chances. The town would have to accept the unbelievable and either grow from it or run from the town of magic. They had to know that the place was filled with magic. The bluffs alone proved that the beauty of magic flowed through them daily. Or maybe it was a witch thing to feel the energy everywhere. Crystal Rock was the Salem of our Wisconsin, and we were the witches that would never be burned.

Well, technically, not again by a dragon that shouldn't even exist... See? How hard will that be to believe when even I am still processing it?

I laughed out loud as we ran, and Freya stopped and looked back at me with worry.

"I'm fine." I stopped running and tried to catch my breath. "I just came back from the dead... I'm totally fine." I swallowed hard and hugged my torso as I tried to inhale more oxygen. "Actually, I think I'm going to be sick." I ran off the path and heaved down the side of the trail.

My dad ran over to me and picked me up, lifting me over his shoulder like a ragdoll. He carried me the rest of the way. I watched as Eric and Freya ran with us and stared at me with worry.

"She's not okay," Eric said to Freya, as they fell behind us.

Freya clicked her tongue and snapped, "We all just died. None of us are okay." She huffed and ran past us, then joined our mom as the cave entrance came into view. My dad rubbed my back as he slowed his jog and began to walk the rest of the way.

"You okay, kid?" he asked when it was just him and I left.

"I feel better. I can walk."

He slowed and bent down to let me gain my balance before we kept walking together.

He looked back at me and waited for me to break the silence.

I smiled, remembering the quiet world we were in and knowing that most conversations started because of me. He was not much of a talker, but you could tell that he loved the company.

"I've just never had to use a lifeline before. And for the longest time, it was just dark. I didn't see anyone or hear anything, and I was... Well, I was terrified."

He stopped walking and looked back at me.

"It was the same for me." He scratched his head and shrugged.

I inhaled heavily. "I keep thinking about it. Like what if there is nothing after this? What if as an Anchor, we die and nothingness consumes us for good?"

He exhaled slowly. "I like to believe that my parents found peace, and peace is with each other and my little sister. Whether that be in Valhalla or anywhere. I believe that peace is much more than just a dark space. I think your body was just searching for your Anchor, and as it happened, we just had to wait."

I shrugged. "I really don't want to find out for real anytime soon."

He huffed. "You won't." He grabbed my hand and pulled me in for a hug. "You and Freya are going to live a long and meaningful life. I promise you two are going to see the world and bring more children into this world. You two... My daughters are going to live amazing long lives. As your father, I owe you that."

I laughed. "Dad, you can't make promises like that. The last twenty-four hours have been horrific, and we may not have another twenty-four to go."

"I just made you a promise. That means something in my world. You may not have grown up with me, but when I make a promise, I keep it."

He let go of me and kissed my forehead.

"I love you, kid."

I felt the tears starting and tried to sniffle them back down.

He smiled and patted my back.

"Come on."

We made it into the cave, and Ezra swooped me up and hugged me tight. His embrace was more than just relief. It was an "I'm never letting you go again" kind of hug.

He set me down and kissed my cheek, then handed me

a bottle of water. I gulped it down without hesitation. He smiled and took the empty container from me.

"You sure you're okay?" he asked.

I nodded and reached up to kiss him. "Now I am."

"Well, I guess Izzy did something good for once in her life. She saved you two."

I half smiled and nodded. "Yeah. I guess so."

Freya walked over to us, and I looked past her at the entire town of Crystal Rock behind us, the lanterns and flashlights illuminating the cave. I watched as the people panicked and were scared.

"Where's Aunt Clara? We need to get them some overload tea. Maybe they will take the info with a grain of salt?" I asked Ezra.

Freya laughed as she pointed back to Aunt Clara already in the back corner with an oversized jug and was already pouring the tea.

"She just told me she saw a vision and started brewing it in huge batches this morning." Freya shrugged. "She made Ezra grab the sleeping bags and other supplies at the break of dawn. She wanted to be prepared."

I made eye contact with her and smiled. She always knew what to do, and for that, I was thankful. She was always so calm and collected, and I wished that I had been more like that hours ago when the dragon came at us. But Freya was frozen, and honestly, so was I. I felt like a coward, and I didn't want to admit that out loud. I felt as if my powers were nothing compared to Freya's, and in that moment, we all needed her, not me.

My eyes shut as I realized where I belonged. I was a

healer, and healers needed to stay with the people. Freya was the one with the true power. Her and Izzy needed to do this. As much as I didn't want to split up the Anchors, we needed to. This fight would not let us all live if we were together. My head spun as my brain began to fire with a plan, but it was as if it were happening in front of me. My legs became wobbly as a vision began. I watched it play out in my head, and as soon as it ended, I opened my eyes. Freya smiling in front of me.

"Please tell me you saw that too?" She grabbed my hands and squeezed them tight.

I smiled and nodded. "You think you can do it?"

Her excitement showed me that she was ready. "I think it's time to send that psycho back to the hell he crawled out of."

Eric heard us talking and finished sipping his tea before he kissed Aunt Lynn and walked over to us.

"Stop with the planning behind my back. We know that I need to be in on this plan. It was what I was made for."

Freya rolled her eyes and clicked her tongue. "You? You are the one trying to get killed to save everyone. *You* think there is no other way. But there is always a loophole." She smiled. "*You* were born and made immortal long before *we* were born. That original plan has sailed, and we're coming up with a new one."

Eric growled. "I am not losing you or your father or your sister or Aisling or even any of your stupid boyfriends at the hands of Ragnar. I am not allowing any of you to take a step toward the city. As soon as the real sword is back here, I am going to finish this myself." He gritted his teeth. "Not with you or your father. This is my job, and I am doing it alone." Before he even knew it, his palms were filled with flames, and his breathing became too heavy. His rage made his fists clench harder as he shook the fire out and began to walk out of the cave.

Freya's eyes were big as she watched him walk away from us.

"Valerian root?" I asked her.

Her smile didn't return, but she nodded. "We can't let him help. We've used the root on him before, and it can definitely put him to sleep for a while. Izzy needs to help me."

I half smiled. "When is Izzy's mother going to jump in?"

Freya grimaced. "Izzy needs to think she's dead for this to work. Nicolai said that Izzy's magic works better with rage and there will be no stopping her once she starts to syphon from him. Her mother thinks that between Izzy and I, we can contain his magic long enough to kill him with the sword."

"What do you do with the chaos magic after?" I asked.

Freya bit her lower lip, and I watched her plan stop there. But then she slowly reached in her back pocket and showed me the small glass bottle containing the squid ink. "Nicolai gave this to me before she left."

"That magic will run just like yours did. It won't destroy it," I said. Freya fidgeted with her necklace. "You guys can't hold on to it forever."

She shook her head. "I know that. I just haven't figured that part out yet."

"Freya... That magic will kill you in the long run... It's unnatural."

She nodded. "I know."

I inhaled and exhaled and tried to think of other options.

"Do you think it was smart for Nicolai to run after Oxana?" I asked her.

She shook her head. "No, but honestly, Oxana needs help too. The bracelet will stop the mind control and then we will have a dragon on our side. Ragnar thinks he killed her so he won't be looking for her. He thinks we all are dead. At least we have that for an advantage."

I nodded and hugged her tight.

"You're staying, aren't you?"

I nodded again. "You saw it in the vision too. I'm not supposed to be there. You need to go talk to Eric."

She inhaled sharply and walked away, slowly letting my hand go. Ezra watched carefully as I filled him in on the plan.

Chapter 33

Freya Chamberlain

The night was cold, the cave damp, but it was all we had. The townspeople were safe and I was forever grateful. The town could be rebuilt, but without the people, what was it good for?

I ran to the opening of the cave and saw Eric pacing back and forth, muttering words under his breath as he kicked the loose gravel.

"Hey." I walked slowly up to him and stopped him from pacing.

"Why do you think you have to be the hero?" he snapped.

I leaned back and glared. "I am not trying to be anything. I want to keep everyone I love alive, and I know for a fact that if you kill Ragnar, then you will die. Especially if you try to use that sword while he has his chaos magic. And I refuse to have your blood on my hands."

He growled and clenched his jaw. "You wanted me dead months ago. Let me choose my fate."

"That was months ago." I pushed his shoulder, and he

barely budged, but it was the meaning behind it. "You deserve to live. You and Aunt Lynn deserve a life together. Please." My hard voice cracked at the end of the sentence, and I watched as his hard face turned soft. "Please... I don't want you to sacrifice any more of your time for everyone else. I want you to take Aunt Lynn and leave this place. I want my mom and dad to do the same. I want you guys to be happy and live. No one has to die tonight."

His eyes began to glisten as his lips opened and then closed, speechless. He looked away and inhaled deep. He stared into the dark sky and shook his head. "Freya... I was made to destroy him, and none of this would have happened if I would've killed him when I was supposed to. It was a task that I was given a thousand years ago, and I never had the courage to fulfill it... Until now. I have a family worth fighting for. I have a reason to save the world. I have you and your sister and my brother and the love of my life, and hell, I even have a descendant whether she likes it or not. I got to raise Declan as my own, and I can't let him not have a life because I'm selfish. I got everything I wanted. It's my time, and I refuse to let anyone else die or get hurt because of my own cowardice."

I sucked in the cold air and shook my head. "Eric, please. I have a plan. You don't have to die. You don't even have to fight. It may have been your fight a thousand years ago, but now... Now, it's my fight. It's my town. It's my family and my loved ones."

He sniffled and cleared his throat. "Damn it, Freya, why do you have to be stubborn like me?"

We both laughed through the tears forming.

"I promised you a peaceful holiday together, and

Thanksgiving was not it. I was mean, and I can't let that be how we end things."

He smirked and inhaled heavily. "Alright," he answered.

I looked back at him and let my lungs release the breath I was holding.

"Thank you."

"Hey, kid... I love you, okay?" His words caught me off guard as he grabbed me and hugged me tight.

"Please don't hate me forever," he whispered in my ear before he snapped my neck, and I fell to the ground, back into darkness.

Chapter 34

Jaxon Oakes

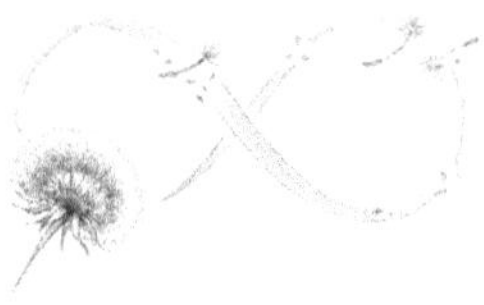

Crystal Rock was on fire as a dragon flew above it, burning the rest of the houses. The cave was right up the bluff, and soon, we would have to make decisions that were life or death. I grabbed my throat and scratched the charred scar that was forming. I gritted my teeth as I thought of Ember and her betrayal as Declan slammed on the brakes and nearly drove us over the side of the bluff.

"What the hell, Declan?" I yelled. My throat felt as if it tore itself back open. I groaned as I looked ahead and saw Eric standing in front of us.

He walked calmly over to us, and Izzy stepped out of the car.

"Are you with me?" he asked her.

She looked back at us and then nodded to him.

Declan jumped out of the car and pushed him back. "What's going on?"

Eric inhaled heavily and reached into his pocket. He handed Declan something small and whispered to him.

Declan stepped back and looked at his hand. He shook his head and placed whatever it was in his pocket.

Eric nodded. "There isn't another way. Everyone else will die trying. I can do this. Izzy will help me. This wasn't meant for any of you."

"Dad, I can't let you do this."

Eric reached out for Declan's shoulders and straightened him up. "I never got to raise a child of my own, but damn if you were one hell of a son. I'm sorry I wasn't better to you. But that girl in there... She's worth keeping. Please take care of her." He pulled Declan in and hugged him tight.

I stepped out of the car and walked over to them.

"Please tell me what's going on."

Eric's eyes looked at my throat, and he shook his head. "Another reason why I can't let you help me. Freya would kill me if I let you fight. Did Ember do that?"

I nodded.

Eric's jaw clenched, matching his fists.

"This ends tonight," he growled. "Jaxon, I'm sorry."

I shrugged. "For what?"

He smirked. "Well, I snapped Freya's neck."

I felt my body jerk forward as I grabbed him and pinned him to the ground. "What did you do?"

He laughed. "Relax. She was stubborn and was trying to be a hero and die for no reason. I saved her."

My breathing slowed as I pushed myself off him.

"She's right outside of the cave. I sat her up nicely, and she has a blanket keeping her warm. Don't worry. She's going to hate me a lot more than you do. But if I didn't do it, she would go on a suicide mission, and me and Izzy already decided to do this ourselves. We made a pact after she got her magic back. We deserve to kill Ragnar after everything he's put us through."

Izzy reached for my shoulder and nodded. "It's all true."

I looked between the two of them and shook my head, realizing that all I had wanted was for them both to be gone from us months, weeks, and days ago, but now in this very moment, I didn't want to lose anyone else. I didn't want my mom to lose her sister again, and I didn't want Eric to leave the Chamberlains again.

"Now, Jaxon, I need you to be the hero boyfriend that you are and go be with Freya and her family. Your parents are in the cave already too. I need you to keep her there when she wakes up. Please keep her there until it's all over. Please. I need you to do this, not for me, but for you and your future with her. All of Crystal Rock's future."

Izzy's hand never left my shoulder, and I felt anger pour through me. I was tired of losing everyone, but I understood where he was coming from.

"I just am thankful that you linked Izzy to the twins. Otherwise, they wouldn't be alive right now."

Aisling gasped.Eric turned to her as she stepped out of the car.

She looked at Izzy and then to Eric and shook her head. "It's not right." She began to cry. "I haven't had enough time to get to know either of you."

Eric reached for her and caressed her cheek. "Your parents are with your Aunt Lynn at the cave. They're safe. Please go be with them."

She shook her head and sniffled. "It's not fair. Why can't everyone have a happy ending?"

Izzy smiled. "Aisling, it's because it's not the end for any of you. You will be happy. All of you will be."

Eric looked back at her and smiled. "She's right."

Aisling looked back at Eric and began to cry. They both pulled her in for a hug, and I stood back, my head spiraling over what was the right thing to do. Eric was right about Freya. But I felt like there was another way. We had too much power on our side to let Ragnar destroy them. We had more witches with us than he did. He had Ember and a dragon. But the dragon could be stopped if we could get Ragnar out of its head.

I looked up toward the direction of the cave and Freya and then back at Crystal Rock, on fire. I felt stuck in the middle of right and wrong.

Declan stepped into the car and pulled the sword from the sheath. He handed it over to Eric with slight hesitation. I watched his hand tremble as he released it. His shoulders fell as he swallowed hard.

Eric's face fell. "It's okay," he said and patted Declan's back.

Declan shook his head. "You're leaving me alone."

Eric cleared his throat, and I watched him swallow his sadness. "My boy, you have the world ahead of you. I was never meant to raise you, but I sure as hell am glad I did. I love you. Always have and always will. But I *need* to do this. For me. I need this to end."

He continued to shake his head as Eric put his hand out to him and waited.

Declan looked back at him, and his nose flared as he

pushed Eric's hand away. "You don't have to die," Declan said with anger and jumped back in the car and slammed the door.

Eric looked at him and then turned to Izzy.

Izzy looked back at Declan, and I could see the pain and regret in her eyes.

"Let's go, Iz," he said, and she looked as if she didn't know which way to go, either.

She nodded and turned to me. "Please keep your mother safe for me. That's all I ask."

I felt that deeper than she realized, and now, I felt like I was wrong to let her go.

"I'm coming with you," I snapped.

Eric glared back at me. "No, you are going to be with Freya. She won't survive a world without you. Now, damn it, go before I snap your neck too."

I clenched my fists and shook my head. "Damn it, Eric. Try to live through this, and her too." I nodded toward Izzy. "Please, for all of us." I held my hand out and waited for his.

We shook, and he stared back at me, and I could see the hurt in his eyes.

Aisling waited for me to let go before she spoke. "His heart. That sword has to pierce his heart but only after the chaos magic is fully syphoned from him."

Eric smiled. "Thanks, kid."

Aisling sniffled and wiped another tear. "Izzy, that chaos magic will be too much inside of you. The only way to destroy it..." Aisling stared at Izzy and cried harder. "The magic must be destroyed right after the blade pierces his heart, or it will try to revive him. It's too much for one person to hold. You will have less than a second to make that happen."

Izzy nodded and smiled. "It'll work."

Aisling nodded. "I know it will. I just wish we would've made it back sooner and things could've been different."

The snow began to fall as if mother nature was trying to heal itself and put the fires out on its own. The cold that came through made me shiver. Izzy's eyes began to well with tears, but I watched her swallow hard and choke them back. "This was never your fight. We were never supposed to live this long." She walked over and wiped the snow from the top of Aisling's head and smiled.

Aisling gritted her teeth and snapped, "Neither of you ever had a chance to live. You both lost everything over and over again because of your father. It's not right."

Izzy half smiled and nodded. "It's okay."

"It's not." Aisling pointed to Declan in the closed car and sobbed harder. "Now Ragnar is destroying *his* life. Taking the only father he's ever known. How am I supposed to mend him? I might have power, but I'm not strong enough for that."

Eric gave me a look, not just any look, but *the* look. The look that it was time and I needed to step in and help them get out of here. I watched as his heart was shattering, knowing no one was going to be happy about any of this.

I nodded and grabbed Aisling.

"Let go of me, Jax!" she screamed through tears, as I forced her back into the car and closed the door. She leaned into me and bawled. "This isn't how it's supposed to happen. Nicolai said we could do this. She told me they didn't need to die."

"Drive," I demanded.

Declan never looked back at Eric as he started the wipers and stepped on the pedal. I grabbed Ais's head and rubbed her long blonde curls and tried to console her. The emotions of everyone were all over the place right now. Our home was being destroyed, and the ground in the center of my old home was crumbling as the flames came up around it. A pathway to literal hell seemed to be opening as Ragnar thought he had won. He would never see Eric and Izzy coming. He thought everyone was dead. It was to our advantage. The only thing we were missing was a better damn plan where we didn't have to lose anyone else.

I looked across to the river and saw the lock and dam rushing through the half frozen Mississippi. I watched the water force its way through the ice and carry on its path. I saw the lights from the dam illuminate the water, and the flow was strong with ice chunks pushing harder against the freezing water. Our fishing float was holding on for dear life with the ice trying to crack through it and drag it with it. But the float stood its ground and never let go of the earth. The fishing float never let the force of nature take it down. It was anchored to the river's flow, and it was going to survive yet another winter.

Anchors...

Anchored...

An Anchor.

"Hey, Declan. What's the one thing every power source needs to work?"

Declan looked at me in the rearview and raised a brow. "A ground wire?"

I nodded. "An anchor or a ground."

He turned around and looked back at me, confused.

"What if when Izzy syphons the chaos magic, she has the twins as anchors holding her in place? What if that is why Anchors were created? What if each one was born to see if they were strong enough to destroy the chaos magic that Ragnar created? What if our lifelines were meant to keep us grounded as we take the magic and destroy it?"

Declan's eyes widened as Aisling sat up.

"No amount of magic is meant to be contained. Look at Ais and Ezra... They are holding on to some extra shit but can only hold it for a little while. What if that's how Izzy survives this? And Eric... I mean, he's immortal still. What if Jim's able to keep him here?"

He shrugged. "I mean it's possible."

"But?" I asked.

The cave came into view, and I saw Freya sitting there with Haven next to her, healing vines wrapped around her neck. My heart sank for a minute while I saw her, but then Freya woke and jumped up, confused and angry.

Declan parked and as I went to jump out to get to her, but he grabbed my arm.

"Jaxon... Whoever pierces the sword will die. There is nothing we can do about it. And Izzy needs to destroy the magic within a second. There is no Anchor strong enough to bring either one of them back from that." He shook his head.

My head started to spin as scenarios played out over and over. I knew I couldn't go into the cave and see my parents right now. I knew if I did, then I would have to tell her of Izzy's suicide mission to be a hero, and I knew that as much as my mother pretended she didn't love her... She has not let her leave her side since she'd been back with us.

I ran to Freya and lifted her into my arms, spinning her around and squeezing her tight. She leaned down, and her lips reached mine. Her heart raced as she kept her hands in my hair and then her eyes widened when she saw my neck.

"I'm okay."

She swallowed hard as I put her down.

"You okay?" I asked, as I examined her neck.

She nodded.

"Where's Eric?" She looked across the field and seemed to panic. "Where's the sword?"

Aisling and Declan met up with us and shook their heads.

"You gave it to him? Why? We have a plan. We don't need him to die." Freya frantically shook her head.

"Izzy and him went after Ragnar." Aisling answered.

"Izzy too? Why? What the hell, you guys... Why didn't you answer us back on the phone? I texted you. We can destroy him from inside his own mind."

Aisling wiped her tears and seemed to have a sliver of hope. "Well, Izzy broke my phone."

Freya looked as if she was going to lose it. She shook with anger.

I stared at her, confused, and Declan and Aisling matched my worry.

"Hey, are you okay?" I asked Freya and grabbed her shoulders, trying to make sure she was still in there.

She pushed me away. "I said I'm fine!" she yelled. "Damn it!" She screamed and dropped to the ground as her magic broke through her emotions and the ground rumbled under us. All the newly fallen snow lifted off the ground and froze midair before it dropped back down and covered the ground again.

Haven stood up and walked over to us. "We have a plan. We need Eric and Izzy to not be heroes today."

"Well, that's not going to happen now. They are halfway there," I answered.

Haven began to laugh, and the night's air sent a shiver down my spine. We all froze and turned to look back at her. Her laughter became louder as she bent over and grabbed her knees. "Sorry," she laughed again. "He's not even going to get far from the bluff before he passes out."

I looked at Freya and back at Haven, confused.

"I had Aunt Lynn slip the Valerian root in his tea before he drank it. Aunt Clara had already seen this in her vision, and she knew that he was going to try and save the world alone. Izzy was not part of the equation, but I'm sure she will be waiting next to his body with the sword."

Freya's eyes widened as she stood up and smiled. "Genius," she whispered to Haven. "We need to get to work. The moon is as high and full as it's going to get. We can harness from the moon as long as it lets us and pray that we are strong enough."

I stepped back and felt the confusion hit me. "Is someone going to fill me in?"

Freya leaned in and kissed my cheek. "Do you trust me?"

My brows lowered, and my lips parted. "Of course."

"Then, do me a favor and take me to the sword and Izzy. I need her for this to work."

I didn't like the idea of Freya getting in the middle of a

battle, but she had a smirk, and I knew she was planning something completely out of her comfort zone, but if she was confident, then I had to believe her.

"Haven, please stay here with everyone. And, Declan, you're not going to like this, but I need you to stay with Eric when we get to him. I need you to keep him from coming to us. We need all the Anchors separated to give us all a chance of surviving this."

"A grounded Anchor." Declan looked at me and smiled. "You two are something else. Yin and Yang." He rolled his eyes and smiled again. "Where is she going?" He pointed to Aisling, and I watched his shoulders tense.

"I need her," Freya said. "She will be out of harm's way, but I need her close."

Declan held his breath and opened his mouth to argue, but Aisling covered it.

"I'm not letting this asshole take our home away," she said, "Ezra is here, so I'll be safe."

Declan released his breath and shook his head. "I don't like this... But I trust you."

Aisling smiled and nodded. "Declan Greystone, I love you so much, and I want you to breathe again knowing that your father is going to live."

He half smiled and grabbed her, lifting her. "I swear I don't deserve you." He kissed her deeply and set her down. "I. Love. You," he said between each peck on the lips.

She blushed and nodded.

"Alright then... What's this new plan?" I asked, as the snow fell and the chill in the air grew.

Chapter 35

Eric Greystone

We ran down the bluffs, our feet carrying us faster with each intention of getting to our destination sooner. Izzy looked over to me and smiled.

"Friends?" she asked.

"Best friends," I answered and grabbed her hand as we made our way to what was left of our old lands.

She lifted her palm. "Ignis." The fire grew as it illuminated our surroundings.

"Where do you think he is?" she asked, as we slowed from a run to a fast pace walk.

I shook my head. "Follow the chaos."

She nodded and pointed ahead, extinguishing the flame she held and took cover behind a building that was half destroyed. We looked down the road of Crystal Rock and saw the buildings and homes destroyed. I looked over and saw my brother's bar still standing and wanted to laugh at the irony of his immortality and the bar lasting forever. Izzy tucked in closer to me as she turned the bracelet around on her wrist, and the pungent smell reminded me of the old days. But then the scent of honey lingering in her hair brought me back to the first time I had seen her after searching for years, and I remembered her standing, shakily, behind the honey stand. I remembered thinking she was a warrior and the strongest person I had ever met, and a part of me was sad that I had blamed her for our past, but when I saw her, it had brought back so many memories of what was and what was supposed to be. She was to be my wife, and we were to bear children. But instead, here we were... ready to kill her father and enter Valhalla together. The universe had a funny way of bringing us back together after all of these centuries.

"Hey, Iz." I whispered in her ear.

She jumped and turned toward me. Her lower lip quivered as she seemed scared for the first time in her life. I grabbed her hand and kissed it before setting it back down.

"You will always be my favorite friend. I am sorry for all you've been through alone, and I promise that I will be by your side from this point on." I smiled at her. "Together?"

She smiled, and her lower lip stopped quivering. I saw the warrior come back into her eyes. "Forever." She spit in her hand and grasped mine, smudging the saliva between our palms. "Who would've thought that you and I would become the heroes?" she asked with a smile.

I laughed and nodded. "Too bad no one is here to see it."

She shrugged and laughed again. She handed me the sword and rubbed her chest. She looked past the building and saw Ragnar standing there with Ember. Oxana had transformed back into her human form and was sitting naked next to them, shivering and covered with ash and snow.

"Stop chattering those damn teeth," Ragnar screamed at Oxana and kicked rubble at her.

Oxana obeyed and wrapped her arms around her body for warmth.

"What's next?" Ember asked with a smile. "They're dead. The town is worthless. Can we leave now? I want to see the world like you promised."

Ragnar looked down at her with disgust. "You don't stop whining, either, do you?" he growled and picked her up by her throat. "We go when *I'm* ready." He spat in her face and then tossed her to the side.

Ember jumped up and rubbed her neck with her hands. "Hey, I thought we were a team."

Ragnar turned around and glared at her. "You were born from magic, so even you are an abomination. You're lucky that I like you enough to *let* you live. But if you keep talking, then I will cut out your tongue."

Ember gasped and covered her mouth.

I could feel a shift in the air as my mind began to unravel. I didn't know what was changing, but something inside of me was starting to ignite. The night's sky shifted from night to day, then back to night, and the chill in the air disappeared. I looked around and noticed that everything seemed different but the same. I straightened myself and clenched my fists as they became clammy.

I shook my head and sucked in a deep breath. "It's time," I whispered to Izzy. She turned and kissed my forehead as we charged Ragnar.

Oxana saw us coming and tried to leap out of our way

as she clawed at the ground to get as far away as possible. Ember seemed oblivious to us as she had her arms crossed and was facing the opposite way. It was Ragnar's scar and glare that made my rage grow even more when he turned around.

"Impossible," he sneered, as we rushed him.

Izzy let the flames grow as she tried to burn him alive, but his chaos magic flickered green and began to circle around us, pulling us closer to him too quickly. I lifted the sword and waved it in the air, slicing across his chest as soon as we reached him. Then, I lifted it and tried to pierce his heart. I could feel his magic trying to push me back, so I pushed through his force shield and almost reached him. But then the earth under me rumbled as his chaos and my magic began to fight against good and evil. After all this time, I finally realized that I was the good one. I smiled and pushed harder against him, reaching him and getting the blade ready to pierce him.

"Izzy, now," I yelled, as Izzy grabbed her father's arm and began to syphon.

Ragnar's eyes bulged as she began to take his magic, and her Mark began to glow bright.

His face hardened as he saw his own magic being taken back from him.

"You've done enough damage," I said to him, as my blade inched closer and closer to his heart. He was pushing back hard enough that it took every ounce of my own strength to get each inch at a time.

Sweat broke out on his forehead before he smirked. He stomped down on the ground, and a section of the town began to crumble, which made us lose our balance. Izzy fell to the side and jumped back up and tried to get her grip back on him.

I took the dragon's blood sword and pushed it hard, piercing his heart. I expected him to collapse or explode or something more damaging to occur, but instead, his scarred face smiled as he pushed me off him and pulled the sword from his chest, the green tar like substance stitching the wound to his heart back up.

Everything happened so fast as Ragnar laughed, an echoing laughter that stormed through the bluffs. I jumped up and stood frozen as the only weapon we had was taken in his hands and dissolved it in front of me. He looked behind me, and his smile grew wider.

"Perfect. They came for you?" He laughed louder. "Clever twins, but stupid Anchors."

I turned behind me and saw Jaxon, Declan, Aisling, Ezra, Haven, and Freya all running toward us. They all had their magic flowing through their palms, charging and ready for the battle. Ezra stopped running and pounded his fist to the ground, and a dome expanded over us and locked us all in place.

My heart sank as I realized what they had just done.

"No," I said under my breath, as I tried to wrap my head around why the hell they were even here.

Ragnar caught me off guard as he came up behind me and grabbed me by my neck. He pushed me down into the dirt with a strength that was beyond my powers. I looked over at Izzy and gasped as her head was already severed from her body. My entire world just came crashing down on me as Ragnar took my head and forced me to face the young witches running toward us.

"Now watch this." He laughed. "This is too easy... Ember, kill them."

Ember stood up and nodded as she pulled a long jagged dagger from her boot and teleported over to them, one by one. She swung hard and didn't miss. It happened so fast that each teen didn't even see it coming. First, Ezra and Haven, and then the dome seemed to shake as Declan and Aisling fell to the ground, lifeless. Freya screamed a blood curdling scream as Jaxon's severed head fell in front of her. She looked back at me, and defeat was all I could see written on her face as she dropped to her knees and sobbed. It was over. The world would be destroyed by one man that I was supposed to kill a thousand years ago. I had failed them... I had failed the world. The tears that I had been holding for years finally started to fall as I watched Ember drag Freya to me, her screams of horror never stopping as Ragnar lifted Jaxon's body and dropped it between myself and her. Freya became frantic and tried to pull her magic from every element of the earth and, instead, became full of rage as her chest exploded with her very own chaos magic. A black tar magic started to flow from her as she released every bit of magic she'd ever syphoned and screamed in horror, but the deafening scream became silent as Ember took the blade and jammed it in Freya's broken heart. Her lifeless body dropped next to me.

"Ember!" Ragnar yelled. "She may have had potential." He rolled his eyes and groaned louder.

I looked around in horror, and the realization hit that I had lost everything I had worked so hard to protect.

Ragnar laughed louder and flipped me over with mere strength that was beyond me.

"Oxana, go and burn the ones left in the cave. This game is over," he sneered.

Oxana nodded and transformed into the dragon I remembered from the worst day of my life as she flapped her wings and flew to the bluffs.

"Did you really think you could beat me? Alone?" Ragnar laughed. "When are you going to learn that you are nothing compared to me? I *am* king."

I shook my head and tried to focus on my task. But it seemed pointless to live on without the ones that were worth fighting for. I thought of Lynn in the cave with my brother and Alex, patiently waiting for the war to be over. They were supposed to step outside tomorrow to a new day, and now they wouldn't make it through the night. My stomach was sick, and the will to live escaped me.

"Do it," I said and waited for the world to end.

Everything went dark as the dome exploded. Oxana broke through it and went to finish the existence of Crystal Rock.

Chapter 36

Freya Chamberlain

"How long do you think he will be out for?" I asked Izzy, as she shrugged.

"We had a long nap with wild dreams the last time you gave us that stuff." She swallowed hard.

"How long has he been out already?"

"Well, he told me we were going to be heroes and no one was going to see it before he dropped and started snoring." She laughed quietly. "Then, my father headed toward the river."

"Should you really be laughing right now?" Aisling asked.

Izzy sucked in a breath and silenced herself. "Sorry, it's been an emotional roller-coaster, and I think I'm ready to get off the ride."

"Agreed," Jaxon said, as he walked back to us after watching Ember grab Oxana a blanket from the half burned house next to them. "They're gone."

I nodded.

"What's he dreaming about?" Jaxon asked me.

I lifted my palms from his temples and shook my head. "It's pretty dark." I left the answer at that and hoped that I would never see anything so heartbreaking ever again. I prayed that tonight would have a different ending than what Eric had strummed up in his nightmares. I rubbed his forehead and hoped that he could get some peace when he woke and the world would be better. I exhaled one last time before Declan lifted him over his shoulder, and we headed for Swig & Jig.

We walked into the bar that was still standing. The others followed me as I went behind the bar and grabbed the bottle of bourbon, pouring a shot for each one of us. I didn't like the idea of alcohol, but my nerves were rapid-firing as I prayed that I had the strength to get into his head. I hoped that Leila was right and that I knew what I was doing.

I sucked in a breath and passed out the small glasses to the others.

"Here's to saving the world." I raised my glass and waited for the others.

They each lifted it one by one with the brown liquid.

"Keep him safe," I added to Declan, as he set Eric down in the office. Ezra walked in and added a dome of protection around the place.

We slung back the shots, and I let it burn my throat as it reached my belly and warmed me. I could feel my nerves relaxing as my fingertips and toes warmed themselves.

"Let's get to the river. Ais, do you have the Valerian root?"

She smiled and pulled out two darts from her pocket, careful not to touch the points of them as she showed the sharp ends glistening with enough of a dose to weaken Ragnar, enough for me to get into his head and Ember to sit still for a little while.

"What about Oxana?" Izzy asked.

"She's going to be okay," I reassured her, hoping that her mother was able to get a bracelet to her before this started.

She nodded. "Freya... My father..." Izzy shook her head. "He's not someone to be reasoned with. When we get the chance, we have to take it."

I had already chosen not to try and change him, but I could see the pain in her eyes as the scenario ran through her mind.

"Let me have the sword," I whispered to her when the others walked away from the counter. "I will help with the syphoning, and when the time comes, I will do it for you."

Izzy hesitated, but then I saw the look in her eyes as she realized she could not do it herself. She slowly handed it over.

Jaxon eyed me carefully as the others began to walk toward the door. "What if you're wrong?"

I swallowed hard and let the emotions reach the surface for only a moment before swallowing back my tears.

I knew I couldn't let Eric do it. It would surely kill him. Plus, I had a theory that a syphon had to do it. Izzy and I were the only ones that were capable of consuming magic. My dad was a syphon, but he didn't know how to do it well enough to control it. I was born for a reason, and this had to be it.

What if the world needed two syphons just for this purpose?

Aisling walked back to us and hugged me tight. "While you're in his head, I'll hold on to the sword. Just in case Ember tries anything teleporty... I will hover it over his heart while he's passed out. If he moves even an inch, I will not hesitate to do it."

I shook my head. "I don't want you to use it at all. We don't know the damage it will do to you."

She raised her eyebrow and frowned. "We don't know what it will do to you, either."

"Izzy said she's going to do it," I reassured her.

Sorry, Ais. I can't lose you.

Aisling nodded and hugged me again.

She walked into the office by Declan.

"I know you have your mind set, but can I tell you a theory of mine?" Jaxon asked.

I laughed nervously and waited.

"Aisling is a descendant of Eric and Izzy, so she has the blood of Ragnar in her system. What if she can do it? What if her magic is meant for this? It has always been a little different from ours."

The thought had never crossed my mind before. I thought about all the times Aisling's magic surprised me and debated on it for a minute. I remembered seeing the green flickering of magic, and it made me wonder if he was onto something. But to put Aisling's life at risk on a theory was too much to handle.

"I'm just saying. Ezra is her Anchor, and he's safe here. Don't hesitate to ask for help."

"You just don't want it to be me."

Jaxon smiled. "I don't want it to be either of you. But especially not you."

I smiled and kissed his lips slowly. I pulled away and exhaled. "I will keep it in mind. I love you."

He smiled and lifted me. "I love you too."

"Please don't hate me."

He set me down and looked back at me confused as Ezra came up behind him and whispered, "Somnum."

He grabbed Jaxon as he fell underneath me and began to snore.

I inhaled heavily and relaxed my shoulders. "Declan, are you ready?" I yelled toward the office. "The river is flowing, and you're better with the water than Jaxon is."

He opened the door and smiled as he walked out of the room with Aisling.

"Thanks, Ezra," I said.

He nodded. "Please be safe." He walked over to me and lifted me in the air and squeezed me tight.

"If this doesn't work—"

"It will," he interrupted.

I swallowed hard and laughed nervously. "Okay, but if it doesn't... Please give this to my parents." I reached in my pocket and pulled out a sealed envelope. I needed them to know why I did what I did and that they deserved happiness together again. "And this to Jaxon, please." I pulled off my tourmaline wrapped necklace that he had re-made for me and handed it to Ezra.

He closed his palm around it and half smiled. "It's gonna work."

I smiled with doubt. "I hope so." I leaned over and kissed Jaxon's forehead one last time before I stepped into the cold with the others.

Aisling and Izzy were chatting softly and stopped

when I stepped out. Declan watched Ragnar and the others stop on the beach. It was our time.

I took the sword, and sheathed the heavy thing, then handed it to Aising who put it on her back. Izzy eyed me carefully with confusion. I shook my head.

I felt wrong leaving Jaxon, but I knew if he was with me, then I would worry the entire time. I did not have it in me to watch him get hurt anymore.

"Hey, Izzy. Remember, Ragnar wanted you and me dead for a reason," I said reassuringly. "We scare him."

She turned and nodded. "Let's go."

We ran down to the beach, and Ragnar's eyes grew wide with disbelief when he saw me standing next to his daughter.

"Impossible," he spat. "I watched you burn, and you," he growled, as he pointed to Izzy. "You are still worthless regardless, ex-syphon." He laughed. "Where's your little twin?"

His scar grew as his smirk widened from ear to ear.

Ember's body lurched, but Ragnar pulled her back. "Not yet."

I looked at Oxana's wrist and exhaled slowly as I realized the bracelet had been delivered to her.

Thank you, Nicolai Cambridge.

I planted my feet and stood my ground. *Don't freeze this time.*

Ragnar lunged at me and ripped me off my feet with an unnatural strength, tugging me toward the train tracks separating the land from the river. I held my breath as I waited for the blow.

"How did you survive?" he spat at me.

I shrugged and stayed silent.

"Well, let's fix that."

I lifted my palms and let the flames grow, feeling my grandparents' magic kick in and help me push him off.

"I am *not* alone."

I turned and watched Ember and the others fighting on the beach, trying to make their way to me. But every time someone would get past her to me, she would teleport them back.

Ragnar stood up and straightened his shirt, dusting the snow off his arms. He seemed surprised by my willingness to stand my ground at all.

"Your twin is hiding, I see... Too scared to face me?" He laughed and walked closer to me.

I lit my palms on fire and clenched my jaw as he inched his way closer, his hands up in defense.

"I don't want to hurt you," he stated and then he came within arm's length and grabbed me by the throat, forcing me to the ground. "I just want to kill you."

I heard the train's whistle, deafening from around the bend, and I choked as I realized this was my shot to get an advantage.

He wrapped both of his hands around my neck and tried to squeeze the life from me.

The whistle blew louder, and I smiled, seeing the headlights right on schedule as it roared sixty miles an hour toward us. I grabbed Ragnar's forearm and syphoned just enough for him to release his grip on me and kicked my legs under him, forcing him in front of the train as it took him away.

I jumped up and rubbed my throat as Ember teleported

from the others and went chasing after the train. The others ran over to me, and we watched as the train disappeared through the tunnel and out of sight. I took a deep breath and relaxed for a minute.

"We need to get off this land," Declan said.

I cleared my throat and pointed to the river and the fishing float by the lock and dam.

"We need a distraction to get the Valerian root in his system. He's too strong without it. Declan, can you get us over there with the water?"

His smile grew as he looked at the water. His eyes, bluer than the ocean, glimmered as he nodded. "Of course."

I inhaled heavily. "Alright, be ready when they get back."

Izzy nodded.

"You sure you're okay?" she asked nervously. "I tried to get to you..."

I nodded. "I know you did."

Oxana ran to us and hugged Izzy, then she faced me with sad eyes. "I'm so sorry. I didn't mean to hurt you. Ragnar was in my head and—"

I covered her mouth. "It's okay. We don't have time for this. Just go along with whatever he says. Don't let him know you can handle yourself."

She nodded and ran off to the side with her blanket covering her.

Then, not a second longer, Ember appeared with Ragnar as he tried to reach us. But a tornado of cold water surrounded us as we zipped through the winter air and landed softly on the fishing float that I had grown up with. I steadied myself as my feet landed on the wooden planks. I watched as Ragnar, Ember and Oxana were pulled through and dropped across from us, keeping a distance from us.

I raised my palm and nodded at Aisling before whispering, "Ignis," letting a fireball grow. Aisling looked at me and readied her dart before I threw the fire at the back of his head, the dart flying right behind it, hitting his head and injecting him before it fell down through the cracks. I smiled when I saw our plan coming together.

Ragnar turned and grabbed his head as he looked around in annoyance.

The snow had slowed, but flurries were still falling as I cleared my throat and yelled to him. "How does it feel?"

He walked closer to me, but I watched him hesitate with each step, and it made the hope inside me grow that maybe I was the reason he was afraid. Maybe the Valerian root was flowing through his system enough for me to get into his head.

"How does *what* feel?"

I smiled and began the game I was playing, trying to distract him from my other motives for this plan to work.

Chapter 37

Aisling Meadows

I stood on the fishing float with my own palms twitching, desperate with the want of releasing my own magic on Ragnar. I wanted him dead for putting my town in danger. He had almost killed my parents, and for that alone I wanted to destroy him. Our lands were burning, and he would need to pay the ultimate price for it.

Declan reached for my hand and steadied the shaking as he gave me a look to stay calm.

I nodded and glared back at Ragnar.

Freya turned and looked at me. She smirked as her eyes glistened, and I could see she was ready to start the torture from within. I winked back at her, and with that Ragnar, Freya, and Izzy disappeared. Freya knew what she was doing, she knew it was time to start toying in the middle with Ragnar's head. I didn't like the idea of them being alone there with Ragnar, but at the same time, I trusted her. If her mind games were as strong as Leila told her... then maybe they could break him in the middle and stop him from imploding our world here.

Ember became frantic as Oxana stood in shock.

"What did you do?" Ember spat.

I shook my head and steadied myself.

"Where did they go?" she asked her mother, who shook her head.

Oxana looked back at me and pleaded with her eyes to save them. She began to walk to us as Ember became crazed. She glared at us and teleported right in front of me, grabbing my throat and trying to terrorize me.

I laughed at her tiny hands and weak grasp. "Ember, you are no fighter. You are a runner. So, run," I said, grabbing her hand and ripping it from my neck.

"Where is he? He made me promises, and I want them kept."

I rolled my eyes. "You don't need a man to give you your freedom. Talk to your mothers. You don't need any promises that he lied to you about."

"He didn't lie." Ember's jaw clenched. "He loves me."

I shook my head. "Like he loves his daughters? Like he loves his wife?"

Ember looked back at her mom, and her rage began to grow. "Ragnar is a good man. You all are evil for trying to kill him. He wants a better world. Why don't all of you want that?"

I readied the second Valerian root dart behind my back when Declan lowered my hand.

Oxana laughed and made her way to us. "Oh, honey... Ragnar has you fooled. You are too much of a child to understand."

Ember glared. "I am a child because you never let me be free."

Oxana shook her head. "You want to see the world? Then, go." Oxana frowned. "I just knew what evil was in the world, and I wanted to keep you safe."

"Safe?" Ember laughed. "You have suffocated me for weeks now."

Oxana took a step back, and even I could see the hurt that caused her.

Ember took a step toward her and slapped her across the face. "You did this to me. You trapped me in a place where there is nothing left for me. I want out. I want adventure, and I want to see the world."

"So, see the world! But if you keep Ragnar alive, there will be no world to see. I can promise you that. You are working with a mad man," Oxana exclaimed.

Ember seemed to have a change of heart, and her eyes saddened. She turned and looked at the burning land of Crystal Rock, and tears began to fall. "I've really messed up this time, haven't I?"

Oxana ran toward her and wrapped her arms around her and pulled her tight. "We can fix this. We can make things better."

Ember looked to us and then her mother and cried harder. "I'm so sorry. He knew exactly what to tell me... I'm a fool."

Oxana rubbed her shoulder, and they sat down on the float.

Declan and I eyed each other as the moment seemed too easy.

Declan shrugged and nodded to Oxana.

I raised my arm and reached for the sword behind my back. I pulled it out and felt the heaviness the sword held. I sat down across from them as we waited for Freya to return. The seconds felt like hours as we listened to Ember and Oxana. They seemed to make future plans and talked about fixing the town. I tried to bite my tongue as I wished Ember would leave town for good. After watching her hurt Jaxon and threaten Declan hours earlier, it made me want to sink the sword into her altogether.

She was too back and forth, and I would never trust her again.

My eyes darted down the river when a boat's light caught my attention, coming toward us too fast as it made its way across the half frozen river. I jumped up and steadied myself with the blade in front of me, ready to battle anyone that Ragnar had played his mind games on.

"Who's that?" Declan asked, standing in front of me, ready to protect me.

Ember and Oxana stood and watched carefully.

"Oh thank the old gods, it's Eric." Oxana released an exhale and waved to me to lower the sword.

My heart began to race faster as I saw not only Eric, but everyone that wasn't supposed to be here approaching.

"No," I whispered, and hope began to disappear as too many Anchors were in the same place at once.

Chapter 38

Freya Chamberlain

I crossed my arms and saw the Valerian root toying with his mind. I watched carefully as his body began to slowly sway, and I knew it was now or never to dive into his crazy mind. I had one shot at this. I grabbed Izzy's arm and nodded to Aisling and Declan, then inhaled heavily and remembered Leila's lecture on how to tap into his mind. I felt the shift very subtly as I watched Ragnar begin to fall and Ember charged us. I closed my eyes and prayed that they could handle her while Izzy and I handled him.

We stood on the float, Ragnar, Izzy and me. The ice was in the river, and it was flowing faster now. My breath was being shown in the air, and I could see it quickening as my heart raced.

Calm down. You've got this.

Ragnar stood and looked around, trying to readjust to his surroundings. I watched as his mind panicked for a second before I felt him trying to get into my head. I looked at Izzy as she taped her bracelet.

"He's trying," she said with a smirk.

"And failing." I began to laugh as my nerves calmed down.

I looked back at Ragnar and continued. "How does it feel? The abandonment... the knowing that you will never be whole again? Your mother left you because she was scared of you." I smirked. "When's the last time you heard from her?" I walked closer to him with confidence. "Did you know that she hides from you in the shadows? She's ready to be free, and you're holding on to every last little grasp of her that you can." I let my smile fade and disgust grow on my face. "While she is pushing you further away."

His eyes glared back at me as we became feet apart. Izzy kept her distance and waited for my call.

"I liked you better when you were dead," he snarled.

"Tell me... How does it feel? To know that the abandonment will never be fixed. The emptiness will only grow. Your wife, your children, your own mother want nothing to do with you. In the midst of trying to recreate a new world, you destroyed your very own."

His nostrils flared as I watched his palm charge with a green flickering rage of chaos. His scarred face began to look tired as he spat, "You shut your mouth. You know nothing about me. You stupid, weak child. You are nothing more than another abomination to this burning world. Twins are nothing more than a carbon copy trying to fix their first mistakes. You are nothing and always will be nothing."

He raised his palms toward us and let his magic try to consume us. Izzy pushed me out of the way and jumped the other direction. We each held on to the wooden rail to keep from falling into the water. She looked back at me and waited for me to let her syphon.

I shook my head and straightened myself. Her rage grew with time. Ragnar stared back at me in anger as he let the flames grow in his palms.

"You killed your wife... Izzy's mother... She was the last person who could tolerate you."

"You will burn, child, along with your town."

I shook my head and waved my finger in front of him. "You really think *we* are nothing to this world?" I lifted my palms to let the flames grow. I focused on the flames and transformed them into a dragon flapping its wings, burning the air above me. I smirked. "You think a *nobody* could do this?" I smiled and flicked my wrists, letting the flame transform the fire dragon into a mirage of his beautiful mother standing in front of him, reaching her palm out to his face and caressing his cheek.

"My sweet boy," she whispered. "You are everything I wished you would never be. You are your father's son, and I never should've come back for you. You evil, sick bastard."

His face went from peace with seeing her to anguish as his rage began to grow. And then I saw it. I saw his chaos magic come to the surface in a moment of weakness, and I knew it was the exact moment we needed to be able to reach it to syphon.

"Izzy, now!" I yelled.

She ran for him and grabbed him from behind and began syphoning. He tried ripping her off, but as soon as he released her grip, I grabbed him and started to syphon with her.

"I am stronger than you both." Ragnar began to laugh and ripped Izzy off him, pushing her to the ground and letting the tar-like chaos try to choke her, pinning her to the boards of the float. I syphoned harder, and Izzy was able to reach him again.

"Keep going," I yelled at her.

"I'm trying." Her voice strained as she kept pulling from him. He turned to face me, and his hands trembled as he tried to get us off him. My body began to shake as his strength was becoming too much. I had hoped that we could weaken him enough to immobilize him, but now I knew that he wouldn't stay restrained for long. I looked at Izzy and panicked as I realized he was stronger than we had planned for. The float began to shake, and the water from the river began to rage under us, sending the water over and splashing us.

He turned to me and smirked. He realized I had messed up. The water hit us, but instead of it being freezing cold water, it was as if nothing touched us at all.

He grabbed my shoulders and shoved me off him, tossing me as if I was weightless across the float. Then, he took Izzy and tried to crush her chest with his foot as he pinned her to the ground with unmatched strength.

"You are trying to mess with my mind... That's a mistake." Ragnar pointed to me and then ripped me from the ground and back to him through the air with only his finger levitating me. "I invited the mind games."

My eyes widened with horror.

"No," I choked. "This is *my* mind."

I threw my arms down to my sides and used them as brakes to stop myself mid-air.

"This is my world," I yelled back to Ragnar. "You don't belong here."

I lifted my palms and let my own anger of my burned town grow inside me.

Ragnar huffed as Izzy kicked from under him and was able to get away from his crushing foot. She stood and came near me as I brought myself back to the ground, steadying myself.

Ragnar laughed. "So, now what? You can't kill me here." He smirked. "What is it that you want?"

I crossed my arms and felt sick as I felt the pull of our world come back. Something was changing, and I could feel my own Anchor getting near me.

Haven, no! What is she doing?

Ragnar grabbed the duplicated sword from behind him and waved it in front of us. "You want this?" He mocked and smiled with his scar face.

I began to lose focus on the illusion, and the float began to lag. Without warning, we were no longer in his head, and Aisling and Declan watched the river with a boat driving in our direction, Ragnar in front of us with his chaos magic still coursing through his veins.

"That was your plan?" He stood up and straightened his jacket. He laughed as he looked back at Oxana and demanded she attack us.

She shook her head and stood her ground. "No more."

Ragnar glared back at Oxana and reached for Ember, pulling her to him by the neck, taking the sword and pointing it at Ember's throat, threatening her life. "I said... transform."

"That I can do." She smiled and stepped forward as she

dropped the blanket and jumped into the air. Her body became scaly as she started flapping her wings high above the sky and then came diving down toward us.

"Move," I yelled to the others, as Oxana flew past us and began to let the flames growl in her throat as she aimed them at Ragnar.

He dove out of the way and grabbed the sides of the wooden float, as the flames began to burn the floorboards we stood on.

"Back up," Izzy yelled.

Oxana came back down for more as Ember was thrown against a loosened floorboard that pierced her lower abdomen. She winced as she tried to stand but fell back down. Her own blood pooling on the wooden planks.

I looked back at Ragnar and shook my head, the Valerian root was either not as potent this time around or his own darkness was able to burn through it too fast.

Ember looked up, losing too much blood as she tried to focus her eyes. She watched as her mother flew high above us.

"You're on the wrong side," Izzy yelled back at Ember.

Ember tried to stand and fell back down as lightheadedness consumed her.

"You lied to me," she yelled at Ragnar, who stood and spat at her. Ember's eyes fell as she grabbed her stomach and tried to pull the jagged board from her body.

"I tried to convince you to switch sides," Izzy said angrily.

Ragnar pulled his duplicated sword from behind his back and aimed it toward Oxana in the sky. As she came swooping back down, the flames along the float began to engulf the old wood. He turned the blade toward the sky and threw it with his unnatural strength, his tar-like green chaos magic forcing the blade to go at a faster speed than lightning.

"No," Ember screamed, as she disappeared from the float and teleported in front of Oxana's body, blocking her mother from the sword that pierced through her skin. As soon as it touched her, the sword transformed back into a piece of driftwood.

Oxana screeched and swooped Ember's bleeding body from midair, wrapping her wings gently around her only daughter, magic or blood, she was hers. She flew to the land near the float, transforming back into her human form, unscathed and trying to tend to her already dead daughter. She screamed in horror, and the chill in the air became frozen as time seemed to stop. The magic that created Ember left her lifeless body and released into the river, glowing brighter than the moon. The magic seemed to evaporate into a million little pieces and floated freely down the river before the glow disappeared. I watched as a womanly figure appeared in the glow of the magic as Ember's soul flowed away in the river freely.

"No... Ember." Izzy's eyes watered as she looked back at me and then her eyes widened. "The water, it's the ground wire... The water can help us."

I looked to the river and back at her, then nodded.

Oxana screamed, and I knew that I could not help her right now. She would need time to heal, and right now, we didn't have time to let that happen. If she wanted to have a world to heal in, we needed to finish this.

Izzy looked at the boat and froze. "Eric is coming. We can't wait."

Ragnar walked through the flames and headed straight for us.

He caught me off guard and gripped my neck, lifting me into the air, and slammed me into the wooden floor boards hard, making the air in my lungs escape as I tried to gasp for a breath.

"You've ruined everything," he sneered. "This was my world to create."

Izzy tried to pull him off me, but Ragnar pinned her down next to me, grabbing a board and pinning our arms away from him.

He began to crush my windpipe with his free hand. "I'm sick of your voice."

My body trembled under him as I was trapped. Izzy thrashed around as he tried to grab her throat.

Declan tried to crash into him but was thrown further down the float. Then, Aisling mimicked him and seemed to get his feet to budge before she was thrown by his chaos and met Declan, he caught her before she was pummeled into the wooden rails.

I couldn't catch a breath and the world began to darken as the night's sky shimmered above us with the stars as clear as ever. Then, one by one... a meteor shower began to fall. I looked up with my eyes wide as I realized it was not stars at all. My limbs began to freeze as my body craved air and then oxygen rushed my lungs as Ragnar was ripped across the float. A loose board came up and pierced into his stomach, holding him in place.

I tried to focus my sight as Declan pulled from the river and extinguished the flames that were getting too close to us. I sat up with Aisling's help as she pointed to the back of the float.

"What is that?" she asked with a shaking voice. Aisling's eyes grew wide as she pulled electricity from her palms and the green flickering grew wider than I had ever seen before.

Izzy jumped up and reached for my arm, pulling me up. I stood and recognized the freed souls that were pinning him back, glowing in the night's sky. I saw as Leila winked at me, and her brother nodded. Levi tipped his cowboy hat, and my late grandparents nodded with affirmation. I grabbed Izzy's hand as she helped pull me to the back of the float. Ragnar choked on his own blood as we each grabbed an arm.

Thanks to the souls, we had an advantage back.

"For all the witches, both living and dead, we are with you," Leila whispered in my ear, as they began to fade slowly, I smiled as they gave me the courage I needed to finish this.

The boat was now coming straight for us and was too close. Eric would be dead in minutes if we didn't hurry.

I closed my eyes and began to syphon. I could feel his chaos magic begin to flow through each of us as the green tar-like substance began to flow along my forearm, but I had never expected the pain that it caused. I opened my eyes and watched as Izzy grimaced with me on his opposite arm. Both of us were careful not to scream. Our legs were weak as we were forced to kneel next to him. The souls one by one disappeared, trying to help us as much as they could, but the chaos magic was strong. We had to do this ourselves.

"Stay focused," Leila whispered before disappearing with the rest of them.

A scream escaped my throat as my entire body burned from the inside and then Izzy did the same. We never let go as we collapsed even lower to the ground, trying to keep syphoning, but the magic was so painful, so evil, so dark that I could feel it killing me from the inside.

"Oh my God," I yelled, as my heart raced from the pain.

Izzy's eyes met mine and began to roll back in her head.

"Stay with me!" I screamed and then pleaded with her. "Please!" I began to cry as the pain was so much that I felt as if my own end was near. I thought of Jaxon and all I wanted was for him to be with me at this very moment. I wanted him alive, but I also didn't want to die alone. I thought we could do this. I didn't think that it would hurt so damn bad.

Ragnar seemed to waken from his injury and tried to claw at us, trying to loosen our grips, but failed with the jagged board gashed through him. He thrashed around as he felt the chaos magic leaving him after just recently getting it back. But the pain was too much, and for him to have it all inside of him was impossible. The evil it held was enough to make anyone psycho from the pain alone. I could feel the magic reaching down to my toes, and it felt like it was going to kill me in a matter of minutes.

Aisling's eyes were watching behind us and widened. I shook my head as I didn't want her near us.

I began to feel dizzy and choked on the tar-like substance flowing through me. "I can't do this."

Izzy's eyes tried to refocus as she nodded.

"Let me do it." She breathed too heavily as her nose began to bleed rapidly. "Let go, Freya." She nodded. "Let go."

I stared back at her in fear of failing and shook my head. Then, I felt the blood begin to drip from my own nose too.

The magic was killing us, both of us.

I looked over to Aisling and watched as Declan kept holding her back.

I needed to finish this and use the sword. I couldn't risk Aisling losing her life over any of this.

"It's not done yet." I kept trying to find my voice to keep her from reaching us.

"It's killing them," Aisling screamed at Declan in horror. "Let me go!"

Declan squeezed her tighter, and she frantically turned around and took his head and zapped him with a quick electric pulse. He released her and tried to stand back up, but it was just enough time for her to run to us with the sword lifted in the air.

"Aisling, don't," I pleaded, tears rolling down my face.

Ragnar's eyes widened with fear as Aisling grabbed his face and began to fry his brain with her own green flickering chaos as he became immobile. My eyes widened as I thought of Jaxon's theory. My heart felt sick, but my mind agreed.

"The others?" I asked.

Aisling ignored me as she nervously placed the blade against Ragnar's heart.

"We need all the chaos out before we can kill him," Declan yelled, grabbing Aisling's arms, steadying them from shaking. "If you die, I die with you."

Aisling looked behind her at Declan's blue eyes staring back at her as he held her arms and wrapped his body around her.

"I'll hold it steady for you," he reassured her.

Her eyes welled with tears as she looked back at me with defeat.

My syphoning continued as the weight of the magic was too much. I felt the world tremble as the float began to rock, and it felt like it was beginning to lean further into the water. We were all going to drown once this was over. The float had nothing left holding it together. I sucked in one last breath as the magic was almost out of him. I saw the last drop roll up my forearm, and then my right shoulder felt heavy, too heavy. I used the last of my strength to turn, and instead of panic, I was relieved to see my dad grab my shoulder. He nodded, and I watched the tar-like substance begin to flow to him.

"No," I whispered weakly. "You can't be here."

"You can't do it alone." My dad half smiled.

I shook my head. "You'll die."

"For you... I would do anything to keep you safe," my dad said as the tar-like substance traveled along his Norse Mark and up his neck.

I looked back at Izzy, and my eyes widened as Eric held her shoulder. The tar-like chaos began to spread to him, and the weight of the evil began to feel lighter in me.

"I've got you, Izzy," he said, as he knelt down next to her.

My lungs began to fill with the air I was gasping for. I closed my eyes and was at a loss for words.

Then, the chaos magic became lighter and lighter inside as it coursed through me. I opened my eyes and saw Aisling release Declan's grip from behind her and nodded toward Eric. Declan shook his head with worried eyes.

"He needs you," she said and nodded.

His shoulders slumped as he didn't dare to argue with her. He kissed her lips gently and slowly released his grip on her before he walked over and knelt behind his dad and took on the tar-like magic, then I looked behind me and saw Jaxon join my dad, then my mom, Haven, and Ezra. I looked back and watched Callum and Margo place their hands on Declan's shoulders.

My heart felt heavy as my eyes welled with tears as the moment became more peaceful than ever expected. I let my shoulders lower as the pain began to subside. I looked behind me as my dad squeezed my shoulder. His smile met mine as I felt whole in a moment that could've killed me. I looked back at Izzy who's breathing relaxed as tears flowed down her cheeks. She looked to her father and back to me.

It was Ragnar's hoarse voice that pulled me back to our mission. "I failed you, child. Please forgive me."

Izzy's bloodied face looked at me as if she was torn between good and evil. She looked at Aisling as she slowly stood and hesitated to take the sword from her. I half smiled and felt her pain as her life had been ruined for so long by a man that was supposed to love her. He pleaded again as the last drop of his chaos magic left his body.

"Isadora, my child. Please forgive me. Please."

Izzy choked back her tears as her hand shook with torment, one hand on her father and the other outstretched for the sword.

I looked at Aisling and nodded sadly, knowing she would know exactly what I meant.

We could not let Izzy sit in torment any longer. I decided it was time to end him and no longer let him manipulate his own child.

Aisling exhaled heavily, nodded, and then held her breath as she forced the dragon's blood sword hard into his heart. An explosion of light came from his chest and blinded me as he screamed in pain. The light faded as quick as it appeared, and Izzy closed her eyes as I could see Ragnar take his last gasp of breath. Then, his body slumped over with the sword pinned into him.

My eyes darted back to Aisling as I watched her begin to crumble to the ground of the wooden float. Right before her head hit the ground, oversized vines spun around her rapidly and cocooned her body as Declan reached her. Haven stood behind Aisling with the tar-like substance still coursing along her arms as she knelt to the ground and whispered incantations under her breath. Everything happened so quickly that it was hard to realize what was happening, and before I could inhale again, I let my shoulders relax as the vines began to unravel. Aisling stood unharmed in front of us, and Haven smiled and exhaled with relief.

Aisling stepped back and checked herself in disbelief. Declan stood in front of her speechless as he dropped to his knees, grabbing her waist and hugging her tight with the substance running along his arms. She hugged him back and then lifted her palms. Her green flickering magic survived and was twice the normal size as she smiled.

"I guess chaos beats chaos with a little help from a healer," she whispered. As she pulled the sword from his heart and dropped and released her grip, it clattered to the wooden planks and seemed to lose its glimmer of magic when she let it go.

She looked at Ezra, and he laughed. "That was a hell of a risk, Aisling."

She smiled. She looked around, and everyone nodded. "We did it."

"Well, almost," Declan said, as he pointed to the black tar swimming along our bodies, but the pain had subsided. Now, it felt like an irritated infection crawling along my skin.

Haven reached in my back pocket and smiled as she pulled out the small black bottle of liquid sloshing around.

"Where did you get that?" Izzy asked in shock, as she inched away from the stuff.

Haven smiled. "The other world. But don't worry... It's not for you."

Declan stood slowly without letting go of his grip on Aisling's hand. "Everyone stay still." He raised his free palm to the river and began to let the river flow through him and along each and every one of us. The freezing water stopped the itchiness along my skin as I watched the tar-like magic get surrounded by the water as if it was scared to be touched by it. Declan enclosed the chaos magic in a water bubble and Haven took the bottle of squid ink and poured it quickly into the center. We stood and watched as the chaos magic tried to fight its way against the substance and water but dissolved slowly and evaporated from within the water bubble.

Haven walked up to Ragnar's dead body and reached into his pocket. She grabbed the magicless Jasper stone and handed it to Ezra with hope.

He picked her up and spun her around, kissing her gently.

Aisling smiled and nodded excitedly. My mom and dad reunited and let their lips meet.

I turned around and watched everyone rid of the chaos magic, and I felt my heart finally slow, and the pain was gone. We stood on the partially destroyed fishing float as a family and survived. The ragged boards would surely need to be repaired this spring, and the charred wood would need to be replaced to have this up and running for business again. I looked behind me at the shore and shook my head as I saw our town—half burned and the ground broken to pieces.

"We will mend it," Jaxon came up behind me and whispered in my ear.

I half smiled and turned around to see him.

"I'm sorry I didn't want you involved."

He laughed. "Do you really think Ezra was going to let me sleep through a battle?" He smirked. "He woke me up as soon as you left, and we got the others. This was not something that could be done alone."

"But how did you find us?" I asked.

He laughed. "Dragons in Crystal Rock are not very subtle."

I laughed and grabbed his neck, reaching up and

smothering his lips with mine. He lifted me up and wrapped my legs around his waist as he squeezed me tighter.

"Miss Freya, you are my world, don't ever try to leave me again."

My eyes never left his as my smile grew, and I agreed.

"I love you, Jaxon."

"I love you more."

My dad interrupted us, "Hey now, it's not a competition." He laughed and pulled us in for a group hug with the others.

A glow caught my eye at the end of the float, and I looked past Jaxon and squinted. Ragnar's mother was glowing bright as she smiled back at me. I seemed to be the only one that saw her. She laid her palm out and reached for a young boy's hand, a boy that did not have a scar along his face anymore, but I knew who he was as they walked into the light together before they disappeared.

Peace after all.

My heart pounded as the surreal moment seemed to be a happy ending for everyone.

Jaxon set me down as we watched Oxana wrap herself in the blanket. She came walking onto the float with her shoulders slumped in defeat and grief, lowering her head as she made her way to us. She was met at the entrance by another woman. Oxana paused, and Lady Cambridge pulled her into her arms and let her sob, consoling her as best as she could.

"Hey, Izzy." I patted her shoulder and nodded toward the two women walking over to us.

She looked back in disbelief as she watched her mother

holding on to Oxana as they took each step carefully along the ragged wooden slates.

She dropped Eric's arm and ran toward them.

Lady Cambridge sucked in a deep breath as Izzy crashed into her, squeezing her and hugging her tight.

The tears flowed between them and with me as I watched the long overdue reunion.

"You did good, kid." Eric walked next to me and smiled. "Come here." He pulled me from Jaxon's arms and squeezed me. "You did all this to save me?" He pulled back and examined me. "Why?"

I laughed. "You don't know yet?" I smiled and hugged him again. "You're family, and you're worth fighting for."

His eyes filled with tears that he had been holding on to for centuries. "Thanks, kid."

"I think it's time to go home," my dad interrupted.

I let go of Eric and pointed to the burnt lands.

"It'll take time," he assured me, "but it's home."

"Swig and Jig?" Jaxon asked.

"I could use some bourbon," my mom answered for us all.

We laughed and headed toward the boat to get back to the land.

I sucked in a deep breath and watched the Mississippi flow fast around us, ice chunks and all. The river saved us today. I looked up at the night's sky and thanked the souls for coming back to us. I looked over at Haven and winked at her. She smiled wide and winked back. And then Aisling came up behind me and hugged me.

"You could've died today." I grabbed her arms and held them tight.

"Not to make light of the situation... but did you see how fast Declan was ready to die with me? Talk about a Shakespeare kind of love." She grabbed her chest and made an exasperated excitement. "I love that man." She had the look of admiration in her eyes as she watched Declan sit on the boat next to Eric and smiled.

I laughed. "You are one of a kind."

Aisling winked. "Truly, I am." She looked at Crystal Rock across the river and back to me. "Can we finally live happily ever after?" She half smiled as reality set back in.

I never let my eyes leave hers as I nodded. "I think it's time."

She smiled and pulled me in for a hug.

"I couldn't have done this without you," I whispered in her ear.

"Guess I'm glad to be in on the secret."

"Witches?" I asked her with a smile.

"Best witches." She laughed and kissed my cheek. "Let's go home."

"Home sounds good."

Chapter 39

Freya Chamberlain

The town was destroyed, but the people of Crystal Rock were safe, and that alone was enough to be happy about. We crossed the river and stepped onto the beach, walking up to Swig and Jig. We looked down the streets, and reality set in that it was going to take time to rebuild our homes, but we *would* rebuild. I glanced at the old movie theater and Rendezvous diner and shook my head at the damage. We could fix the walls of the buildings, but it would be the townspeople that would bring Crystal Rock back to life.

We called Aunt Clara and Aunt Lynn right away to let them know we were safe. They decided to start heading back down by us. My dad said that drinks were on him if anyone wanted to join us. Of course, Jack and the other regulars didn't hesitate to say they were on their way.

Ezra walked over to me and handed me the Jasper stone. "It's fixed. I'm letting you decide where it ends up these days." The half stone felt heavy in my palm as he closed my fist around it. "Aisling and I were able to send the magic back into it. I'll leave it up to you if you want to destroy it or keep it safe."

I looked down at it. Haven leaned in and whispered into my ear, and the thought never crossed my mind until she said it.

"Ezra said it's up to you. So, whatever you decide, I support you." She hugged me and smiled.

I stared at the stone and watched the tiny dragon fossil inside of it flutter as I held it. I could feel the magic, and it felt pure and good. The tingling in my palm was of happiness and light. I looked across the bar at Izzy sitting with her mother, Margo, and Oxana, and without hesitation, I walked over to her with the stone. Eric watched me carefully as I approached them.

"Hey, Izzy... Thank you for today." I cleared my throat. "I couldn't have done it without you."

She half smiled and opened her mouth, but no words came out. Her mother rubbed her shoulders as she exhaled heavily. "Thank you for trusting me." She wiped her tears and stood from the booth. She leaned over and hugged me.

My first instinct was to retract, but then I thought of her pain and rough upbringing, and I felt the goodness growing inside of her. I looked down at the Jasper stone and back at Haven and smiled.

"Here." I patted her back and released the hug. "You deserve *this* second chance." I took her palm and closed the stone in her hand.

Eric's eyes bulged as he watched us.

"You deserve to be a mom if you decide to again. This stone will give you what you've always wanted."

Izzy's eyes filled with the waterworks as she looked

down at her mother and smiled. Oxana wiped her own tears and nodded happily. Then, she looked back at Eric, and he took a step toward us.

He took her hand and closed the stone inside of hers. "My longest friend, you deserve this." He smiled, and his jaw clenched as he held his own tears back. He pulled her into him and hugged her tight.

I looked around the bar and smiled. The cold winter air was blowing outside, but it seemed calm in the bar. I walked into the office and dragged the fake tree out to the corner of the bar. I grabbed the pre-lit string lights and plugged them into the wall. I stepped back and looked at it. My dad walked out of the office with the box of ornaments that we would put on the tree each year and set it down.

He stood on the chair next to us and whistled.

He raised a glass. "Crystal Rock is our home, and we will rebuild it to be better. I am happy to have served so many of you and call each and every one of you my friends. Stay as long as you want or need, *my* bar is *your* bar until our town is back to normal. If anyone wants to gather and place an ornament, then please join us. And thank you for the years of happiness." He toasted the air, and everyone raised a glass back to him. "Now, if you don't mind me, I'm going to kiss my wife under that mistletoe for the rest of the night."

Everyone cheered as the chatter started back up.

Eric walked over to me. "Christmas dinner at your house this year?" He smirked, and the thought of my home burned to the ground made my stomach hurt.

"It'll be somewhere that's for sure. And don't worry,

you're invited." I patted his shoulder, and he huffed and then smiled.

"Thanks, niece."

I winked and began to decorate the tree with others. I watched as he walked over to Declan and pulled out the small figure from his pocket. I saw the ring from his mother glimmer, and I watched him whisper into his ear. Declan pulled back in surprise and smiled wide from ear to ear as he nodded in agreement. Then, Eric walked over to Aisling and her parents and kissed Aunt Lynn before Declan joined them with excitement.

I smiled watching our life become happy again.

After some time in the bar, celebrating with the hundred and fifty townsfolk and my friends and family, I could hear them telling stories of our magical world, and some were intrigued while others were still in disbelief. What I knew for certain was that I would never have to hide my magic again. The town was going to be rebuilt, and it was going to be built on magic and be better than ever before.

I looked at Jaxon and nodded toward the door.

He walked over with me, and we began to walk outside.

"Hey, wait." Margo's voice caught me off guard.

I turned around and waited to be hated or scorned by her. But instead, she hugged me. She wiped her tears and then hugged me again.

"You are everything my son needs in his life." She kissed my cheek. "I heard what you did to try and keep him safe." She smiled. "I'm damn glad he didn't let you do it alone, but it was the thought that counts. You are the best thing that's ever happened to him." She wiped another tear, and I smiled as her words sunk in. "Forgive me?"

I choked back the tears that I wanted to cry for the last two years and nodded. "Fresh start is good." I hugged her again and nodded.

"Welcome to the family, Freya."

Jaxon's shoulders relaxed as he grabbed both of us and bear hugged us. "About damn time." He laughed as he set us down. He winked at his mom before we began to walk away from the bar. I stopped us in our tracks when I heard the purring of an animal, lurking in the shadows near the bar. I squinted and dropped down to the ground and waited for Tinker to jump into my arms.

"You made it!" I smiled, patting her softly before turning around and handing her to Margo.

"Looks like she's going to be sticking around for a while." Margo smiled and took her back into the warm bar with her.

Jaxon exhaled with relief as he grabbed my hand and rubbed my thumb gently. "So, where are we headed?"

I looked up at him and leaned my head into his shoulder and shrugged. "I kind of wanted to check my home."

He nodded as we walked slowly toward it.

The few blocks that we had to go made my heart race the closer we got. When we took the turn for the final block, my eyes widened with hope.

He looked down at me in amazement. "He never got to this street. Look... Aisling's house and yours are still standing."

My jaw dropped as I ran for the house, him following close behind me.

I pushed the door open, and relief washed over me as everything was left untouched. I turned around and jumped into his arms. The excitement we had was enough to let the hope grow that maybe everything wasn't as destroyed as we had thought. He carried me along to each room and then hesitated as he opened the side door to the garage. He exhaled and turned the handle.

And there it was... the Camaro that he had promised to fix for my dad. He set me down, and we walked into the garage together. I walked to the driver seat and opened the door, sitting down and readjusting the rear-view mirror. He joined me in the passenger seat. We both seemed to be speechless as he reached for my hand. I stopped him, flicking my wrist and giving the car a little magic to try and start it. The car didn't roar to life but it was enough juice for the clock to turn on. He shrugged and reached for my hand again, rubbing it gently. I stared in disbelief at the time of 11:29 p.m. on the dash. My heart quickened as a flash of memories hit me. I remembered sitting in the exact spot years ago contemplating on sneaking out of my home, which ultimately changed my world. Then the only other time I recall was when I saw Jaxon for the first time since the accident. The time itself was irrelevant but yet, in this moment, it meant so much to me. I knew it was the universe giving me a sign that tonight was going to be the start of our new beginning. Only this time it would be forever.

"I promise I'll always be here for you." he said.

My heart settled when I looked over at him, as his

words hit me differently than before. Because this time, I knew he meant it, and there were no magical mishaps that could get between us anymore. The Immortals were no longer an evil duo, and Ragnar, the man and all his chaos, was destroyed. I stared at our hands together and then looked back at him and smiled, wiping a tear, only this time it was a happy one.

"You think we can fix this?" he asked.

I squeezed his hand tighter and nodded.

He winked back at me and smiled. He leaned over the shifter and pulled me close to him, tucking my hair behind my ear and lifting my chin gently. His lips parted as they met mine and I felt the moment of our future start. We had a long road ahead of us, but I knew we would never be alone again.

"Together?" he asked.

"Forever."

"And ever." He kissed me.

The End

Epilogue

After two summers of rebuilding our town and too many weddings and other celebrations to count, the town was finally better than ever. It was helpful to use our magic to help with the construction. I stared out of the window and smiled at the town. Aisling and Declan were expecting their first child in the next few weeks, and here I was, sitting on the cold table in a small room that overlooked the town in the bluffs, waiting for the OBGYN to come in. Jaxon was running late but promised he had just parked the Jeep and was running up the stairs. I waited patiently for the door to open with either the doctor or Jaxon bursting into the room.

My heart raced as I waited for the cold gel and ultrasound to let me know how well our baby was doing. It had been a long year of hoping and praying that we could conceive since Aisling's wedding last year. Aisling and I had hoped to be pregnant at the same time, but it looked like this was as close as we could get.

I turned my wedding band nervously. Even though we

were newly pregnant, it was beginning to get tight already. I twisted it gently and hoped that everything was going to be good news today.

The door creaked open and in walked Jaxon. I exhaled with relief as he walked over and kissed me.

"Did I miss anything yet?" He tried to catch his breath but struggled from the three flights of stairs he had to run up, the elevator having maintenance work done today.

I shook my head and smiled.

The door opened again as the doctor walked in. A petite woman with dark hair in a bun. Her glasses hung on her chest by a string. She smiled bright, sliding her chair across the room to us.

"Hi, I'm Dr. Vorwald. I'm your prenatal doctor, if you'll have me." She reached her hand out to shake ours as we both nodded, knowing that she was the only prenatal doctor in Crystal Rock. "Well, then... Let's get started. I will need your husband to move to your left side so he can view this little one too."

Jaxon moved over and grabbed my hand with both excitement and nervousness.

"This gel will be a bit cold."

I nodded and braced myself as she began to rub the gel along my almost flat belly. I could hardly believe there was anything inside there yet, but the little white stick and two pink lines were a giveaway that I was not alone.

She swirled the wand around, and her smile grew wider. I turned and looked at the screen, at the gray matter moving around, trying to see the little bouncing baby.

"Here, listen..." She reached for the machine and turned the volume up. "There is one heartbeat..." *Thump,*

thump, thump. I smiled with relief to hear the little life growing. "And then there is the second one." She moved the wand around, and I watched as two little sacks appeared on the screen next to one another. "Looks like you two are having a set of identical twins."

Jaxon's hand squeezed mine hard as I looked over to him in shock. His usual calm and collective face seemed to go pale, and he looked dizzy. "Twins?" he questioned.

Hearing him say it out loud finally made it *feel* more real.

The doctor nodded. "Congratulations, you two. You both will definitely have your hands full with these two little ones." She smiled. "Do twins run in your family?"

I turned my head away from the screen, and away from Jaxon, and stared blankly at the doctor and swallowed hard.

"Freya, do twins run in your family or in Jaxon's?" the doctor asked again.

Once the shock dissipated, my smile began to form as I realized what was happening. "Both sides... actually." I looked back at Jaxon, and his face became more colored as his smile grew with mine.

"Is this really happening?" he asked me.

"Seems so," the doctor answered. "Let me give you two some privacy. I will be back in a few minutes." She nodded before she turned to walk out of the room.

Jaxon leaned down bond kissed my forehead. He stared at the ultrasound picture in awe, and I watched as his excitement grew. "Best day of my life," he exclaimed.

"Bestest." I smiled as happy tears fell down my cheeks.

My phone rang after a moment of blissful happiness. Jaxon reached for it on the counter and answered it.

"Hello?" Jaxon smiled. "Yep, your vision was right." He laughed. "Here, you can talk to her." He changed the phone to a video call and handed it to me. "It's your family."

I put the phone in front of me and smiled excitedly. "Hey, guys—"

"Twins?" Aunt Clara, Haven, and my mom squealed with excitement. "Aunt Clara kept saying it, but I didn't believe her," Haven said. "Do you think they're Anchors?"

I watched my dad in the background as he steadied himself against the back wall. His hand to his head as he processed. I looked at Jaxon and then down at my belly and smiled. I put my hand to them and concentrated on any growing magic inside me. All of a sudden, I felt the tingling begin as my Mark began to glow subtly. Jaxon looked back at me with wide eyes.

"I think they are."

Jaxon's jaw dropped. "Anchors?" he mouthed.

I smiled from ear to ear. "The next generation. Only this time... *We* won't let these two grow up without magic. Right, Auntie Haven?"

She smiled and cleared her throat as she swallowed her happy tears. "So right... Congratulations, Jaxon and Freya. We can't wait to meet the little ones."

I nodded. "Same. Love you guys."

"Love you too."

My dad came and grabbed the phone from them. He wiped his tears away and smiled. "Hey, kid, congratulations."

I could tell he wanted to say more but he had such a mix of emotions that I figured I'd do the talking for him. "Thanks, Dad. I'm more excited to watch you and Mom be grandparents more than anything."

He looked back at the video and laughed. "Grandpa Jim? Huh?" He choked back more tears as my mom came and patted his back and wrapped her arms around his shoulders.

"That sounds good on you," she smiled.

"It does, doesn't it?" he smiled and nodded. "You two will be amazing parents. I love you, kid. Proud of you."

I felt it in that very moment, the emotional hormones, and the feeling that after everything, I had done something right. I felt what Izzy had been looking for her whole life, and a moment of peace washed over me as I realized that everything was happening just as it should.

I thought of Izzy raising baby Ember Lynn with her mother near Oxana, and thought of how the world could be happy if everyone worked together. I had doubts when I handed her the Jasper stone, but when I saw her hold her daughter in her arms, I saw the Izzy that she was supposed to be all along. A normal woman with a warrior's heart. She had been through so much, and now she was living out her dream of being a mother, and she had her mother to help guide her. Even Eric and Aunt Lynn found time to spend with them between their travels with Aisling's parents.

My parents' vow renewal had really been the icing on the cake for the fresh start. When we stood under the tree at JFK and my mom handed me the bouquet and Haven handed my dad the rings, it was a moment where our family was as one. Jaxon watched us from the audience, and that night, he proposed to me. It was one of the best days of my life, until today. We were going to be parents. At first, I was waiting for bad news to follow, but instead, there wasn't any. We had the rest of our lives to live a semi-normal, but still a very magical life, and I was ready for it.

"Hey, babe." Jaxon helped me sit up and sat next to me on the bed. "You think Eric is going to be thrilled, or is he going to try and steal our babies?" He laughed.

I chuckled and shook my head. "He's going to have to help protect them. The world is much bigger than Crystal Rock."

Jaxon looked back at me with worry.

"But for now... We need to figure out their names."

His worry faded as his smile came back. He leaned over me and kissed my belly and then met my lips with his. "Let's head home, we can think of some on our way to JFK." He jingled our house keys to our newly built home next to the tree and smiled. "Plus, now I need to make room for the second baby in the nursery."

I smiled and rubbed my belly gently. "You two are going to be so protected and so loved."

Jaxon smiled and kissed me. "As are you, Freya. Now, let's go home."

Thank you for all of the love and support

For more information on the series and for future updates
check out the author website:
https://stephanievorwald.wixsite.com/website

About the Author

Stephanie Vorwald is the author of the Witches &
Immortals Series. She found her passion for writing long
before she achieved writing 'The End' for her debut novel.
She loves writing fantasy books where she can create her
own world of magic in everyday, ordinary life. When she is
not writing, she is a Registered Dental Hygienist. She loves
being a mother to her kids and having family time.

facebook.com/StephanieVorwaldWriter

tiktok.com/@stephanievorwaldauthor44

amazon.com/author/StephanieVorwald